Assault and Matrimony

Assault and Matrimony

JAMES ANDERSON

PUBLISHED FOR THE CRIME CLUB BY
DOUBLEDAY & COMPANY, INC.
GARDEN CITY, NEW YORK
1981

Library of Congress Cataloging in Publication Data

Anderson, James, 1936–
Assault and matrimony.

I. Title.
PR6051.N393A8   1981   823'.914
AACR2
ISBN 0-385-17799-2
Library of Congress Catalog Card Number 81–43249

Assault and Matrimony

CHAPTER 1

It was on a Wednesday that Sylvia Gascoigne-Chalmers decided to murder her husband.

What she didn't know was that on Tuesday her husband, Edgar, had decided to murder her.

Once they had made up their minds, both Sylvia and Edgar felt extremely relieved, and they were especially charming to each other during the days that followed. Not that there was a very marked difference from their normal manner, for they were habitually charming to each other—and not merely in public, but in private as well. It was largely this characteristic that had led all who knew them to consider them an ideal couple. They were good-looking, healthy, apparently prosperous, socially successful and highly respected.

Nobody, least of all Sylvia, knew that Edgar had detested her for at least five years; and nobody, least of all Edgar, knew that Sylvia had abominated him for at least six.

They had, though, lived together peacefully for a long time, and the cause of these sudden homicidal impulses was a decision made by Sylvia's second cousin, Charles Inchcape. The ultimate responsibility, though, might just as well have been laid on Charles's great-grandfather, Silas Inchcape—or even on Horatio Dimsdale, the Victorian man of letters, who really started the whole business. However, Dimsdale's only fault was to be struck by a Great Thought during a country weekend and subsequently write a book about it, so to lay the blame on him would be a little unfair. It will, then, be best to jump from that weekend in the mid-eighteen-eighties to a Friday morning in July, just about ninety years later, when Edgar entered the dining-room of his home, *The Elms,* a large detached country house near the small Wiltshire market town of Cornfield, to find Sylvia seated at the breakfast table, reading a letter and wearing a pensive expression.

"Good morning, dear," he said cheerfully, kissing her on the cheek.

She smiled prettily. "Good morning, darling. Sleep well?"

"Like a top." He sat down at the highly polished Victorian mahogany table, unfolded his crisp white napkin and poured milk from a delicate Royal Worcester jug on to his cornflakes. Sylvia watched carefully, ready to spring forward with a tissue if any milk descended to the surface of the table. But all was well.

If once, if just once in his life, she thought, he would say, "like a log," or "like a baby," or even "mind your own business." And, of course, not a word about the fact that even though Mrs. Thring was away, breakfast was bang on time and everything as clean and bright as usual.

Edgar glanced at her letter and recognized the handwriting. "And what does *dear* cousin Charles have to say?"

"Oh, he's just invited himself to dinner, that's all."

"Really? When?"

"Sunday. A mere two days' notice, you see, and me without a servant. Did you ever hear of such cheek? It will mean several hours' hard slog in the kitchen for me. I was thinking we'd have something very simple on Sunday, too."

"Well, why not stick to that? A simple meal won't hurt him for once."

"Oh no! Only the best is good enough for our rich relation. I'm not having him going round complaining about the dinner I gave him."

The silly little twit, thought Edgar. He disliked Charles as much as she did. But he did know that, gourmet though Charles was, he'd be perfectly happy with bread and cheese and a glass of beer.

"Why's he coming, anyway?" he asked.

"I don't know. He's going to spend a day or two at *The Firs,* and he's not bringing the Bruntons. He says he's got something very important to discuss with us. I hope it's the party wall at the back. I've mentioned it several times to him, but of course, with three homes, what does he care if one falls to the ground? Listen to this, 'So, dear second-cuz and second-cuz-in-law, would be greatly obliged if you could spare the odd crust from your humble repast on Sunday e'en for your most obedient and devoted kinsman.' I ask you, how facetious can you be?"

Edgar said, " 'Something very important'? I can't imagine Charles considering a party wall very important."

Sylvia looked a little alarmed. "Then what do you think it can be?"

"I haven't a clue, my dear. If *you* can't read between the lines, how do you expect me to?"

"Do you want to read it, darling?"

"No thank you, dear, he's your cousin."

"But he's *our* next-door neighbour, too."

"He is when he deigns to spend a few weeks there."

"As a neighbour, that's the best thing about him—the fact that he's practically never in residence."

Inwardly Edgar groaned. How many scores of times had the trite little moron made that crack? Still, she only had about three jokes—and this one was the best of them. He chuckled appreciatively. "Well, let's hope he doesn't stay too long this time."

"He'll certainly be an utter pest as long as he's here. I'll have to ask him to at least one more meal, and then no doubt he'll expect us to go in there and eat some foul concoction he's cooked himself from a recipe one of his weird foreign friends has given him." She shuddered.

Edgar said, "I hate the way he behaves as though *The Elms* is his home, too—wandering in and out at all hours, settling down in my chair with one of my books."

"Yes—and going into the kitchen, helping himself to a glass of milk from the fridge, with hardly so much as a by your leave. And apparently expecting us to behave in just the same way in *The Firs.*"

"Well, at least we've never done so. Though he seems too obtuse to realize we're trying to set him an example in correct behaviour."

"Mind you, he's the same with everybody. All his friends behave like that. Do you remember that ghastly weekend at *High Tors?* Never did I think I'd find a ballerina, a professional boxer, a Salvation Army officer and an Oxford professor of physics—not to mention that peculiar Burmese person, who never spoke—all under the same roof, and all apparently quite at home."

"*Apparently* is the operative word, dear."

"Of course it is. We must never forget Charles's money. He wouldn't get away with his behaviour if he wasn't so wealthy."

"Now there I think I must disagree with you, darling. I have a sneaking feeling that he'd get away with the most outrageous behaviour even if he were penniless."

"Perhaps you're right, darling."

Funny, she thought: it was only at times like this, when they were discussing somebody they both disliked, that she found Edgar's presence bearable. For a moment or two then she had almost felt a rapport with him.

Edgar said, "I must go." He stood up. "No one coming tonight, is there?"

"No, of course not, darling. I'm not having anybody here until Mrs. Thring gets back. It was to have been the Craythornes and the Willoughby-Grants tonight, but I had to put them off."

"Oh well, I can't say I'm sorry."

"Of course, I can't stand them myself. But the Craythornes have never Seen Over; and the Willoughby-Grants not for five years. It's really infuriating of the woman to have walked out at this time."

"Did she say how long this benighted sister of hers expects to be ill? I can't remember."

"Five or six weeks at least."

Edgar gave a tut. "And I suppose Thring will insist on staying with the husband and children until the bitter end?"

"Oh, naturally—and until the woman has finished a long convalescence, I shouldn't wonder. No thought for me—absolutely no sense of duty."

"Any chance of getting a temporary replacement—just a daily?"

"I doubt if there's a spare cleaning woman in the whole of Cornfield. Besides, I wouldn't want to leave a stranger here alone."

"I suppose not. Still, I'm sure you'll manage beautifully, as usual." He bent and kissed her.

"Thank you, darling. I'll do my best—as usual."

Edgar left the house. It was another blazingly hot morning. How long could this fine spell possibly last? He never thought he'd get tired of sunshine, but this one really was too much. The grass in the meadow opposite was beginning to look more like straw. It threw into sharp contrast the bright green of their lawn, where George, their aged and intermittent gardener, had just started the sprinkler again. He wondered how long they would be allowed to go on doing that.

Edgar gave a sudden grin as he walked to the garage. The little snob wouldn't like it if the appearance of her precious garden was spoilt. She'd be willing Mrs. Thring to stay away, then—just so she would have an excuse not to have guests.

He got the Rover out and started the short drive to his office. What a loathsome woman she was! Smug, self-centred, proud, prim. He had, of course, often thought about divorce. But in the end he had always decided that as long as he could stick it, it was better to put up with her. It wasn't as though he wanted to marry somebody else. (There had been other women from time to time, but nothing he'd wished to make permanent.) Divorce would be bad for his image. In these country districts they still preferred their County Councillors and JPs happily married. And to give the little prig her due, she was an excellent housekeeper and charming hostess.

However, outweighing all others, there was one overriding objection to divorce: he was determined, never, under any circumstances, to pay her alimony. He could just imagine, if once she knew his true opinion of her, how she would screw him for every last halfpenny.

Surely she hadn't been like she was now when he married her twenty-four years ago? Of course, she had been very beautiful. In fact, she still was extremely attractive. One would never take her for forty-three. (But then, no one would take him for forty-seven, either.) So had he really been in love with her? Or had he, as the saying went, simply been captivated by her beauty and blinded to her faults? He'd certainly *believed* he loved her—and had gone on for many a year telling himself he did. For, as no man likes to admit that the car he has just bought isn't the best in its class, thus acknowledging his own lack of judgement, so few men, early on in their married life, are willing to admit even to themselves that the new wife isn't all she might be.

It had certainly taken Edgar a long time to face the fact that he didn't love Sylvia. But once he'd let go—made that acknowledgement—it had been but a tiny step to recognizing that he hated her.

It was impossible now to pinpoint the exact moment that it had happened. Though, strangely, he could put his finger on the much earlier occasion when the seeds of hatred had been sown: the day twenty-two years ago, when, after looking over that dreary, dilapidated mausoleum of a house, she had turned to him, her eyes gleaming, and said with utter determination,

"Edgar—my great-grandfather built this house. I'm going to live here."

CHAPTER 2

It was in the year 1881 that Sidney Inchcape and his twin brother Silas entered into a joint purchase of an acre and a quarter of building land near the small market town of Cornfield. Shortly afterwards they legally divided it between them and commenced building themselves rambling, and rather ugly houses. Sidney planted some elms, Silas a row of firs, and with what was for her a startling touch of originality Mrs. Sidney suggested the two names which were later adopted.

For many years Sidney and Silas had prospered exceedingly in Cornfield as respectively corn merchant and saddler, but the moment the houses were completed, each sold his business, and they both settled down to acquire the reputations, not of country gentlemen—that would have been aiming too high—but of cultivated upper-middle-class burgesses.

Now, Sidney and Silas were snobs—though snobs of the largely harmless kind. Neither having received more than the bare minimum of formal schooling, they both possessed great reverence for book learning, culture, and the Arts. And with time starting to hang a little heavily on their hands, they began to develop a fascination with artistic, musical, and literary people. It wasn't long before the idea came to them that they might actually aspire to the rank of Patrons of the Arts. Neither of them, of course, wanted to go to the absurd length of actually spending good money in supporting struggling young writers or painters or composers. No, what Sidney and Silas sought was the friendship of Famous Creative Men. They wanted Famous Creative Men around them. And especially they wanted them in their homes—in *The Elms* and *The Firs*. They became in effect collectors—collectors of Famous Creative Men. And soon, inevitably, they became rival collectors.

The Railway had brought Cornfield within two hours or so of London, and in London Sidney and Silas began spending more and more time. They bought and wangled introductions and invitations. They scoured the salons and smoking-rooms of the metropolis for

Famous Creative Men. Their persistence paid off in so far that both succeeded in *meeting* many of their quarries. Sadly, though, in spite of scattering invitations to their homes like confetti, neither was ever as successful a collector as he would have wished. However, this is not to say that their hunting expeditions were complete failures. They may have failed to get the Most Famous Creative Men, but those somewhat lesser names who were among the first to accept invitations, returned to town reporting good air, pleasant countryside, exceedingly comfortable accommodation, excellent food, attentive and most respectful hosts, and large circles of admiring dinner guests hanging on to their words each evening.

Although, therefore, at various times, Wilde and Meredith and Browning and Gilbert and Sullivan and Millais and many others all refused invitations, over the years a good number of poets, playwrights, novelists, composers, painters and sculptors did spend varying periods under one roof or the other. Roden Noel, for instance, stayed at *The Elms,* Alfred Cellier at *The Firs,* Birket Foster at *The Elms,* George R. Sims at *The Firs,* Harry Bates at *The Elms,* Horatio Dimsdale at *The Firs,* and so on.

The phrase "under one roof or the other" is important. For Sidney and Silas were true collectors, and the words "Roden Noel visited *The Elms,*" mean he visited *only* that house. Likewise, the phrase "Alfred Cellier visited *The Firs*" means equally that *The Firs* was the only house Cellier visited. Nor would any member of either Inchcape family make a call on the next-door relatives during the visit of a captured lion. The only way, in fact, that the brothers exhibited their triumphs to each other was through the medium of photographs, and the solitary and mediocre Cornfield photographer made a handsome profit from frequent visits to the two Inchcape houses for the purpose of capturing the likenesses of the sometimes strangely undistinguished-looking guests and their hosts.

Both families played the game fairly, and neither would have dreamed of poaching one of the other's captures. As a result, and because their success rates were roughly equal, not too much illfeeling was engendered, and although there were occasional fallingsout, these were strictly temporary.

Sidney and Silas eventually passed into history, having achieved the minute peripheral fame of occasional passing references in a few works of literary or artistic biography. *The Elms* and *The Firs* passed to their heirs. By a strange chance, *The Firs* descended in a direct male line, coming eventually, in 1950, to Silas's great-grandson, Charles Inchcape; while *The Elms* passed exclusively from female to female—first to Sidney's daughter, Ethel, then to her daughter, Maude, while the latter, never marrying, left the house in her will to her niece, Sylvia Gascoigne-Chalmers, *née* Inchcape-Briggs, the great-granddaughter of Sidney.

Sylvia and Edgar had been married two years at the time of their first visit to her inheritance, and were living in two rooms in Paddington. He had just completed his articles with a firm of chartered accountants and was looking eagerly round for a job in the City. So her announcement that she intended to live at *The Elms* came as a shock to him. When they'd first heard that she'd been left the house in the will of her Aunt Maude, her late mother's maiden sister, they had both speculated excitedly on what it might fetch. Sylvia had visited the house when she was younger, and had never given Edgar the impression of thinking much of the place. But now, looking at it with the knowledge that it belonged to her, she seemed to see it with different eyes.

In vain he had protested that he didn't like the country, didn't want to live here, would never be able to get a job in the area and would have to spend four or five hours a day commuting. In vain he pointed out how isolated the house was, with *The Firs* next door the only other building for half a mile in either direction, how lonely and quiet she would find it, how absurdly large it was for two people, how much work would need to be done on it and on the garden.

Sylvia had remained adamant. Every argument he put against the house was for her an argument in its favour. She wanted solitude. She longed for space. She welcomed the challenge of making something really special out of the house. Besides, it was *her* inheritance; it had been in her family over seventy years. She had a duty to live here and restore it.

And he had let himself be won over, had convinced himself that what she wanted, he wanted. They had moved in. And immediately it was as if some form of mania overtook her. Her life became almost exclusively taken up with the place. She had time for nothing else. The house seemed never free of the smell of paint and turps. She was always tired out.

Edgar meanwhile, at her instigation, had borrowed some money from an uncle and set up in business for himself in Cornfield. There was only one other firm of accountants in the town, and after a shaky start he had begun to do pretty well.

But—only ever pretty well; never outstandingly so. For auditing the books of farmers and small shopkeepers was not what he'd wanted, and after the initial excitement of being his own boss had worn off, he knew he'd never be able to put his all into his work. He'd always longed to be rich. But more than that, he'd yearned to be important. His day-dreams were of oak-panelled City board-rooms, of takeover bids, chauffeur-driven Rolls-Royces, of flights to Zürich, New York, Tokyo, of being Sir Edgar Gascoigne-Chalmers and being interviewed on television about the state of the pound.

But that sort of life would never be his now. Thanks to Her . . .

Edgar reached Cornfield, parked the car, and walked to his office. It was on the first floor of a somewhat depressing Victorian building with echoing stone-floored and tile-walled corridors—the only office building of any size in the town. His secretary, Beryl Nash, was already there.

She gave him his mail and said, "Mr. Brownlow phoned just now. He's received another letter from Amalgamated Farm Equipment and wanted an appointment with you as early as possible next week."

She was plain and plump, about thirty-five, pleasant in manner and efficient. She had been with him for six years since being left a widow with no insurance and two small children. These were now looked after during the day by her mother, who lived with them, and whom Beryl also supported.

"What time did you give him?" Edgar asked.

"I couldn't fit him in early in the week at all. Monday morning you're on the Bench and you have the County Council meeting in the afternoon. Tuesday morning you're tied up with other clients. Then there's the Rotary club lunch—you know how they drag on, and at four-thirty you have the appointment with Mr. Whittal—he wants your advice about his expansion plans for the farm. Wednesday morning you're giving your Treasurer's report at the meeting of the Trustees of the Handicapped Persons' Charitable Society, and on Wednesday afternoon you have the meeting of the Board of Governors of Greenhill school. The earliest time I could work Mr. Brownlow in was Thursday morning at ten. He wasn't very pleased. He suggested you might see him tomorrow morning, but I thought you wouldn't want to give up your golf."

"Quite right, Beryl. It won't do him any harm to wait for a few days."

"It seems a pity to antagonize him, though. He'll still be a valuable client even if he does sell one side of his business. If you change your mind about tomorrow, I could ring him back."

"No, don't bother."

Edgar went into his private office and sat down. She was right, of course. Brownlow, though a vulgarian, was an important man in

Cornfield. He ought to find time to see him before next Thursday. Why had he let himself get tied up in all these activities? To compensate for his failure to become rich and important? If he couldn't be a big fish in a big pool, at least he'd be a big fish in a little one?

When he and Sylvia had first moved to the area he had tried to become a countryman—taken up angling, bought a shotgun and gone shooting, even had a few riding lessons. But he'd never got on with any of it. Then he had thrown himself into these other things. And he had undoubtedly become a person of importance in the district. People did look up to him. But who really wanted to be looked up to by minnows?

And he was certainly out of pocket as a result of it all. Probably only Beryl knew just how much. If he'd really put all he'd got into his professional work over the years, the business could have been expanded enormously. He could have been a comparatively rich man by now—instead of just getting by.

Of course, it would have helped if Sylvia hadn't used up every spare penny on that blasted house. There had been a good deal of nice old furniture in the house when they'd moved in; but there had been a lot of modern stuff as well. Just about the time he had started to make a reasonable living, she had got it into her head that all the modern had to go and be replaced by period pieces, which would "blend," "be fitting." That was when her roving had started; she'd seemed always to be off somewhere, at auctions or antique shops. Piece by piece and at ever-increasing cost the stuff had been gathered. And after the furniture—paintings.

He had been looking forward to throwing some money around himself—travelling a bit, gambling on some speculative shares, laying down a cellar, perhaps getting a cruiser on the Thames—once the initial struggle to get established was over. Maybe if he'd known there was a chance of those things, and others, he'd have had the incentive to work harder. But he'd always been aware that every extra pound he made would go on the house. So why bother?

In heaven's name, how much had she spent over the years? He'd always been frightened to keep a running total. Anyway, the way things had appreciated in value recently, it had to be worth many times more now. So it had been a good investment, he supposed. There was no chance of ever cashing in on this, though—getting a bit of pleasure as a dividend.

No, it would all continue to moulder in that great dead empty house—a house at which nobody ever dropped in, but to which people were invited in small manageable groups to "see over."

Like a museum—with Her as the curator.

CHAPTER 3

After Edgar left for the office, Sylvia cleared away the breakfast things, washed up, made the beds and then did an hour's cleaning. In spite of her words at breakfast, she wasn't altogether sorry that Mrs. Thring was away. Doing the work herself brought back her early years there, when they hadn't been able to afford a domestic—although she knew this nostalgia would have long passed by the time Mrs. Thring returned. It was nice, too, to have the house completely to herself. That was how she really liked it.

Her work finished, she wandered from room to room, smoothing a vase here, straightening a picture infinitesimally there, picking a speck of fluff from the carpet. The house really was almost perfect now. My, but it had been hard work, the years of toil—painting, papering, laying lino, making curtains—in later years the constant visits of workmen; then the scouring of salerooms and antique shops —she must be known in every one in a radius of fifty miles, let alone London. But it had been well, well worth it.

There were still a few things she wanted—a dressing-table for the third bedroom, for instance; the present one was too modern. But that could wait until she saw one that was absolutely right.

Of course, *The Elms* would never be completely perfect. There would always be some further effect to strive for. And that was perhaps a good thing. To achieve the ultimate was to have no goal left and to stagnate.

She went downstairs, made herself a cup of coffee and took it outside to drink. She sat down in a wicker chair and surveyed the scene. The garden was really looking lovely—in spite of the drought. It had been a wilderness when they'd come here first. There'd been no question of a gardener then. She'd knocked it into shape—as she had the inside—with her own hands and at the cost of her own sweat.

About the only thing that was unchanged since those days was the old well—said to have been sunk in Elizabethan times—which made such a delightful centrepiece for the garden. It might turn out to be extremely useful, too, if this weather continued.

How beautifully, beautifully peaceful it was. She could hear no sound but the buzz of insects and the song of birds, smell nothing but the scent of flowers. It was so lucky that there'd been no development nearby. They were still surrounded by open farmland—and now certain to remain so. The road outside had never really become more than a country lane, and—apart from Whittal's farm, over a mile away—didn't lead anywhere that couldn't be reached more conveniently by other routes. So except for tradesmen's vans, farm vehicles, and the occasional car of exploring tourists during the summer months, traffic on it was rare.

Sylvia sat, as she'd done thousands of times before, and gloried in her privacy and seclusion. Nothing about her home gave her greater joy than this. And although it still made her shudder to think of her young days, there was always a grim satisfaction in keeping alive the remembrance of what she'd escaped from . . .

Sylvia's mother, as she never tired of informing her only child, had married beneath her. Cliff Briggs, although from a lower-middle-class background, was the kind of man who left to himself would have drifted into unskilled semi-manual work and been quite content. But his wife had pushed him towards higher things. The particular high thing where her pushes had finally landed him had been the proprietorship of a rented fish-and-chip shop, "with residential accommodation" in Bermondsey.

The accommodation consisted of four rooms over the shop. Here Sylvia was born and brought up. On one side was a cinema, on the other a pub. A large tenement overlooked the rear, and a bus station was opposite. In spite of the commercially favourable position, however, and notwithstanding the Briggses staying open until eleven o'clock six nights a week, the shop was never successful enough to enable them to live elsewhere. Mr. and Mrs. Briggs were never able to understand why this was so. (It was only many years later Sylvia suddenly realized that the reason had undoubtedly been the highly unpleasant fish and chips they sold.) Rather than puzzle over the problem any longer, Cliff Briggs eventually died, Sylvia then still only nine. Mrs. Briggs had struggled on alone to the end of the war —a thing she seemed to consider organized specifically to inconvenience her—and through the grim years following, only to be knocked down and killed by a speeding ambulance in 1951.

In some miraculous way she had managed to pay for Sylvia's education at a private day school—though the utter impossibility of ever asking another girl home, or even letting any of them know her address, had made her very much of a loner there. Thus she was left with a good accent; £160 from the sale of the fixtures, fittings and non-existent "goodwill" of the shop; and a double-barrel surname. (Her mother had been proud of her Inchcape ancestry and had insisted on Sylvia tacking it on officially in front of Briggs as soon as she was old enough.) She had no training, but being quite determined not to take a "poor class" job, was going through the £160 at a rate of knots when she met Edgar. Marriage came in the nick of time for her.

Apart from the absence of the smell of stale cooking fat, the two rooms in Paddington were no real improvement on the flat over the shop. But then had come Aunt Maude's death—and *The Elms.*

She had been somewhat disgruntled at first to find—a fact she'd once known but forgotten—that her wealthy and cultured cousin Charles owned the next-door house. She had met him only once previously, at a funeral, and although then had been mightily impressed by his urbanity and *savoir vivre,* had, too, been irritated by his unconscious air of calm superiority. He was older than she was, a genuine cosmopolitan, widely travelled and, it was believed, very well off. (Silas's descendants had managed their financial affairs a good deal better than Sidney's, and in addition Charles's mother had been wealthy in her own right.) Sylvia had feared that Charles would look down on her and that as a result other locals would do the same. His presence there would be an intrusion on her beautiful new private world. She was anxious, too, in case it turned out that he entertained a lot of rowdy guests, or family parties swarming with children and young people. She was moreover irrationally resentful of the fact that he had been in possession of *The Firs* several years longer than she of *The Elms.* She coveted *The Firs* herself.

She was, therefore, immensely relieved to discover, as the months passed, that for nine-tenths of the year *The Firs* remained unoccupied. Charles, it transpired, owned several properties and spent but brief and irregular spells at *The Firs.* On the rare occasions that he was present, he couldn't have been more friendly or welcoming. So in this respect her fears turned out to be groundless, and although she always retained an obscurely uneasy dislike of her cousin, she was forced to admit that if anybody else had to own *The Firs,* it couldn't really be anyone more satisfactory than Charles.

All the same, she did hope he didn't stay too long this time. Merely having one person next door always spoilt things for her. It was probably the absence of other buildings nearby that made *The Firs* and its occupants seem so close, for the two houses certainly

were not near together by town standards; but somehow when anybody was living there she always felt she was being overlooked.

However, at the moment things were quite perfect. In fact, with
The Firs empty, Edgar at the office, Mrs. Thring away, and even old
George out of sight and earshot round the front, they had really
never been better.

If only she could always have it like this. If only she could live
completely alone—watching television, reading; entertaining a couple of times a week—elegant little dinner parties—people who
would come, admire, and go away again. She didn't need somebody
there all the time.

Least of all Edgar. He had no appreciation of what she'd done
here, of the lovely home she'd created. Precious little help he'd ever
given her, except when he absolutely couldn't get out of it. All he
was interested in were his blasted committees and things.

It was this that had led her to hate him. It must have happened
gradually. There must have been a long period when her feelings for
him were changing from affection (they'd never been more than
that) to indifference, and then—because you can't go on living with
someone for long in a state of complete indifference to him—from
indifference to positive dislike. But she hadn't been conscious of the
change. She just remembered now the moment of realization: sitting
opposite him one day, looking at him eating lemon meringue, and
suddenly thinking, without surprise, "I don't like you." From then
on, she had been aware of dislike intensifying into hatred, until now
the process had gone about as far as it could go.

She had disguised her feelings well, though. The creep still
thought she was crazy about him. And in spite of everything she
wanted to keep things that way. She certainly didn't want to split up.
He kept her in an extremely comfortable way of life. He was still attractive—and very charming. She was much envied locally—and
that was nice. His professional, charitable and social activities, too,
brought many contacts; without them there would be very few people she could invite to the house. Besides, divorce was so unpleasant
and, in their circle, still, even today, slightly shocking. No, it was far
better to put up with him, smiling through gritted teeth the while,
and maintain her local reputation and standing—not to mention his
income.

Though these days it was awfully hard going to keep up the
façade. She was certain that one day her nerve would snap, and
she'd scream and throw things at him. So far she'd managed to control herself. But sometimes only just.

CHAPTER 4

"Well, this is very nice," said Charles Inchcape.

He was sprawling back in a deep armchair in the sitting-room of *The Elms*. A cigarette in his mouth had liberally shed its ash on his shirt-front, and Sylvia was waiting in anguish for the moment Charles would rise and transfer it all to the carpet; he had already missed the ashtray twice with inaccurate flicks.

Charles was a large, ungainly, untidy man of about fifty-five with wispy grey hair and a round, pink-complexioned, good-natured face. The dark lounge suit which he wore (he knew that Edgar and Sylvia liked their dinner guests to maintain a certain degree of formality) was backed up by light brown suede shoes, old and with bald patches, green socks (odd, Edgar believed, though he didn't like to peer too closely), and a bright red knitted tie, crumpled and very narrow. A glass of brandy was in his hand. He had just enjoyed an excellent dinner and was feeling content; but then, he nearly always did. And, as he was the first to admit, he had no reason not to.

After war service in the RAF, Charles had had a brilliant academic career at Oxford, culminating in a double first. He had just been elected a Fellow of his college when he inherited a substantial fortune, together with a large country house on the north Devon coast, from his mother. A few months later he resigned his Fellowship, rented an elegant flat in central London, and settled down to spend the next twenty-five years making an enormous circle of friends, entertaining, travelling, collecting first editions and French impressionists (referred to always as his FEs and FIs), patronizing the arts in a way undreamt of by his great-grandfather, and writing an immensely long book, which no one had ever seen or even knew the theme of. He spent about four months of the year abroad and the other eight divided mostly between his London flat and his Devon house, *High Tors*, where he kept his collections and did most of his writing. The greater part of his time there was spent alone, apart from the Bruntons, the couple who looked after him, though two or three times a year he threw lavish house parties.

He looked now from Sylvia to Edgar, both of whom were sitting upright, very neat and spruce, and he chuckled.

"What's the matter?" Edgar asked—a trifle sharply. He'd been a little on edge the whole evening, and at that moment was in addition being obscurely irritated by the sudden realization that in the impossible event of *his* going out in odd socks, and the highly unlikely one of Charles noticing the fact, Charles would have said loudly, "Hey, me old chum, you've got odd socks on."

"Sorry," Charles said unapologetically. "I was just contemplating you two."

Edgar said, "And you find us amusing?"

"No offence, no offence. I find nearly everyone amusing, you know—myself most of all."

"And what do you find amusing about us?"

Charles tugged at his earlobe, seeming by the action to precipitate another shower of cigarette ash on to his tie. He flapped at it absently. "Well, amusing's not perhaps the right word for you two. It's just that you're too good to be true."

Sylvia looked pleased. "Us? Too good to be true? Why, Charles, how nice."

Edgar asked, "How do you mean exactly?"

"Dunno. You're just too perfect. Beautiful house, beautifully furnished; beautiful garden. Rover and Mini. Ed" (he was the only person ever to call Edgar this) "a successful professional man, and on the Council and the Bench and all that jazz. And you're both so elegant and good-looking and charming and popular. You're like something out of a colour supplement. I just feel there ought to be some flaws somewhere."

Edgar laughed cordially. He was annoyed with himself for the touch of asperity in his voice earlier. "Oh, there are many of those, Charles, I assure you," he said.

"Well, they're not obvious." He stubbed out his cigarette. Sylvia's relief was short-lived, for he immediately lit another.

"So you think the garden's looking nice, do you, Charles?" she asked.

"Super. Who wouldn't think so? Bit of a difference from mine at *High Tors.*"

"It's more grounds than garden at *High Tors,*" Edgar said.

"Yes, it needs a full-time man. That's the trouble—my bloke Pilger walked out and I can't get a replacement."

"Doesn't that cottage inside the gates go with the job?" Sylvia asked.

" 'Course it does. And I spent a fortune on that place—had it done up top to bottom, put a phone in, television, the lot. But can I get anyone? It's small, of course—only room for one comfortably—and it's lonely—wild bit of country, that—but all the same, you'd think there'd be fellows who wouldn't mind that. Know why Pilger packed it in? Scared of burglars."

Sylvia said, "Burglars? Who on earth would burgle a gardener's cottage?"

"His idea was that with all the valuables I've got up at the house, my FEs and FIs, and so on, somebody might try to break in there—as has been attempted in the past."

Edgar said, "But didn't you tell us once that you were virtually burglar-proof?"

"That sounds rather like tempting providence, though I'm certainly as secure as the best firm in the business can make me. But that was the point that worried Pilger. He thought that some thief who failed to break into *High Tors* could be so disgruntled he might have a go at the cottage as a consolation prize, or just out of spite. He had a sort of point, I suppose—it's the kind of thing thieves do. However, I drew the line at fitting a burglar alarm to the cottage too—which was what he wanted. But I'm waffling. I didn't call tonight to discuss the minor irritations of my life."

Sylvia said, "We were wondering what the very important thing is that you want to discuss."

Charles shifted in his chair. "I know. Actually, it's less discussion as having to tell you something. Now, I don't want to be a bore, but if I'm not to confuse you unconscionably I'm going to have to tell you rather a long story."

"Go ahead," said Edgar.

"Thanks. Difficult to know where to start, actually. Either of you heard of Horatio Dimsdale?"

Edgar shook his head. Sylvia, about to, suddenly paused. "Yes, I think I have. I don't know who mentioned him—Mother, or Aunt Maude, or somebody else but the name stuck in my mind at the time: wasn't he one of the celebrities who stayed here in Sidney's day?"

"You're not far out: actually he stayed at *The Firs,* with Silas and family. But he *was* one of their celebrities—though a celebrity in a very minor sort of way. I'm not surprised Edgar hasn't heard of him."

"What was he?" Edgar asked.

"A typical late Victorian all-rounder in the general field of culture and the Arts; dabbled in everything—composed music, painted, and tried his hand at every branch of literature: poetry, plays, essays, criticism. Most of his stuff's pretty bad. Fortunately he had money, so he didn't need to make his living at it. He did write a couple of quite decent novels, though. So he had talent, but obviously no concentration—spread his gifts too thinly."

He noticed the polite lack of interest on their faces. "Don't worry. I'm coming to the important part. About two months ago I received a letter from a firm of London solicitors, acting on behalf of the Horatio Dimsdale Trust, saying they understood that I was the owner of *The Firs,* near Cornfield, Wilts, and asking if I could confirm that that was the house, referred to by Horatio Dimsdale in his Journal, at which he had stayed as the guest of Mr. and Mrs. S. Inchcape in the year 1886. I wrote back, saying I had no knowledge of the exact year, but I was the great-grandson of Silas Inchcape, who built *The Firs,* and that I'd always known, from old family tradition, that Dimsdale had indeed stayed at the house in the late nineteenth century. Incidentally, I remembered afterwards that I had a photo somewhere, showing Dimsdale standing in the garden with Silas."

"Of course!" Sylvia said. "That's where I saw the name. Aunt Maude had a copy of that same photo. The name was written on it. They were posing in front of that big privet hedge that used to divide the gardens. But I thought the other man was *Sidney."*

"No—Dimsdale was one of Silas's captures. My grandfather told me all about those visitors they had when he was a boy. Don't forget Sidney and Silas were identical twins. Again, that photographer they always employed had very little imagination and used that hedge for almost all his backgrounds; one side of it looked much the same as the other. Then, of course, the families were in the habit of giving each other copies of every photo they had taken."

"Oh, I know," Sylvia said. "Aunt Maude must have had hundreds of them—family groups, individuals, couples, and scores of them with just Sidney or Silas with an eminent guest. As you say, they're nearly all standing in front of the hedge."

"I've *still* got hundreds," Charles said, "stuffed in a big cardboard box in the attic at *High Tors."*

"Yes, you showed it to me, years ago—said you were going to sort them all out soon."

Charles chuckled. "Needless to say, I never did. It's never been touched. I haven't seen that photo for years—but I'm sure Dimsdale's name isn't written on my copy, so I guess Silas wrote it on before he gave it to Sidney. Dimsdale was one of his more eminent guests, and he wanted to be sure Sidney got the point."

"Weren't there other people in the photo as well?"

"I don't think so."

"I seem to remember two others—one a woman, perhaps."

Charles frowned. "Maybe you're right. I don't really remember."

"Possibly I'm getting it mixed up with another one."

"You don't still have the photo?"

"I don't think so. I threw most of them away years ago—just kept a few of the immediate family."

"I see. Still, I'm digressing. Where was I? Oh yes. A few weeks after I'd answered the solicitors' letter, I received another one from them, saying that their clients, the Horatio Dimsdale Trust, were interested in the possibility of purchasing the property in question, and would I be prepared to consider selling it."

Sylvia drew her breath in sharply. "You told them no, of course."

"Well, not straight away. You see, the fact is that I often *have* considered getting rid of it."

Sylvia looked aghast. "Charles, you haven't!"

"My dear, who needs three homes? In fact, for a bachelor to have even two is pretty immoral, when you come to think of it. I've got a big, lonely country house and a flat in town. What man could want more?"

She stammered. "But—but you never *have* sold it, in all these years."

"I know. One reason is that property is probably the best investment there is; I knew the house could only increase in value, so I hung on to it. But in other circumstances I certainly would have let it go years ago. The only thing that held me back was knowing how you two felt about your privacy here. I've never really needed the rent it would bring in, so I salved my conscience about owning the place at all by letting it remain empty most of the year. But frankly, for twenty years it's been nothing but a liability—rates to pay, repairs to make—but no return. At one time that didn't matter. But unfortunately, I can't say that any more."

"Why is that, Charles?" Edgar asked quietly.

"Inflation, old boy. I've been hit."

"Who hasn't?"

"Agreed. Fact is, though, I'm a member of the despised and dwindling leisured class and I've been hit more than most."

"I'm sorry," Edgar said. "We've always thought that you were, um
. . ."

"Stinking rich? Well, I suppose I was, once. But not any more. Oh, I'm not on the breadline—far from it. But the situation has looked worrying enough to occupy my mind more than somewhat. I'm a selfish swine. I want to keep my FEs and FIs and *High Tors,* and my flat, and the Bruntons, and my travel and entertaining: but earlier this year I'd come to the conclusion that I wouldn't be able to much longer if I couldn't raise a really substantial sum pretty quickly. I spoke to Watkins, the estate agent in Cornfield, about *The Firs,* and asked him for an unofficial valuation. I was hoping he might say roughly thirty-five thousand. But he was extremely pessimistic—said houses like that were a glut on the market just now and I'd be very lucky to get thirty-five thousand for it. I was still pondering on what was the best thing to do when I had that second letter from the solicitors.

"What did you do?" Edgar asked.

"Told them I had no wish to sell *The Firs*—true—but that if their clients cared to make me an offer I'd be prepared to consider selling it. Anyway, to make a long story a bit less long, three members of the Trust arranged to come down and have a look over it. I tried to phone you then, to let you know what was happening, but there was no reply. I learnt later that you'd just gone away on holiday."

Edgar nodded. "Yes, we took ours earlier than usual this year."

"Well, anyway, you weren't here when they came down. I showed them over *The Firs,* waxing sentimental about how the house had been in my family since it was built, and how greatly attached I was to it, and so on. And they made the mistake of letting me see how very keen they were to get hold of the place—and also that they seemed to be not at all short of funds. As a result, when I received a letter a few days later making me a firm offer, I turned it down. They immediately increased the offer. I rejected it again—and again they upped it. By now I was very curious to see just how far they'd go. Guess."

Edgar looked blank. "What?"

"Guess how far?"

"I've no idea, Charles. Obviously at least to thirty-five thousand—probably a good bit more. Forty?"

"Sixty-five."

Edgar's eyes bulged. "You're—you're joking!"

"Never been more serious. I've got a written offer in my pocket from the solicitors. Here, you can see it, if you like." He took a bundle of papers from his pocket, selected one and passed it across.

Edgar unfolded it and read it dazedly. "It's—it's incredible, Charles. Who are these Dimsdale Trust people? Why do they want the house? And why on earth are they willing to give nearly double the market value for it? Are they mad?"

Charles nodded. "I'm afraid they are," he said.

Edgar gave a start.

"Oh, don't get me wrong. They're not certifiable or anything like that. They're just eccentric—and with far more money than sense. But they're perfectly genuine. I've checked up on them and on their solicitors—who are a highly reputable firm and I'm told certainly wouldn't handle any business that wasn't absolutely straight and above board."

"Then why?"

"Here's where I have to go back to Dimsdale himself. In middle age he developed a great interest in the whole theory and philosophy of the Arts: the origins of creative talent, the nature of genius, all that sort of thing. He lectured about it and wrote about it at exhaustive length. Most of it's sound stuff—dull, plodding, but perfectly conventional. Then you gradually find his ideas becoming rather eccentric. Soon they're neither dull nor conventional—and then suddenly he hits you with the theory of Conductorism."

"The theory of what?"

"Conductorism."

"What on earth is that?"

"You may well ask. To my mind it's absolutely bonkers."

"You mean Dimsdale was mad?"

"As far as this theory is concerned, I can't escape the conclusion. No doubt in every other respect he was quite normal. There was a biography of him, and there's no suggestion in that, or in his published Journal, that his behaviour was in any way odd. I certainly never heard there was anything strange about him when he stayed at *The Firs.*"

"Was that when he formulated this theory?"

"Yes. Though he didn't work out all the details or coin the word until later."

"Yes, but what is Conductorism? Something to do with music, presumably."

"Not exclusively music—oh, I see what you mean. No, it's nothing at all to do with chaps waving batons in front of orchestras. Basically, and very briefly, it's an extension of the idea of the creative artist being inspired. The Greeks, of course, had the concept of the Muses, and we talk today of a poet, say, or a composer, 'working like a man possessed.' Many artists have talked of producing work almost automatically, without conscious effort—of words, or notes, just pouring out of them, or of a painter's hand being controlled. I don't know the explanation, and I don't think anybody does."

"But Dimsdale thought he did?"

"Precisely. The answer seems to have come to him in a flash while he was staying next door. His theory was that no great artist ever actually creates anything himself. He merely acts as a sort of conductor for works which are already in existence."

"In existence where?" Edgar asked.

"Somewhere else in the Universe—in some other dimension or parallel cosmos—somewhere out there." Charles made an expansive gesture with his arm. "Or if you like, right here in this room, but out of sight. I can't explain these metaphysical things, but somewhere there are infinite numbers of poems and symphonies and so on, just floating about waiting to be—well, transcribed. The great poet, say, is a man with a special ability to act as a sort of poetry conductor— like a lightning conductor. He can, as it were, reach out, and some passing poem will attach itself to him and flow through him, and he's simply got to perform the mechanical act of writing it down. Though mostly he doesn't realize this and thinks he's creating it himself."

Edgar said, "But that's insane!"

"I told you it was. But in a small way it did catch on. Naturally, it wasn't popular with real creative people, who didn't like being reduced to mere stenographers. But it was a fine excuse for the unsuccessful ones. If you weren't as good a poet as Swinburne, it was simply that you were not lucky enough to have the conductive gift. For a while Horatio gathered quite a little following around him. I've always been mildly interested in Dimsdale—largely through hearing my grandfather speak of him—and I read a lot of his stuff years ago. I wrote off Conductorism, of course, and I always imagined that the theory had died with him. What I didn't know until recently was that all these years he has had his serious disciples."

"You mean, people who actually believe in Conductorism—don't just admire his other work?"

"Exactly. They even exist in America. In fact, it seems that in California he's beginning to become quite a minor cult figure."

"Good lord! And this Trust wants to buy *The Firs* because that was where Conductorism was born?"

"There's a bit more to it than that, but basically, yes."

"You mean they want to turn it into a museum, or something?"

"I'm afraid not. If that was all there was to it, I wouldn't be feeling so guilty about all this now. No, the idea is to turn the house into a centre for the study and practice of Conductorism."

Since Charles had first mentioned the possibility of his selling *The Firs,* Sylvia had spoken only once and hadn't moved at all. A sort of numbness had seemed to descend on her. She might have just been put into an instantaneous hypnotic trance. Her face had set into a

waxwork-like expression of polite attention. It was a face she tended
to use at social functions, when she wanted to leave her mind free to
work without displaying any emotion. To Edgar she always looked
an idiot. He hated the expression and avoided looking at her when
she was wearing it. By paying close attention to Charles during the
previous few minutes, he had not only avoided letting his own eyes
fall on her for more than a second, but had diverted Charles from
looking at her too. Now, however, she spoke again, in a careful,
controlled way, without altering her expression, as if her face was
made of porcelain, and she had to avoid breaking it.

"A—centre—you—say?"

Charles looked at her and for a moment was startled by the
blankness of her expression. He hesitated. "I'm afraid if you're
going to make sense of this, I'm going to have to talk a bit more
about the theory."

He got to his feet suddenly and stood making little gestures with
his hands as he groped for words. "It's all so weird that it's terribly
difficult to explain. I'm not at all sure I understand it myself, and
even what I do understand I'm going to have to simplify absurdly if
I'm going to get it across. However, it seems Horatio believed that
there were certain locations from which this other world was particularly accessible—where the barrier between the worlds is thin—
and that if by chance some people who had this gift in a small degree happened to be together in such a location, they could develop
a sort of group power to tap this other world—a power which would
be greater than the sum of its parts. (This would apply even though
they didn't act consciously as a group.) Consequently, they could
get through more easily. He thought this was the reason for great
outpourings of great creative work at certain places and times, various schools of literature or art. The Italian renaissance is his
supreme example, but he gives many others. The nub of the theory,
though, is that if a group of people who might have the gift slightly
deliberately came together at one of these locations, and consciously
and systematically attempted to tap this other dimension—well, then
they might succeed in starting another renaissance. Now—and this is
the crucial factor from our viewpoint—the basic idea struck him
while he was actually staying at *The Firs*. He was convinced it came
as a direct revelation from the other dimension—and he later became convinced also that the house itself was partly to thank. He
writes in his Journal later about the remarkable atmosphere of the
place and of feeling inspired the whole time he was there."

Edgar said, "And you mean these people want to use *The Firs* as
a place for their experiments?"

"That's it. The idea is to bring together ten or a dozen people who will then act in unison to try and break through to all the great art that's floating around out there."

"But how will they try to break through, for heaven's sake?"

"I just don't know, Ed. Horatio left no precise directions on that point. Concentration or meditation or hypnotism. Perhaps rituals or ceremonies of some kind."

"But why *just The Firs?* I mean, the Italian renaissance didn't take place in one house."

"As far as I can make out, Dimsdale thought it may actually have *started* in one house! But it seems that individual buildings are very important. As I understood it, the idea is that the barrier may be narrower over a whole area, but that in one precise point—mostly indoors—it is narrowest of all, and that's the point you've got to start your tapping. It's like a hole in a dyke: once you've broken through at the weakest spot the water will first start to trickle through. But then the hole will get bigger and bigger and more and more water will gush out until you've got a torrent. Eventually, of course, it will dry up, and you'll never get an outpouring at that point again. But that might take a hundred years or more, and I think, before that happens, the Trust visualize the whole of Cornfield, the whole of Wiltshire, becoming a sort of cultural oasis as a result of what they do here. It was, though, at *The Firs* that the Master received his revelation. They have his word that it is an especially propitious spot, so that's where they must start."

"But suppose you'd turned down their offer? Would they have scrapped the whole thing?"

"No, there are a few other locations that Dimsdale mentions as having inspirational value. But *The Firs* is far and away their Number One choice."

Edgar shook his head in bafflement. "Who are these lunatics, anyway? Who's going to pay for all this?"

"A couple of very rich old maids, who met Dimsdale when he was an old man and they were young girls, and who've been disciples ever since. They got together with a lot of other admirers and eventually the Trust was set up, with a Board that includes a representative of the old girls' bank, some University of London professor, a psychologist, and a couple of actual authors or painters. It may be nutty, but it's all highly respectable and deadly serious."

"And these are the people who'll be doing the experiments?"

"Oh no—they'd be no good."

"Why not?"

"For the theory to be proved, the experiments will have to be done by people who *want* to produce great works, who have tried to do so—but have failed. So the Trust are only interested in *unsuccessful* writers and painters and so on. What they intend to do is bring group after group of failed dramatists, say, for a couple of months at a time, in the hope that eventually another *Hamlet* or *Cherry Orchard* will be produced. Later they'll go on to novelists, poets, composers, painters, sculptors, or anything else you can think of."

"And they'll give these people free accommodation?"

"Oh yes."

"How are they going to get hold of them?"

"Advertise—all over the world."

"Advertise for unsuccessful poets, and so on?"

"That's right."

"But they'll be inundated with applications—from cranks, confidence tricksters, people who just want a month's free board and lodging."

"I'm sure they will—at least in the beginning. They'll probably learn to sort the sheep from the goats in time."

"It's utterly insane!"

"I know. The press and TV people are going to have a field day when they hear about it. I'm afraid they'll be here in force."

Charles paused, as if waiting for Sylvia or Edgar to say something. But neither of them did. He sat down again and said quietly, "Well, that's it. The next-door neighbours with whom I'm proposing to saddle you will be a constantly changing, multi-racial, mixed-sex crowd of hippies, hoboes, weirdos and freeloaders. By your standards many of them will be dirty, scruffy, immoral and noisy. They won't generally be well-mannered. No doubt there'll be a lot of drinking, jazz music, and altogether way-out behaviour. I'm extremely sorry to do this to you, but I just cannot afford to turn down sixty-five thousand pounds. If you want to throw things at me, now's the time to do it."

He glanced from one to the other, trying to gauge their reactions. Edgar was just looking bemused. But Sylvia's mask had at last broken. It was as if the full ghastly horror of the situation had finally put too great a strain on the porcelain façade. Her face was anguished, stricken, like a woman who has just received a death sentence. It frightened Charles somewhat. Hastily he said,

"Of course, I've deliberately painted the picture as black as I can, so there'll be no misunderstandings. However, they may not be quite as bad as I've made out. These people will probably be friendly, easy-going, helpful—even fun, if you accept them on their own terms."

His eyes still fixed on Sylvia's face, he paused, then added, "But I see I'm not cheering you up much. So I'd better say quickly that there's no need for you to despair yet. You may be able to avoid the situation."

Edgar said sharply, "Avoid? Just what do you mean, Charles?"

"Well, there are two possible courses of action you could take. Firstly, I haven't sold the house yet. I've made no agreement, verbal or written."

Sylvia jerked her head round and stared at him with an intensity that momentarily distracted him. "You—you mean you may not?"

"I've explained my financial position, my dear. But before I accept the Trust's offer, I think it's only fair that I give you an opportunity to purchase the place yourselves."

Sylvia's eyes gave an odd sort of flicker. She opened her mouth to speak, but before she could do so Edgar said, "For sixty-five thousand pounds?"

"No; I'd be willing to drop a bit."

"Why?"

Charles shrugged. "Family solidarity. Guilt offering."

"How much would you drop?" Sylvia asked.

"Five thousand, say."

Edgar said, "But good lord, Charles, we'd still be paying around twenty-five thousand more than the market value."

"I know that, old boy. I thought you might just think it worth while. I'm sorry I can't drop more, but five thousand is about my limit, I'm afraid. It's just a gesture, really."

"Appreciate it, I'm sure," Edgar said, stressing the words just enough to reverse their meaning. "And what's our second possible course of action?"

Charles smiled. "Hang on to your hats, children. I've kept the biggest bombshell till last."

They stared at him, Sylvia holding her breath.

"The Trust are willing to buy this house, too," Charles said, "—and for the same price as *The Firs.*"

Edgar seemed to rise about three inches from his chair. He gaped and for several seconds appeared to have difficulty in speaking. Then he managed to get out: "Six—"

"Sixty-five thousand pounds—that's right."

Edgar had gone white. "But—but they've never seen the place!"

"Not the inside, no; but I've assured them that it's very similar to *The Firs* and that it's in first-class condition. Naturally, the offer is dependent on a satisfactory surveyor's report, and I took the liberty of letting them examine the outside and look round your garden when they came to see over *The Firs*. They liked everything very much. You would have had a letter from the solicitors by now, except that I asked them to let me make the first approach on their behalf. I wanted to fill you in and prepare you. They'll be in touch with you immediately after their next meeting, if I tell them you're willing to talk turkey. You can take my word that they're dead serious and very keen."

"But what on earth do they want it for?" Edgar still seemed in a sort of daze.

"Extra accommodation. The two old maids want to live here, so as to be on hand to observe the experiments. Then there's to be a full-time Warden or Director—the domestic staff, a secretary, and visitors. If you turn them down—not, of course, that they expect you to—they'll look for another house in the Cornfield area though nothing could be so handy to *The Firs* as this one—"

Then he noticed that both Edgar and Sylvia had obviously stopped listening. He broke off, looked at his watch, and got to his feet.

"Well, I fancy I've given you enough earth-shattering pieces of news for one evening. I'll leave you now to mull them over. You've got seven weeks to decide what you want to do, so don't panic. Many thanks for a delightful meal—and again my sincere apologies for subjecting you to this upheaval."

"Oh—that's all right." Edgar spoke rather jerkily.

Sylvia said flatly, "Thank you for coming."

They went out with him to the hall. In the porch he turned. "For the next day or two I'll be going through the house, deciding what to do with everything, so if there's anything else you want to know, I'll be on hand. Good night."

He started to leave, then turned back a second time. "By the way, it may be I've been thoroughly unfair to old Horatio and to the Trust. Conductorism is a remarkably complex and subtle theory, and maybe it's just too clever for me. After all, serious physicists talk about the possibility of disappearing through a black hole in space into another universe, there's the German *doppelgänger* theory, which has had many respectable adherents; and cleverer men than I have believed in the spirit world. Maybe Conductorism isn't any more way-out than some of these ideas. So because I've been taking the mickey out of these people there's no need for you to write them off as complete fools. One day they may be laughing at me. Perhaps all these years I should have been writing my book next door, rather than at *High Tors*. 'Night."

CHAPTER 5

"But, darling—sixty-five thousand pounds! It's a fantastic offer!"

"Darling, you know perfectly well I'd never consider selling this house."

"Not normally, of course—but sixty-five thousand pounds! It's the opportunity of a lifetime."

"Not for a hundred thousand! Not for five hundred thousand! *The Elms* is mine."

Edgar stared at her, intense, brain-bursting exasperation welling up inside him, as it had been doing so frequently for so many years. He longed to smash his fist into that stupid, stubborn, self-satisfied face. He was often scared that one day he might actually do it.

They were at breakfast on Monday morning. Neither of them had felt able to talk after Charles had left the previous evening, and this was the first time they'd discussed his news.

By a pure effort of will that became harder to make each time, Edgar battened down his temper, gave a resigned smile, shrugged, and said, "Well, of course, my dear, you know I'd never try to press you."

She gave his hand a squeeze, restraining the shudder that touching him was always on the brink of inducing in her these days. "I know you wouldn't, Edgar, and I do appreciate it. I realize this house doesn't mean as much to you as it does to me. But you are fond of it, aren't you?"

"Of course I am. But I don't want to live next door to these dreadful people."

"Well, naturally, neither do I. And I have no intention of doing anything of the kind."

"But what's the alternative?"

"We've got to think how best to raise that sixty thousand, of course."

He gasped, "But, Sylvia, it's out of the question!"

She stared. "Why?"

"I can't raise sixty thousand pounds!"

"But a mortgage—we've got this house for security . . ."

"Nobody would loan us sixty thousand on *The Elms:* we'd only get the market value. We'd still be at least twenty-five thousand short. We'd have to apply for a second mortgage—on *The Firs* itself —for that. And I don't think for a moment we'd get a second one on my income. Think of the repayments on sixty thousand worth of mortgages—and the amount of interest!"

She said nothing and he hastened to ram home his advantage. "Besides, what would we do with the place? Just keep it empty?"

"Oh, that's something we could decide later. Perhaps we could find some nice elderly couple we might let it to, if absolutely necessary."

"Darling, can you imagine any elderly couple wanting to rent a place that size? No, Sylvia, you must forget it. I'd love to buy you *The Firs,* I really would, but it's just not on."

Sylvia felt an almost irresistible urge to snatch up the pot of scalding coffee from the table and hurl it into his unbearably complacent and self-confident face. One day, she was sure, she would. But she must resist now. She took a firm grip on herself and let the eagerness die out of her expression to be replaced by a wry, slightly sad smile.

"I see. I suppose you're right, darling. You usually are."

"Far from usually, my dear. But I am in the present case."

"So—what *do* we do? You said yourself you don't want to live next door to these people."

"I did. And at the moment I just can't think of an answer. It seems an impasse. However, a way out may occur to one of us at any moment. All we can do for now, I think, is put our minds to work. Charles said we don't have to decide anything immediately. So let's just both work on the problem quietly for a few weeks, eh, and see if either of us comes up with a brainwave?"

"All right, darling, I suppose that is best. And thank you for being so nice about it."

Edgar kissed her.

Sixty-five thousand. Throughout Monday and most of Tuesday the figures filled Edgar's mind to the exclusion of almost everything else. He did his work like an automaton, thinking, thinking, thinking of just what he could do with that money. On Tuesday afternoon he was brought back to his senses by finding himself assuring the Commissioners of Inland Revenue (in the course of dictating a stiff letter) that his client could prove beyond question that he had spent sixty-five thousand pounds on business lunches during the previous financial year; and it was shortly after this that the Great Idea came to him.

At the time he was in the middle of his interview with Mr. Whittal, who had been complaining about some difficulty in raising a bank loan. Edgar was trying to reassure him.

"Oh, I'm sure I can . . . murder her," he said.

Fortunately, Whittal was a little deaf. "I beg your pardon?"

"I—er, said I'm sure I can murmur a few persuasive words to your bank manager," Edgar said hurriedly.

But his heart was racing and he could hardly get through the rest of the interview. "Don't disturb me under any circumstances, Beryl," he said when Whittal had departed. Then he sat at his desk, staring unseeingly at his blotter.

Well, why not? It would solve everything. *The Elms* would become his automatically—it wasn't entailed or anything like that. He'd be rid of the foul woman and her miserable house for ever.

And then he'd have sixty-five thousand pounds to do with what he liked. No—more. He was forgetting the contents of the house, not to mention her jewellery and furs and things.

It was perfect—if he could only find the nerve. Could he? He thought he could. Yes—he was *sure* he could. In fact—in fact, it would be a pleasure.

Naturally, he would have to be very, very careful. They always suspected the husband first, particularly when there were large sums of money involved. What luck that he'd never let her know what he really thought of her. She still believed he loved her. And if *she* believed that, then certainly everybody else did.

But it was vital that nobody should get the idea in advance that he wanted to sell at *this* time. Had he given Charles that impression? If so, he must correct it—convince Charles that he loved the house and was determined to remain there. However, after Sylvia's death things, naturally, would be very different. What more natural than that a man would want to dispose of a home, in which he'd spent over twenty blissful years, immediately after the demise of his beloved wife?

All the same, not the faintest shadow of suspicion could be allowed to fall on him. He would need an extremely clever plan. But, of course, he was undoubtedly far cleverer than the average murderer. And his training had given him the right sort of mind; analytical, dispassionate, able to spot discrepancies, to examine facts without being distracted by frills, to weigh up and balance.

Yes, he was the ideal man to murder his wife.

And Sylvia was the ideal wife to be murdered.

Edgar called in at *The Firs* on his way home that evening. Charles came to the door in his shirt-sleeves, looking hot and grubby.

"Hullo, old boy. I was just wishing somebody'd drop in—give me an excuse to stop work. Come on in and have a drink."

They went into the drawing-room and Edgar sat down while Charles got busy with bottles and glasses at the sideboard. "How's it going?" Edgar asked.

"Oh, slowly. I'd forgotten how much stuff there is here. I was hoping to complete it today, but I'll have to go home and come back to finish off next week before I go abroad."

"Oh, you off again? Where?"

"North Africa." He handed Edgar a glass.

"For how long?"

"About a month. Then I'm toddling down to *High Tors* to spend a monastic autumn working on my book. As for the furniture here, though, I think I'll leave most of it for the Trust to do what they like with—just take a few pieces down to *High Tors*. But, of course, I hope you and Sylvia will pick out anything you particularly fancy." He sat down.

"That's very nice of you, Charles, but we might want to leave it all here."

"Leave it all here? How do you mean?"

"Well, I'm considering taking up your offer to sell us this place for sixty thousand."

Charles stopped dead, his glass halfway to his lips. "You serious?"

"Yes—though not finally committed. Surprised?"

"Very. I got the distinct impression Sunday night that you thought it would be a real pig in a poke."

"I'm sorry if I gave you that idea—or if I appeared ungrateful at your generosity at offering to drop five thousand. It did all rather come as a bolt from the blue and I didn't really have time to collect my thoughts."

"Yes, I can appreciate that." Charles sipped thoughtfully.

"On consideration, though, I think it might be quite a good investment—even at sixty thousand," Edgar continued. "If prices go on rising as they have been, it may well have a market value of sixty thousand in a few years' time, so we wouldn't really be out of pocket at all."

"But what would you do with it?"

"I'm not sure—probably let it. Perhaps convert it into four or five flats for elderly couples—of the right sort."

"I see. Sylvia's very much in favour of the scheme, I suppose?"

It was clear that he believed the whole idea was hers. Edgar shook his head. "Not really. In fact, at the moment she's leaning slightly towards selling out to the Trust."

Charles looked at him sharply. "Indeed? You do surprise me. I always thought she was really in love with the house."

"I wouldn't say that. She's very fond of it, of course—and very much torn; but I think she'll come round to my way of thinking eventually. In fact, Charles, I'd be obliged if you wouldn't mention to her what I've said to you. *The Elms* is her house, after all—and the final decision must be entirely hers, without any pressure from me. I'd hate her to think I'd been making plans in advance—as though the whole thing were cut and dried."

"I understand."

"Thanks. I'm only telling you this so that, after our reaction on Sunday evening, you don't misconstrue our position and accept the Trust's offer straight away."

"Oh, there's no danger of that. As I explained, we all have seven weeks' grace."

"That's definite, is it?"

"Quite definite. The board members will all be holidaying in different parts of the world until the end of August. They're not meeting again until the first week in September. I promised them a firm answer then, and that I'd let you know the deadline too."

"I see—fine." He paused, then added casually, "So, if by any chance, Sylvia doesn't change her mind and wants to sell out to them after all, there's no possibility of their making an offer for some other property before then?"

"None whatsoever."

"And these solicitors aren't expecting some immediate reaction from us?"

"No. I'll write and tell them I've passed on their message to you— but, of course, you can get in touch with them yourself if you like."

"Yes, I think I will—just to acknowledge the offer. It'll be only polite—and one does like to do the correct thing."

"One does," said Charles.

Sixty thousand pounds. Throughout Monday and Tuesday Sylvia was obsessed with the thought of this sum. She went about oblivious to her surroundings, hardly noticing a strange preoccupation in Edgar's manner.

She had to get the money. She had to. Because she couldn't let her life be ruined like this. But how? How? How?

The idea of killing him didn't come to her with the same blinding flash as the idea of murdering her had come to him. It dawned on her quite calmly, and her first reaction was how stupid she was not to have thought of it before. It was so obvious.

There followed no wrestling with her conscience. Within minutes of getting the idea, she knew she was going to do it. Her second reaction was what a mercy it was that she'd never asked him for a divorce. If she had, there'd be no insurance now.

Insurance. Lovely word. What luck he'd insisted on taking out such a big one all those years ago.

One hundred thousand pounds . . .

His life assurance policy was, in fact, a source of constant irritation to Edgar. The thought that if he did die before her the creature would come into a hundred thousand, had for years annoyed him intensely. But there was nothing he could do about it. He'd taken it out years before, during the period when he'd been trying to convince himself he still loved her as much as ever. He'd kept buying her expensive presents—gestures to himself more than to her—and the insurance policy had been just another of these—though by far the most extravagant of them. The premium was much greater than he could afford.

But by the time he'd stopped trying to fool himself about his marriage, it had been too late to discontinue the policy. Apart from having to explain to her why the premiums had disappeared from their bank statements (which she always studied like an art expert verifying a Rembrandt), the broker through whom he'd taken out the policy was both a business friend and a bit of a gossip. If the policy lapsed, the news—together with the general assumption that he couldn't afford to keep up the premiums—would have been all over the small and tightly-knit Cornfield business community in days. By now, he would have been delighted to leave Sylvia penniless. It would almost be worth dying for. But with every year that passed, it had become more impossible to let the policy lapse. So he paid up grimly, his only consolation being that the premiums were at least met by standing order, so he didn't have to keep writing cheques all the time.

To her surprise, Sylvia began to find herself developing feelings of gratitude to Edgar—gratitude partly for his having taken out the policy in the first place, but partly for his being so hateful: if he were a nice person, she wouldn't be able to kill him—or, at least, not so happily, not with such a clear conscience.

Perhaps "happily" was not the right word, though. For the prospect, though in one way very pleasant, was also rather daunting. She realized she was going to have constantly to boost her courage by thoughts of what life would be like afterwards: *The Elms* AND *The Firs* completely to herself, with forty thousand pounds (plus whatever she could get for the sale of the business) to live on. Bliss.

If she got away with it. For she must face the possibility of being caught. This was a risk, though, that had to be taken. Because if she didn't get the money, life wouldn't be worth living anyway. However, if she used her brain, and took every conceivable precaution, she ought to be all right.

And the first precaution must be to make absolutely sure Edgar suspected nothing in advance. She would have to be very nice to him from now on. That would be difficult, because she was always so nice to him anyway. She would, also, have to be extremely careful not to drop the smallest hint of having, at this stage, plans for spending sixty thousand pounds. Nobody must know she wanted to buy *The Firs*. It must later appear to have been a decision made only after Edgar's death. A memorial to him. That was it—a grief-stricken widow, determined to preserve unchanged an area her husband had deeply loved . . .

Now—on Sunday evening, had she displayed too much interest in Charles's offer to sell them *The Firs?* If so, she must undo that impression of interest—make Charles believe that she had not the least intention of buying. And the best way to do that would be to convince him that, on the contrary, she had made up her mind to sell *The Elms*.

Charles was having his morning coffee when Sylvia's ring came at the door. He let her in and offered her a cup, which she refused.

"Finished your sorting out, Charles?" she asked.

"Far from it, my dear. But as you know I don't believe in wearing myself out. I'm off back to London this afternoon. But I'll be down again shortly—though probably not to stay overnight."

"So Edgar said. He mentioned that he dropped in here for a drink yesterday—and that you offered us a choice of some furniture."

"That's right."

"It's very kind of you, Charles, and I do appreciate it. But honestly, if we're moving from *The Elms*, we'll almost certainly take a rather smaller place and I doubt very much if we'll have the space.

Perhaps I could choose just one or two very small pieces—as mementos."

He looked at her curiously. "That's settled, is it? You will be selling out?"

"Well, I'm sure it's the best thing to do. Trouble is, Edgar loves it here so much. At present he wants to stay. I'd *like* to, of course. But I can see it's not going to be pleasant with this weird gang moving in; and buying this place from you—handsome though your offer is —would be quite impracticable. I think Edgar will come round to my way of thinking shortly. Don't tell him I said so, though, will you? Legally, *The Elms* is mine. But I want the decision to move to be his own."

"I quite understand," Charles said.

"You did say we have seven weeks before we need to let them know, didn't you?"

"That's right." He repeated what he had told Edgar the previous day.

She nodded. "Good. I just wanted to make sure there was no chance of them buying another place in the interim." She hesitated. "And, of course, that means you won't be completing the sale of *this* house to them before September, either, doesn't it?"

"It does. But that won't affect you, will it?"

"No, of course not," she said hastily. "I was just thinking aloud."

"A dangerous habit, my dear."

She gave the slightest of starts. "What do you mean?"

"Oh, nothing in particular. Just that it can be advisable to keep your thoughts to yourself."

CHAPTER 6

How to do it?

It was really much harder to decide than Sylvia had first anticipated. There were so many snags. Ideally, she would like it to happen when he was far away from her. A road accident would be perfect—if only she knew how to sabotage the car. So often in films
and on television she'd seen men reaching into an engine or under a
car and fiddling about. Then, later, just as the victim started to go
downhill the brakes failed . . . But even if she knew what to do
there were no steep hills near, and Edgar always drove so cautiously
since he'd been made a JP that he'd probably have no difficulty in
simply coasting to a sedate halt. Besides, it would really be a shame
to wreck the Rover. It was such a pretty car, and she'd hardly ever
had a chance to drive it flat out.

What about poisoning? She liked the idea of this very much.
Poison was always reputed to be a woman's weapon, and she supposed it was because she was such a very feminine person that the
thought of it had such appeal. The almost insurmountable problem
here, however, was that she and Edgar lived together; she did all the
cooking; and if Edgar was poisoned and she weren't she was sure to
be suspected; people had such nasty minds. She'd heard of murderers poisoning themselves, just a little, as a blind. But she wasn't
going to risk that. Of course, there were the sort of poisoning inci-
dents in which a person swallowed something by mistake, or took an
overdose of medicine. But no one would believe that of Edgar; he
was so infuriatingly careful about such things.

A fire? No—positively not at *The Elms*. It might get out of control. Electrocution? There again you needed technical knowledge.
Drowning? Edgar didn't swim, and there were no lakes or rivers
nearby where he was in the habit of walking and might fall in. Of
course, people did drown in their baths, but they had to be held
down; and while she thought she'd quite enjoy holding Edgar down,
it would be awfully risky. Falling? That was a possibility. But to be
certain of killing him, it would have to be a really long fall, not just

a tumble downstairs, say. Supposing, though, that she did take a risk and managed to manoeuvre him to the edge of a cliff (highly difficult in itself), and then gave him a push? The same snag would apply as with some of the other methods: he was such an unlikely person to fall over, that the local police, who knew him well, would surely never believe it was an accident.

Oh dear, who would think it could be such a problem? People were getting killed every day, by the thousand, and yet it seemed absolutely impossible to arrange for Edgar to be one of them. Why did he have to be such a revoltingly cautious person? He actually deserved to be murdered for taking such care of his precious skin. He really was a perfect murderee—the sort of man who in books and films was always getting murdered. A professional man, an accountant, with access to company books, having the opportunity to expose fraud—and in addition a JP, who'd sat on the Bench and sentenced people to prison—people who might later come out seeking revenge. In short, he was the sort of person whom men were actually paid to eliminate.

Sylvia's mental train pulled up with a jolt. A hit man. Did such people exist in Britain? She knew they did in America, she'd seen them many times in films on TV. Cold-eyed men. They carried rifles in sections in suitcases, and they went up into high buildings and fired down to the street as their victims came out of doors. Professional killers. There must be such people in England too. Could she possibly find one?

Of course, his death wouldn't then be taken as an accident. It would be plain murder. On the other hand, surely nobody would suspect her of having hired the killer. Wives didn't do that sort of thing—at least, not in England. They poisoned their husbands or stabbed them with carving knives. No, a professional killing was far more likely to be arranged by some crooked business man Edgar was in a position to expose, or by someone he'd sent to prison.

She wondered how much it would cost. She'd seen a film on TV recently in which a hit man had been paid ten thousand dollars. That was about five thousand pounds. An awful lot of money . . . But perhaps charges were lower in this country. The maddening thing was that there was no way of finding out. She wouldn't know if she was being overcharged. She doubted if she'd have any chance to shop around. Anyway, she certainly didn't fancy the idea of trying to beat the man down, as she would an antique dealer. The only answer was to decide how much the job was worth to her, and resolve to spend not a penny more.

Five thousand pounds. That would be it. She knew, though, that she'd be furious with herself if she ever discovered she could have got it done cheaper.

She supposed the man would be willing to wait for the insurance money to come through. Well, he'd have to—she'd make that clear from the start.

Now—where to find a good man?

London, obviously. Soho? Wasn't it in the pubs and clubs there that all the crooks gathered? Yes, Soho would be the place.

It took Sylvia two days to reach this stage in her planning, and two more to steel herself to take the first step. But by Sunday she was ready.

"Darling," she said, while they were drinking their after-lunch coffee, "I thought I might drive up to town tomorrow, if you don't mind."

He gave a slight start, as though he had forgotten she was present. Strange, he'd seemed rather withdrawn and preoccupied for a day or two. He was sitting now with the *Sunday Telegraph* crossword on his knee, but he hadn't done any of it. She wondered if he had any business worry. If so, it was fortunate, as he'd be less likely to notice if her behaviour was different from usual—and she'd be a miracle woman if it wasn't.

He blinked at her, as if trying to take in what she was saying. Then his face changed. For a moment it seemed to her that he was pleased by her words. The next second the impression was gone, and she decided she had imagined it.

He raised his eyebrows and gave her the quizzical smile which he believed was one of his most charming and attractive mannerisms. She always thought he looked like a secret police chief contemplating a new form of torture.

"Mind, darling?" he said. "Of course not. Why should I?"

"Well, you'll have to make your own arrangements for lunch and dinner."

"Oh, don't worry about that. I'm playing golf, and I'll dine at the club. Any particular reason for the trip, though?"

"There's a sale on I'm interested in."

"My word—quite like the old days, when you were gallivanting off to auctions every week. You haven't been to one for a long time now."

"That's true, but as you know, I've been looking for a dressing table for the third bedroom for ages, and I hear there's just the thing coming up tomorrow."

"Fine. You don't get away from this place enough. Go and enjoy yourself."

"I'm sure I shall, dear."

She went away, and Edgar sat quite still, his heart beating fast. He could hardly believe his good luck. She was playing right into his hands—actually driving to London, along the M4, the very next day, just after he'd decided on this scheme. It was positively providential . . .

That night he told her he had some paperwork to get through, and he stayed up after she'd gone to bed. Actually, he did no work, merely sat in his study, waiting and visualizing her going through all the boring routine with which he was so horribly familiar—brushing her hair a hundred times, smearing muck on her face, and so on. He waited until he thought she'd be asleep, then went out to the hall. Just to be on the safe side, he crept up the stairs until he could see that no light was showing under their bedroom door, went down again, fetched a torch, and quietly left the house. Not that it would matter greatly if she did hear him. If she mentioned it tomorrow, he'd only have to tell her that he'd needed some papers which he'd left in the car.

He walked across to the garage, opened the door and went in. He always carried a key to the Mini, as she did to the Rover, and with it he opened the boot. He took out a wheelbrace and went to the front. With his penknife, bending and then breaking the blade in the process, he at last managed to get the hubcap off the right wheel. Then he loosened the four wheel nuts. It was difficult to judge how far to unscrew them. He didn't want the wheel to come off too soon—while she was still on the road to Cornfield, say, and not going very fast. That wouldn't do at all. On the other hand, if he didn't loosen them enough, the wheel might not ever come off. In the end, he could only hope that he'd got it right. He replaced the hubcap, put the wheelbrace back in the boot of the car, locked it, picked up the torch and left the garage, locking the door after him. Then he went back indoors.

It was done! He felt exhilarated. This sort of thing was remarkably stimulating. He went to the kitchen and washed his hands carefully at the sink, before returning to his study and pouring himself a celebratory whisky and soda.

Would it work? It was, he knew, a hit-and-miss way of attempting murder. But he had to try this method first. Because for Sylvia to be killed in a car crash would cause far less surprise than if she died by any other means: she was a notoriously reckless driver—she'd picked up several endorsements in her younger days, once only narrowly escaping disqualification—and always refused point blank to wear a seat belt. About five miles the other side of Cornfield she would join the M4, which would take her all the way to London. She certainly wouldn't be doing less than seventy from then on, and probably considerably more. And to lose a front wheel at that speed on the motorway . . . It was a beautiful thought.

Another favourable factor was that on long stretches of this motorway there was no central barrier. So with a bit of luck, she might even cross right over into the westbound lane and meet another vehicle head on. There'd be no chance of getting alive out of that! But he mustn't be greedy and bank on this. An ordinary overturn would do fine.

Of course, the danger was that she wouldn't be killed, merely seriously injured—and would be in hospital until the Trust's deadline was passed. But unless he killed her with his bare hands, that would be a risk with almost any method.

On the credit side, too, was the fact that it was the *only* risk. For he could never be suspected. Sylvia had had a new set of tyres fitted to her car less than two weeks ago. Since then she had only pottered around in it. So the blame for the loose nuts would fall on Hillier's, the garage in Cornfield who did all their work. Afterwards, he would accuse them of criminal negligence. He might even sue them! Edgar chuckled. What a delicious idea. How much would he get for the loss of a loving wife?

He finished his drink, turned out the lights and went upstairs. Sylvia was sleeping like a log when he entered the bedroom. He undressed quietly and was pulling back the sheets, thinking with pleasure that, given ordinary luck, this would be the last time he'd ever have to sleep with her, when she stirred.

"Edgar?" she murmured.

"Yes, darling. Sorry to wake you."

"That's all right. Haven't you been an awfully long time?"

"I'm afraid so. But it was something that just had to be done."

"You work too hard, dear. Good night."

"Good night, darling." He bent over and kissed her.

That night they both had exceptionally pleasant dreams.

CHAPTER 7

Sylvia felt only very slightly nervous the following morning. It wasn't an altogether unpleasant nervousness, either—more like the feeling before an important date in her teens, than the apprehension she might feel before a visit to the doctor. Moreover, it was another glorious day. She set off at about nine, and by the time she'd reached Cornfield, she was humming to herself.

Then suddenly she felt the smooth progress of the Mini falter. There was a moment's bumpy jerkiness, and, startled, she braked sharply.

It took only a second or two for her to recognize the symptoms. She got out. Yes—a flat. The front offside. She swore out loud. Fortunately, however, she was only a couple of hundred yards from Hillier's. She locked the car and started walking.

All the mechanics at the garage were engaged on other jobs when she got there, but Hillier himself immediately offered to come and change the wheel for her. Mr. and Mrs. Gascoigne-Chalmers were good customers. He drove her back to where she'd left the Mini, took out the jack and wheelbrace and removed the hubcap. Sylvia had started to pace impatiently up and down. Hillier fitted the brace on to the first nut and pulled strongly. Sylvia at that moment had her back to him, but had she been looking towards him she would have seen a startled expression appear on his face. Quickly he tried each of the nuts in turn and his startled expression deepened to one of utter horror. Then he hastily composed his features and said, "Didn't, er, have a go at starting to change the wheel yourself, before calling me, did you, Mrs. Gascoigne-Chalmers?"

"In this outfit? Hardly!"

"Nobody else has touched it?"

"Not since you fitted the new tyres. Why?"

"Oh, the, er, hubcap wasn't on properly. I don't think there was any danger of your losing it, but I must speak to my mechanics about it."

He hastily unscrewed all four nuts and removed the wheel. He examined the tyre for a moment, then said, "Here's your culprit, Mrs. Gascoigne-Chalmers."

Sylvia came forward and he pointed out to her the twisted blade of a small penknife embedded in the rubber.

Sylvia gave a tut of disgust. "Practically a brand new tyre, too."

Hillier finished changing the wheel and let the car down. Then he said, "Mind if I take a quick dekko at the other wheels while I'm at it?"

"What on earth for?"

"Well, a few Mini owners have been having trouble with, er, the bearings recently, and I—"

"I'm in rather a hurry. I'm just off to London."

Hillier closed his eyes for a second. "On the M4?"

"Naturally. How else?"

"Of course—silly of me. But this won't take a minute and it's all the more important if you're going any distance. We don't want you breaking down. Mr. Gascoigne-Chalmers would never forgive me. You can sit inside, if you like."

Sylvia did so, and waited while he went hurriedly round to the other three wheels. She heard him remove the hubcaps each time and replace them some seconds later. Then he came to the driver's window. "Well," she asked, "bearings all right?"

"Bear—? Oh—yes—the bearings are fine."

"Good. Thank you, Mr. Hillier. Stick it on the account, please. I must get on now."

"Hang on, ma'am. You'd better not go all that way without a spare. Stop at the garage and I'll lend you one."

"Oh, very well. Thank you."

Ten minutes later Sylvia at last drove out of Cornfield. Hillier watched her speed away. Then he went grimly into his office, searched through some record cards for a minute, returned to the door and gave a yell. "Barry—get in here! Now!"

Sylvia stayed on the motorway for an hour, and then turned off at a point where it passed through some heavily wooded countryside. She found an obviously little-used lane and drove along it until she came to a spot where a path, just wide enough to take the Mini, led into the cover of some trees. Here she stopped. She went to the boot and took out an overnight bag, which she'd packed before leaving. She opened it and extracted from it a plum-coloured trouser suit. She grimaced slightly as she looked at it. It had been a "snip" in a sale three years ago and she'd bought it on impulse, the colour looking more subdued under the shop lights. She had regretted the purchase almost immediately, had never worn it, and even Edgar didn't know she owned it. But at last it was going to serve a purpose. She looked carefully round to make sure there was no one about, then took off her grey dress and donned the trouser suit. Next she delved into her bag again and brought out a long, flowing blonde wig. This also had been an impulse-buy, several years previously, but she'd never had the nerve to let anyone see her wearing it. She put it on carefully, with the aid of a largish hand mirror. Then she got out her make-up kit and started to paint her face. Normally she wore very little make-up, but now she plastered it on, giving herself heavily rouged cheeks and very full, scarlet lips. When she was satisfied she put on a pair of dark glasses.

She studied herself in the mirror. Yes, she'd achieved her aim. She looked brassy and common: a barmaid in the worst type of pub, starting to go to seed. Certainly no one would recognize her.

She folded her grey dress, put it in the bag, and twelve minutes later was back on the M4, speeding towards London—and Soho.

Sylvia left the Mini in a car park, when she was still a few miles from central London, walked some distance and caught a tube. She got out at Picadilly Circus, walked up Shaftesbury Avenue, took a street on the left, turned off a couple more times, and was in the heart of Soho. She continued walking until she came to a pub, licked her lips, took a deep breath and went in.

It was just about lunchtime and crowded inside. Sylvia went to the bar and ordered a pork pie and a light ale. She disliked any sort of beer, but this seemed a drink that would be in character. She spotted a spare chair at a table occupied by a couple of girls, and sat down. The girls were giggling over some half-whispered anecdote, and ignored her. Sylvia looked around. But with her dark glasses on, it was too dim to see much. She risked raising them a little and surveyed the clientele. Everyone present looked depressingly respectable. She might have been in the Duke, back in Cornfield. She felt that she herself looked more like a criminal than any of them. Fool, she said to herself, did you expect them all to be wearing stocking masks and carrying coshes?

She was hungry, so she ate her pork pie. She drank half the ale and sat at the table for about five more minutes. Then she left. There was no point in remaining there. It was plainly the wrong sort of pub. She'd have to find one of the sort frequented by crooks.

Then followed two or three of the most tiring, boring and unpleasant hours of Sylvia's life. She hated crowds, and Soho teemed with people. She disliked foreigners, and every other person seemed to be speaking in broken English. It was horribly hot, and from the multitude of shops selling strange exotic foods wafted strong, exotic smells. Strip-club barkers touted for custom, and pop music blared forth from porn shops, inside the entrances of which tired-looking men sat reading racing papers.

Sylvia went into pub after pub. She drank in turn part-glasses of lager, sherry, gin and orange, and port, and then, beginning to feel the effects of these, alternated between ginger ale and tomato juice.

But nothing happened. Nowhere did she see anyone who looked remotely criminal, or who acted in the least suspiciously. Thinking it over, she realized that what she'd been expecting and hoping to see were groups of tough-looking men, talking with heads close together. Or she might have seen one man pass an envelope or a packet furtively to another. Or in one of the pubs there might have been a door through which people slipped occasionally, after being given a terse nod by the barman. If she'd witnessed anything like that, she could have waited until one of the men left and followed him. Then she might have slipped him a note. As soon as she'd got in touch with somebody—anybody—who had criminal connections she ought to be able to buy herself an introduction to a man who'd be willing to take on—as she intended to put it in the first place—"a dangerous job, which would pay well." But it was becoming plain that she just wasn't going to see any men of the right type. She was wasting her time. It might have been an idea to try and get an introduction to the sort of man she wanted through another woman. She'd seen many girls during the afternoon whose profession she'd been in no doubt about. Certainly many of them would at some time have been in trouble with the police; and anyway, weren't they always controlled by men who were part of organized crime—what films and television always referred to rather vaguely as "the Syndicate?" Vice, drugs, protection, contract murder—they were all tied up. But the trouble was that she just couldn't bring herself to go up and talk to a woman of that type. It would be too degrading. She had to draw the line somewhere. Besides, did she really want to get involved with the Syndicate? She might never get out of their clutches again if she did. No, some lone wolf would be a far better type of criminal for her purpose, some small-time crook, who would act as go-between. Perhaps she would have been more likely to find that sort of man in the East End, rather than Soho. It wasn't too late to go there now. But the prospect of spending the evening trudging through the East End on the type of pub crawl she'd been on in Soho appalled her.

She hailed a taxi, went to Fortnum and Mason, ordered a pot of tea and some fancy pastries, and sat and brooded on the débâcle. What was she going to do now? If only she had access to Scotland Yard's criminal records. But they were never revealed to the general public—

Wait a minute, though. On certain occasions they were—in court. Whenever a man was found guilty of a crime, a list of his previous convictions was read out.

Sylvia thought hard. Suppose she went along to a court—a magistrates' court—Bow Street, say—and waited until someone with the right sort of record was in the dock. . . . The snag there was that they didn't read out the prisoners' records until after they were convicted, and obviously if a man with a long record was found guilty of another crime, he'd usually be sent to prison. On the other hand, if there were extenuating circumstances they did sometimes just fine them or bind them over.

It would be a long shot. But she had to try it. Because there was just nothing else she could think of. It was too late to do anything today. But she would be at Bow Street when they started proceedings tomorrow morning. That meant either staying in London overnight or going home and leaving again very early in the morning. Better to stay. It would be much less tiring, and she could easily explain to Edgar that there was some private sale on first thing tomorrow that she just had to attend.

She finished her tea and then rang up and booked a room at the Alendale Hotel, where she and Edgar usually stayed when they were in London. Afterwards she took the tube to where she had parked her car. There was nobody near, and with some difficulty she changed back into her dress sitting in the car. She removed most of her make-up with tissues, took off the wig, then drove to the Alendale, stopping off only to buy a toothbrush and a few other necessities for an overnight stay. She had dinner at the hotel and spent most of the evening watching TV in the lounge. At about nine-thirty she went up to her room and phoned home.

Edgar answered immediately. To her surprise, he sounded breathless—almost frightened.

"It's me," she said.

"Sylvia." The word came in a gasp.

"Yes—what's the matter?"

"What's happened to you?"

"Nothing's happened to me. Why? Are you all right, Edgar?"

"Yes—yes, I'm fine."

"Then what's wrong?"

"I—I've been worried about you."

"I'm sorry, dear. I would have rung before, but I thought you'd be at the golf club."

"Where are you?"

"At the Alendale. I've decided to stay overnight." She ran through her fiction about the next morning's sale.

"I see," was all he said when she'd finished.

"You don't mind, darling, do you?"

"No, of course not."

"I'll be home tomorrow—late afternoon or early evening, without fail."

"That's all right. Enjoy yourself. Have you had a good day?"

"Well, you'll be pleased to know I haven't bought anything. But it was quite interesting."

"Er—good trip up?"

"Average. What sort of day have you had?"

"What? Oh, so-so."

He seemed oddly constrained, but she knew it was essential that she behaved perfectly normally. She searched her mind for something trivial and everyday to talk about. "Oh, I nearly forgot: I had a puncture."

"A puncture?" From the oaf's reaction to this, one might have thought he'd been told she'd had triplets.

"Where?" he asked.

"In Cornfield."

"Which—which wheel?"

"Front right. Why?"

"Oh." There was a pause. "No reason. Just interested. Did you change the wheel yourself?"

"Certainly not. I wasn't far from Hillier's. I walked there and Hillier himself came and changed it for me."

There was silence again. "Edgar? Are you there?"

"Yes, darling, I'm here. Er, what did Hillier say?"

"Say?"

"About the puncture—what caused it."

"Oh, a broken penknife blade. It was embedded right in."

"I see. And Hillier changed it for you?"

"I just said he did."

"Sorry, darling. The line's not very good this end. I keep missing words. I thought I heard you begin to say something about another thing Hillier did—or said."

"No. Though he did check the other wheels, actually. Said some customers had been having trouble with the—bearings, is it? He wanted to make sure mine were OK. It only took a minute or two. He was very nice—lent me a spare tyre. Well, darling, I think that's everything. I'll see you tomorrow."

"All right, Sylvia. Have a nice time. Look, give me a ring tomorrow, will you, and let me know more precisely what time you'll be arriving."

"I will."

"Thanks. Take care of yourself, then, dear. Bye."

"Good night, Edgar."

Edgar put the receiver down slowly. He was shaking.

He had had an awful day, waiting at every second—at home, at the office, at the golf club—for news, for the arrival of the police, telling him that Sylvia was dead or in hospital; or even for a call from Sylvia herself to report some miraculous escape. As the hours had passed he had been unable to understand why he heard nothing. Because the wheel must, surely, have come off long ago. The nervous strain had grown almost unbearable. When the phone had eventually rung, he'd been at the end of his tether.

And now this! What absolutely appalling luck. That accursed penknife blade—and in that very tyre. The odds against such a thing must have been astronomical. And what made things even worse was the knowledge that now he could never use the method again.

Edgar hardly ever swore out loud, but for several minutes he thought every swear word he knew.

The question now, though, was whether Hillier suspected anything —or whether he had assumed that the blame lay with his own mechanics. The fact that he had checked the other wheel nuts (bearings, indeed!) suggested that he might think the fault lay with his workers. Edgar decided to speak to him first thing the next day. It wouldn't be possible to ask him anything outright, but he could catch the man alone and thank him casually for helping Sylvia. Then, if Hillier was confident about his men's work, he would surely mention the loose nuts. If he didn't say anything, it would be a certain bet that he felt responsible.

And in that event, it would be safe to start planning attempt number two. . . .

Something a little more elaborate was going to be needed next time. Edgar already had the vague outline of a plan in his head. But it was one that needed Sylvia out of the house for several hours, and there was no telling now when that would happen again. In recent years she'd seemed to cling to the house for weeks after spending even one night away from it. This was the first time since their holidays in early June that she'd gone further than Cornfield. It was al-

most as though any absence from *The Elms* actually weakened her
—physically and mentally—and that in some odd way she drew
renewed strength from the house itself. Weird, if there really was
something in old Dimsdale's theory. . . .

However—it meant there was little chance, after tomorrow, of her
being away—

A thought struck him. Tomorrow. She wouldn't be home till early
evening. Could he possibly set things up by then? It would be
rushing things absurdly, of course—particularly as he hadn't got any
of the details of the plot worked out yet. On the other hand, if he
could plan everything tonight, there would be very little actually to
do in preparation.

Yes, he might just be able to make it. And it would be rather nice
to have everything waiting for the dear girl when she got back.

CHAPTER 8

After her pub crawl of the previous day, Sylvia found Bow Street magistrates' court blessedly restful and quiet. However, it wasn't long before she started wondering if she would have been wiser to go to the Old Bailey. She was quite familiar with magistrates' courts, having many times seen Edgar on the Bench, so she had been prepared for the steady stream of motoring and other petty offences; she had known that there would be a higher proportion of genuine criminals on trial at the Old Bailey. Against that, though, was the fact that there would be far fewer cases dealt with there, and the trials would take longer; so the odds against her being present when one ended in the way she wanted were in fact probably greater at the higher court.

At Bow Street, though, she was forced to watch defendant after defendant not even remotely suitable for her purpose, and she was just thinking of giving up and going to get some lunch when the case came up that seemed an answer to her prayers.

Two men who had elected to be tried by the magistrate on a shopbreaking charge came into the dock. There seemed no doubt about their guilt. They had been caught red-handed, one inside the shop—an electrical dealer's—the other, whose name was Nokes, with his hand on the door of a van, belonging to the first man, which was parked near the shop's rear entrance. Inside the van were found several stolen radios and tape-recorders.

The man who'd been caught inside pleaded guilty. But Nokes claimed to have been merely passing at the time and to have stopped because he recognized the van as belonging to his friend. This claim, Sylvia noticed, was greeted by subdued chuckles from one or two knowing-looking people near her in the gallery, and by some grins from the press box. The defence was, however, supported by the first man, who maintained that he'd planned and carried out the raid single-handed. Another point that Sylvia noted was that in his evidence the Detective-Sergeant who was the chief prosecution witness testified that when making the arrest he'd crept up behind Nokes, put a hand on his shoulder and said, "Come along, Duggie, it's all over." There couldn't, it seemed to her, have been a much stronger indication that Nokes had a criminal record.

He was a weasly little man with greased-down hair, a small moustache, and long sideburns. In the dock he looked depressed and resigned. But then there arose some question as to whether he'd been properly cautioned at the time of his arrest. This, coming on top of the first man's evidence, and the lack of any more positive link between Nokes and the robbery, clearly sowed a doubt in the magistrate's mind, and shortly afterwards he found Nokes Not Guilty.

The look of amazed delight on Nokes's face, the expression of utter disgust on the Detective-Sergeant's, and the hastily suppressed chortles from the gallery, were proof enough for Sylvia. She waited just long enough to hear the Clerk start to read out a long list of previous convictions sustained by the first man, then hurried out after Nokes.

She saw him joined and comprehensively embraced by a large, frizzy-haired woman some three inches taller than him, who then walked off with him. Sylvia, who was again wearing her disguise, followed them.

Her car was parked some distance away, and she was anxious in case they got into a car of their own and disappeared. But fortunately they remained on foot. After a hundred yards they entered a pub. Sylvia gave them a couple of minutes and went in after them.

As she entered, she saw them just settling themselves each side of a table in a corner booth. She took a deep breath and walked across to them. As she reached them they were just raising their glasses in a toast. Sylvia came to a quick decision—and addressed herself to the woman.

"Mrs. Nokes?" (There was a wedding ring on the woman's finger.)

They both looked up, the man with a flicker of interest, the woman with definite suspicion. "That's as may be," she said. " 'Oo wants to know?"

"My name is Mrs. Smith." It wasn't an original pseudonym, but they'd soon realize, anyway, that she wasn't using her real name.

"Oh yes. What would you be wanting—Mrs. Smith?"

"Can I sit down? I'd like to speak to you both for just a minute."

"What abaht?"

Taking their assent for granted, Sylvia slipped into the seat. She looked at the woman. "Mrs. Nokes—I'd like to talk to your husband in private. Would you object?"

Mr. Nokes stared. "Well, you got a nerve!"

"I'm sorry. But you needn't get the wrong idea. I'm all fixed up in that line. This is strictly business."

Nokes spoke for the first time. "What sort of business?"

Sylvia looked at him closely. He had small watery eyes and a pointed nose. She said, "Easy business. No risk. You could probably do it all on the phone. And you'll earn a hundred pounds."

Nokes glanced at his wife, who then looked sharply at Sylvia. "Why d'you want to speak to 'im alone?"

"I'll talk to both of you if you like," Sylvia said to her. "Only I thought you might prefer not to know what we're discussing. Isn't it safer for you like that—in his line of work?"

Again the Nokeses exchanged glances before Mrs. Nokes said, "We could use a hundred now. How long would this talk take?"

"A few minutes," Sylvia said.

"All right. I'll go and do some shopping. I'll be back in quarter of an hour." She finished her drink, got heavily to her feet and squeezed herself out from behind the table. "Now, don't you go agreeing to anything silly," she said sternly to Nokes. Then she went out.

"OK, lidy," Nokes said, "what's this all abaht? Whatd'yer want me to do?"

Sylvia glanced around. Nobody was within earshot. Yet almost unconsciously she leaned forward and lowered her voice as she said, "I just want you to introduce me to someone."

" 'Oo?"

"I don't know. I'll leave that to you. What I want is a villain."

Nokes picked up his glass of beer and sipped from it. "What makes you fink I know any villains?"

"I was in court just now. I heard your friend's record read out."

"So—I know one villain. And 'e ain't going to be no use to you for a bit. It don't mean I knows no others."

"Oh, Mr. Nokes, come on! I saw the expression on that policeman's face when you got off. He was furious about it. He wanted you. I'd bet a pound to a penny you've been on the opposite side of the fence from him all your life. You can't live like that without getting to know plenty of villains."

The ease and fluency with which she found herself talking amazed her. She had always been stiff with strangers. Yet here she was, talking to a criminal as though she'd known him and mixed with the underworld all her life. She'd tried to let her voice grow coarser to match her appearance and was surprised, too, to find how simple this was. Although she wasn't aware of it, she was now speaking in the accent her father had once used.

Nokes said, "OK, I gotta bit of form. I ain't denying it. That's why the cops pulled me in on that shop heist. But I'm going straight nah. I knew a few villains once, but I ain't in touch wiv 'em any more."

"But you could be. You know where to find them."

"Why me, lidy? Why d'yer come to me?"

"Because *I* don't know any villains. I'm what might be called respectable. All my friends are respectable, too. I tried to think where would be the best place to find villains, and I thought of a law court. I guessed that if the sort of man I wanted wasn't actually there, there'd be somebody who'd know where to find the right man. Then I saw you and your friend. I decided that if you knew one villain, you'd probably know others too."

Nokes was silent. He finished his beer, then lit a cigarette. "It's a specialist you want, innit?" he said. "You want me to put you in touch wiv a specialist?"

"I suppose you could say that."

"Well, what's 'e gotta be? Peterman? Cat? Electronics? What?"

"None of those things. I want a—a hard man."

"You just want someone worked over? That shouldn't be no problem—"

"No." Sylvia interrupted him. "I mean a *really* hard man. The hardest you know." She paused. "Somebody who can use a gun."

"Blimey!" Nokes's jaw dropped. "You're looking for a killer," he whispered.

Sylvia said nothing.

"Look," he said. "I don't want nuffin to do wiv it." He made to stand up.

Sylvia put a hand on his arm. "You haven't got to have anything to do with it. There's no law against introducing two people to each other, is there—or just passing over an address or phone number? Once you've done that you're out of it. You can forget the whole thing."

"For that I'd get an 'undred nicker?"

"You put me in touch with the right man and I'll make it two hundred."

Nokes lit a second cigarette from the first, not yet half-smoked. "These blokes—the sort you're looking for—they cost, you know."

"I'm willing to pay him five thousand pounds."

Nokes jerked his head up. "Five thahsand?"

"That's right. But there's to be no bargaining. Five is the absolute maximum. Either he takes the job or he doesn't."

Nokes was still looking shaken. Then he rallied a little. "Two hundred isn't much for setting up a deal worth five thahsand."

"There's nothing to stop you doing a deal wiv—with the other party too. I don't see why you shouldn't ask, say, five per cent from him for putting him in touch with me. That would be four hundred and fifty pounds altogether—just for making a few phone calls."

"Look, that's all very well, lidy, but I ain't sure as I knows anyone as'd fill your bill."

"OK." Sylvia stood up. "Forget the whole thing. I'll find someone else. Sorry to have bothered you." She started to move away.

Nokes caught hold of her sleeve. "Nah hold on. I didn't say I defin'ly couldn't find a bloke, did I? Hah soon would you want 'im?"

"Very soon. Next week."

Nokes thought for a moment. "OK—look, leave it wiv me. Give me a number and I'll phone you in a day or two—"

"No." Sylvia shook her head firmly. "I'll ring you. You give me a number."

Nokes hesitated. Then he nodded and started to fumble through his pockets.

"Here." Sylvia opened her bag and took out a notebook and pencil, which she passed to him. "Write it down in there."

Nokes scribbled down a number and handed the notebook back. Sylvia looked at it. "Right. I'll ring you Thursday afternoon—OK?"

He nodded. "When do I get me money?"

"When I've seen your man and he's agreed to do the job."

"But, lidy, I'll have expenses. It won't be a matter of just making calls on the blower, whatever you fink. I'll 'av to get around, see people, buy a few drinks. . . ."

"All right." Sylvia reached into her bag again, and took out two five-pound notes. "Here's something on account. Don't ask for any more because I won't pay it."

Nokes took the money with a look of disgust. "I won't get far on a perishing tenner."

"Just do your best," said Sylvia.

She walked away from the table and left the pub without looking back. She could hardly believe what she had just done. Already, after only a few minutes, the whole conversation was beginning to take on the air of a dream. Well, until something happened, perhaps it would be best to pretend that that was exactly what it had been.

She found a café, had some lunch, then, as she'd promised, phoned Edgar. There was no reply from *The Elms,* so she rang the office. He'd just got back from lunch.

"Darling," she said, "I'm starting for home now. Should be there between four and half past."

"Counting the minutes, darling," he said.

CHAPTER 9

Edgar rang off and looked at his watch. Just gone two. Counting the minutes had been right, for timing was going to be crucial. He mustn't act too soon.

He ran through the plan yet again. He had been awake until the early hours the previous night, working it out. He couldn't see any flaws in it—though, ultimately, of course, it all depended on Willie. . . .

Willie Morgan was employed as a janitor and general handyman in the office building where Edgar had his premises. He was about twenty-four, six feet two inches tall and broad to match. He was good-natured, happy, anxious to please—and very simple.

Willie's chief joy in life was make-believe crime, and he was an avid watcher of all the television police series—though Edgar was sure he was quite incapable of following the plots. His tiny cubbyhole at the rear of the building on the ground floor was plastered with pictures of the TV cops—Kojak, Columbo, McGarret, Starsky and Hutch, and dozens of others. As his job consisted of little more than unlocking the building in the morning, sweeping the corridors, changing light bulbs and locking up at night, he spent the bulk of his working day in this little room, poring over crime comics, slowly tracing the words with his finger. His only other hobby was cycling. In the summer he was out on his bicycle each weekend, and seemed to know intimately every foot of road for miles around.

Willie had once been in trouble with the police. Three or four years before, he had become the butt of a gang of teenage louts, who had started to follow him along the street, yelling insults, and jumping out at him when he cycled past, trying to push sticks in his spokes. One day, after a month or two of this, maddened beyond endurance, Willie had pounced on the gang leader, picked him up and hurled him bodily through a shop window.

He had come up before the magistrates when Edgar was on the Bench, and in view of the provocation had been put on probation. For some reason he seemed to believe that it was Edgar who had recommended leniency; and when shortly afterwards his probation officer had obtained the janitor's job for him, Willie had got it firmly —and quite falsely—fixed in his head that Edgar had been responsible.

Since then Edgar had been able to do anything with Willie, and often used him—entirely unofficially, Willie being employed by the owners of the building—as an unpaid, but quick and reliable, messenger boy. Nobody ever seemed to notice Willie's absence on these occasions.

Edgar's plan had required very little advance preparation—merely thought. That morning he had brought to the office in his brief-case one of two heavy silver candlesticks that normally stood on his study mantelpiece. Next to the other one he had left his own key to Sylvia's car, and had opened the study window a few inches. Apart from stopping to check that the nearest phone box to *The Elms*— about a mile towards Cornfield—was in working order, that had been the extent of what he'd had to do.

It *ought* to work. Certainly no one would suspect him—the doting husband. He'd already, in fact, received an encouraging indication that in Cornfield at least he might well be above suspicion. For Hillier's manner, when Edgar had called at the garage that morning and thanked him for attending to Sylvia—just a little over-friendly, almost hearty, yet at the same time noticeably embarrassed, a shade apprehensive—had made it clear that he had accepted blame for the loose wheel and didn't harbour the slightest suspicion of Edgar. This portended well.

Edgar forced himself to wait until three o'clock, then called Beryl into his office and handed her some papers. "I'd like you to drive out to Mr. Andrews and get him to sign these," he said. "It's important I have them back tomorrow, so I can't wait for the post. I've phoned him and he is expecting you."

Beryl looked at her watch. "He lives about twenty-five miles away. It'll take me all of an hour and a half to drive there, see him, and get back."

"I know. I don't expect you back here tonight. I can manage on my own. Bring the papers in first thing in the morning."

Beryl left within five minutes. As soon as the outer door closed behind her, Edgar took the candlestick from his case, wiped it over with a duster, and put it on the window-ledge. Then he went downstairs to Willie's cubby-hole.

"Willie," he said, "I'd like you to come up to my office a minute. I want to show you something."

"Oh yes, sir, right away." Willie threw down his comic and followed Edgar upstairs. Edgar took him through to the inner office and pointed to the window-ledge. "See that candlestick?"

"Yessir."

"Have a good look at it." Willie went across. "Pick it up," Edgar said. "Examine it really closely."

Willie did so, holding it about four inches from his nose, twisting it back and forth.

"What do you think of it?" Edgar asked.

"It's lovely, sir."

"I've got another one exactly the same at home."

"Have you, sir? They must look lovely together."

"Yes, they do. And I've been told they might be very valuable."

"Oh." Willie put the candlestick down hurriedly.

"Willie, I'm going to let you into a secret." Willie looked excited. "There's an American millionaire staying at Polchester, who may be willing to buy them—for thousands of pounds."

"Cor." Willie's eyes grew big.

"Now, I've promised him that I'll take one of them to show him tonight. If he likes it, I thought I'd take the other over tomorrow. I reckoned it would be safer than carrying them both together. Do you follow?"

"Oh yes, sir, I do."

"Now, can you guess what's happened?"

Willie shook his head.

"The millionaire's rung me up to say he's leaving Polchester this evening and I must have the candlesticks there by 6 P.M. Well, the other candlestick's at my home. See my problem?"

"Well, sir . . ." Willie looked doubtful.

"I've got to stay here working until half past five, Willie—every second is tied up. I'll just have time to take that candlestick to Polchester, but I haven't got time to go home and get the other one first."

Willie tried hard to look wise. "Oh, that's bad, Mr. Chalmers." (He'd long since given up trying to get his tongue round Gascoigne-Chalmers.)

"Yes, it is bad, Willie. I stand to lose a lot of money. And—well, frankly, I'm wondering if you can help me out."

"Me?"

"Yes. You see, what I need is someone to go to my home for me, collect that candlestick from my wife and take it to Polchester. Would you do that for me, Willie?"

"Polchester!" Willie said the word as though the town were two thousand miles away. "But—but how would I get there? Take a powerful long time to bike, and buses only runs every couple of hours."

"Can you drive, Willie?" Edgar knew the answer to this question, as Willie had once told him.

"Well, I *can,* Mr. Chalmers. Me dad taught me. But I ain't got a licence. I couldn't never pass the test."

"Don't worry about that. You can take my wife's car. I'm a magistrate, as you know, so I've got the authority to give you permission to drive without passing the test."

"You have?" Willie scratched his head. "I didn't know that. No one never told me that before."

"It's not widely known, but you can take my word for it. If the police stop you, you can tell them you've got special permission from me. This is what I thought you might do for me. You know my house?"

"Oh yes, sir, passed it a few times on me bike."

"Well, I'd like you to cycle out there now and wait for my wife. Do you know her?" He was pretty sure of the answer he'd get to this, too, as Sylvia very rarely called at the office these days.

"No, sir. Well, I sort of caught sight of her coming up the stairs here once, just for a second, but I can't say as how I'd know her again."

"Well, she's driving a little white Mini car. You go inside the front gate of my house and wait until she arrives—at about half past four. Then you tell her you want the candlestick—and you've got to have her car. If there's any question, she can telephone me here. Then when you've got the candlestick drive to Polchester, to the Crown Hotel, and leave it with the receptionist. I'll drive straight there, pick it up, and I'll have time to show them both to the American and try to do a deal with him before he has to leave. Meanwhile you can drive back to my house, pick up your bicycle and ride back here. What do you say?"

Edgar waited, banking—correctly—on Willie not thinking to ask why Sylvia couldn't take the candlestick to Polchester, nor working out that it would take Edgar not more than an extra ten minutes to go to Polchester via *The Elms* and collect the candlestick himself.

"Well," Willie said slowly, "I'd be awful pleased to help you, Mr. Chalmers, but what about me work here?"

"Don't worry, Willie. I'll see you don't get into trouble. And you can put a notice on the door of your office, saying 'all inquiries to Mr. Gascoigne-Chalmers, first floor.'"

"But I'd have to be back by half past six to lock up."

"You would be. If you like you could come straight back here in my wife's car after going to Polchester, lock up, and then drive out to my place and pick up your bike. You'd really be helping me out of a jam. I'd be most grateful. And I'd make it worth your while. I'll give you twenty-five pounds."

"Oh, you've no call to do that, Mr. Chalmers. I don't want money."

"But I want to pay you, Willie. It'll be only fair. So, will you do it?"

Willie paused—for a long, long time. Edgar could almost see his brain slowly ticking over. Then he reached the great decision.

"Yes, sir, Mr. Chalmers. I'll be proud to help you."

"Good man, Willie! I knew you wouldn't let me down. Now, let's just go through it again."

He went over the instructions carefully, until he was sure Willie had everything straight. He ended up by saying, "If anything goes wrong—if for any reason at all you can't get the candlestick—you phone me here. There's a public call box about a mile from my house—by the crossroads."

"I know it."

"Well, if you can't get the candlestick, nip back on your bike to that phone box and ring me. Here, I'll write my number down for you."

Edgar scribbled the office number on a piece of paper and gave it to Willie, together with a few coins. "And here's some change for the phone. All clear?"

"Yes, Mr. Chalmers, I understand everything. Would you be so good as to write out that notice for me office door, sir?"

Edgar hastily did so and Willie hurried out. As soon as he'd gone, Edgar took a square white silk cravat from his pocket, wrapped it carefully around the candlestick and put it in his brief-case. Then he sat down. There was nothing to do now except wait. It was going to seem an awfully long time. One certain fact, though, was that he couldn't possibly concentrate on work.

He closed his eyes and for the twentieth time visualized just what was going to happen during the next couple of hours. . . .

Willie dismounted outside *The Elms,* opened the gate and pushed his bicycle through. He walked up the drive to the house, leaned the bicycle carefully against the wall, and sat down on the step. He took a comic from his pocket and started to read.

Ten minutes passed. Then there was the sound of a car engine in the lane and a moment later Sylvia's Mini stopped outside. Sylvia got out, opened the gate, returned to the car and drove it up to the front door. It was only after she switched off the engine that she saw Willie, now standing with his comic in his hand, staring at her. She felt a twinge of alarm. She didn't get out, just opened the window and called, "What do you want?"

Willie ambled forward. "You Mrs. Chalmers?"

"Gascoigne-Chalmers, yes."

"I've got to have the candlestick."

"What's that?"

"The candlestick—I've got to have it."

"I don't know what you're talking about. Which candlestick?"

"The silver one."

"You want one of my silver candlesticks? What on earth for?"

"Mr. Chalmers sent me. I got to take it to Polchester. And he said as how I got to have your car to take it in. I'll bring it back."

Sylvia was staring at him incredulously. "My husband said I had to give you one of the silver candlesticks—and my car—to drive to Polchester?"

Willie looked pleased at this manifestation of intelligence. "Ay, that's right."

"I've never heard such nonsense. Go away at once, or I'll call the police."

Willie's face fell. "But it's awful important. He said as how you was to phone him to explain."

Sylvia eyed him doubtfully. It was in the highest degree unlikely that there was a word of truth in this halfwit's story, but could it just be . . . ?

"He wants me to phone him?" she asked.

"Ay, if there's any question. And if I don't get it, *I* got to ring him. Look, he gave me his phone number."

Willie plunged his hand into his pocket and for a second Sylvia flinched. But he only brought out a piece of paper and held it up for her to see. It was Edgar's office number—and certainly his writing.

She said, "Very well, I'll phone him now. But I'm not getting out with you here. Kindly wait in the lane."

Looking puzzled, Willie ambled down the drive and out to the lane, where he stood looking up at the house. Keeping a careful eye on him, Sylvia got hurriedly out of the car, locked it, ran up the few steps to the front door, let herself in and closed it behind her. Feeling considerably safer now, she went straight to the phone and rang Edgar's office.

He answered himself.

"Edgar? It's me."

"Darling! Are you home?"

119507

"Yes, just this minute."

"Oh, fine. Everything go well?"

"Edgar, there's a most peculiar young man here. He wants one of the silver candlesticks. Did you send him?"

"Candlesticks? What on earth are you talking about, darling?"

"You didn't send him, then?"

"No, of course not. Look, tell me exactly what's happened."

"He was waiting by the front door when I drove up. He said he wanted one of our silver candlesticks, that you'd said he had to take it to Polchester, and that he was to have my car to do it."

"Your car?"

"Yes, he said it was very urgent and that I was to phone you. He had your office number on a piece of paper in your writing, and he said that if I didn't ring you, he had to."

Edgar was silent for a moment, before saying, "This is mad. I don't know anything about it. Where is he now?" Then there was a sudden note of alarm in his voice. "Not in the house, is he?"

"No—he's waiting in the lane. Edgar, I'm sure it was your writing on the paper. Have you written down your number for anybody recently?"

"No, I don't—" Edgar stopped short. "Hang on a minute. What's he look like?"

"Oh, he's young, tall, well-built. Dark, curly hair. Quite nice-looking, actually. But quite half-witted, I'd say."

"It sounds like Willie," Edgar said.

"The boy who works in your building?"

"That's right. I did write the office number down for him the other day, now I come to think of it. He was doing a message for me, and I thought he might have to report back. Tell me, has he got a bike?"

"Yes—he has. I only noticed it sort of half-consciously. It was leaning against the side of the house."

"What did he call you—Mrs. Chalmers?"

"Yes."

"That's Willie, for sure. But what the deuce is he up to? He hasn't even got a driving licence."

"Edgar—he isn't violent, is he? You told me he was up before the Bench for throwing somebody through a window."

"Oh, that was years ago. He seems as gentle as a kitten now. I can't think what he's playing at, but the likeliest explanation is that he's got muddled. Probably somebody else has sent him on an errand, and as he does a lot of them for me, he's got confused and come to the wrong house. After all, plenty of people have got silver candlesticks."

"Well, what shall I do?"

"Go upstairs and call to him out of the window. Tell him I know nothing about it, and that if he doesn't go away you'll call the police."

"Do you think I *should* call the police?"

"No; at least, not unless he still refuses to go. Now, don't worry. I'll be home soon."

"All right, Edgar."

He rang off and sat tensely by the phone, waiting. Six, nearly seven minutes passed before it rang. Edgar snatched up the receiver. "Yes?"

There was a short silence. Then Edgar heard a coin being put in the box, and the pips. This was followed by another pause. Edgar said, "Hullo? This is Mr. Chalmers."

"Mr. Chalmers?" Willie spoke a little uncertainly.

"Yes, Willie. What's wrong?"

"She won't let me have it, sir."

"Won't let you have it? My wife won't?"

"No, sir."

"But why not? Didn't you tell her to phone me?"

"She said she did, sir—and that you didn't know anything about it."

"She didn't phone me," Edgar said.

"Well, she said she had. She called out of the window and said she'd spoken to you and you said as how I was to go away or she'd call the police."

"But this is incredible!" Edgar said. "I don't understand it. Why should she lie like that?" Suddenly he changed the tone of his voice, speaking urgently. "Willie, what was she like, this woman?"

"Like, sir?"

"What did she look like?"

"Well, I wouldn't rightly know, sir."

"Did she have red hair?"

"Oh no, sir—kind of brown."

"That wasn't my wife!" Edgar exclaimed. "My wife has got red hair—ginger. Willie, that woman's an impostor."

This was a word Willie had heard often enough in his television shows to know the meaning of. He gave a gasp.

"She's a thief," Edgar said excitedly. "She's after the candlestick."

"Cor," Willie said.

"She must have stolen my wife's car," Edgar went on. "Willie, we must stop her getting away with that candlestick. And it's up to you. You've got to get it first."

"But how—?"

"You said the woman was upstairs?"

"Yes, sir."

"Well, she obviously doesn't know where the candlestick is kept and she's looking for it upstairs. Actually, it's downstairs—in my study. There's a good chance she won't have found it yet. Now, this is what I want you to do. Are you listening?"

"Yes, sir."

"Right, ride back there now as fast as you can. Go round to the side of the house—the left—by the red rose bush. Got that?"

"Red rose bush. Yes, sir."

"By the rose bush is my study window. It's open. Climb in and get the candlestick off the mantelpiece. Will you do that for me?"

"Yes, sir—you bet."

"Good. Now, next to the candlestick on the mantelpiece is a key to my wife's car. Take the key, too—and drive away in the Mini. That'll stop the woman escaping. Can you manage all that?"

"I can manage, Mr. Chalmers."

"One more thing, don't come back here towards Cornfield. Go the other way—down towards Whittal's farm. You'll join the Polchester road eventually. Go on there as arranged."

"Right, sir."

"OK—I'll go through it once more. Window by the red roses. Candlestick and key off mantelpiece. Take the Mini and drive towards Whittal's farm and then on to Polchester."

"I got it, Mr. Chalmers."

"Good lad. Now be as quick as you can. I'm going to call the police."

Edgar put the receiver down, took a few deep breaths to calm himself, then immediately lifted it again and dialled *The Elms*. Sylvia answered almost immediately. Edgar said, "It's me. What's happened to Willie?"

"He went away."

"Well, listen, darling. I've just learnt something about him from somebody else in the building and I think you *should* call the police, after all."

"But why? You said—"

"I know what I said, and I'll explain when I see you, but do that quickly now."

"But what shall I say?"

"Just that a man called Willie Morgan has been bothering you. Tell them he seemed to be after a pair of silver candlesticks and that he demanded your car. When you've done that, go upstairs, lock yourself in the bathroom and stay there until you hear me—or the police."

"Edgar, what is this? I'm frightened."

"Sylvia—just ring the police now—at once—and then go upstairs. Please."

"Well, all right."

"Good girl. I'll be with you in ten or fifteen minutes. Bye."

Edgar rang off again. Then he grabbed up the case containing the candlestick, rushed out of the office, slamming the door after him, ran down the stairs and along to Willie's room. The notice which he'd written out was pinned to the door. He snatched it off and thrust it in his pocket, before hurrying to his car. The time element was going to be crucial. He was sure the police couldn't get to *The Elms* in less than fifteen minutes. There were no regular patrols in that area. They'd either have to divert a car from the motorway, or send one especially from the station. Whichever course they took, he was nearer to *The Elms* than they were, he had a fast car and once out of Cornfield it was open country all the way. On an average day he could reach home in ten minutes, on a good one eight. So, given reasonable luck, he ought to be there at least five minutes before them. Which should be ample.

Eight minutes later Edgar, doing about sixty, approached the cottage of their nearest neighbour, Miss Killigrew. As was her invariable custom at this time on fine days, she was working in her garden. She heard his car and straightened up to watch him pass. Sometimes he stopped to speak to her, always he at least gave her a wave. But today he ignored her. Let the old bag see that something was wrong. He caught a glimpse of her face staring stupidly at him, then was past. Half a mile to go.

He reached the last hundred-yard stretch leading to *The Elms,* pulled on to the verge, so the car was screened from the house, got out and fixed his eyes on the front gate. Had Willie already gone? Or would he have to wait for him to leave? The next moment, he saw Sylvia's car shoot out into the road, turn away from him, half-mount the bank, sway wildly back to the other side of the road, then accelerate to disappear round the next bend.

Edgar jumped back into the Rover, started the engine, roared up to the house in bottom gear, swept in through the open gates, giving a loud trumpet on his horn, and up the driveway to skid to a halt outside the front door. He opened his brief-case and took out the candlestick, still wrapped in the silk cravat. He got out and ran up the steps to the door. He opened it with his key and burst into the hall. A white-faced Sylvia was on the stairs.

She gasped, "I heard a noise from the study."

Edgar threw open the study door. The window of the room was wide open. Sylvia joined him in the doorway and her eyes went straight to the mantelpiece. She pointed. "He's taken the candlesticks."

Edgar said, "Did you ring the police and tell them about Willie—like I told you to?"

"Yes."

"Then do it again now—they can look out for him on their way."

Sylvia hurried across to the phone and dialled 999. "Police," she said.

"Just tell them that Willie Morgan—the man you phoned about earlier—has broken in here."

Sylvia nodded. Into the phone she said: "This is Mrs. Gascoigne-Chalmers again—from *The Elms*. That man I called about a few minutes ago—Willie Morgan—he's broken in here. Please hurry. He's—"

Edgar put his hand on the receiver rest.

CHAPTER 10

Sylvia stared at him in amazement. "What did you do that for? I was just going to tell them he'd taken the candlesticks."

"I couldn't let you do that, dear."

"Why not?"

"Because he hasn't."

"What do you mean? They're gone—"

"Yes, but you see, I've got one of them." Edgar held up the candlestick, pulling back the silk covering from the base, but still holding the other end with the cravat.

She gave a gasp. "Where did you get that?"

"From the mantelpiece, this morning."

"But what did you want it for?"

"For this, my dear Sylvia." And Edgar raised the candlestick above his head.

The sudden look of terror—and understanding—in her eyes was a moment immeasurably sweet to him before he brought the heavy base of the candlestick crashing down on to her skull.

She crumpled silently on to the floor, the telephone receiver falling with a clatter on to the table. To make quite sure, he struck her twice more, as hard as he could. Then he bent down and felt her pulse. Nothing.

He let the candlestick fall free of the cravat on to the floor, beside the body. Then he folded the cravat neatly and put it in the pocket of a coat hanging on the hallstand.

He went outside, closed the front door behind him and hurried down the steps to his car. He got in and backed half-way down the drive. He sat in the driving-seat, listening intently until, from the lane behind, he heard the sound of a police bell. Then he accelerated up to the front door again.

As the two constables in the police car pulled in through the gateway, they were just in time to see the Rover sliding to an abrupt halt.

Edgar got out, turned, saw their car and ran towards it as it stopped and the two policemen hurriedly emerged. "You've had a call from my wife?" he asked.

"Yes, sir—she reported a prowler."

"I think he may have stolen her car—I just saw it disappearing down the lane. Let's find her."

He strode up to the front door, fumbling for his keys, the two constables at his heels. He thrust the key into the lock, pushed the door open and stepped into the hall. Then he stopped dead. He gave an anguished shout, "Sylvia!" and fell on his knees beside her body.

One of the constables turned on his heels and ran back towards the police car, while the other knelt down by Edgar and felt for Sylvia's pulse.

His eyes met Edgar's. "I'm very sorry, sir. I'm afraid—I'm afraid she's dead."

"You've got him, then?" Edgar said dully the following day.

The Inspector nodded. "Yes, sir. No problems there. He was picked up half-way to Polchester in your wife's car. He didn't resist at all."

"I blame myself for this, you know," Edgar said bitterly.

"Oh, I shouldn't do that, sir."

"But I should, Inspector! I knew Willie had a history of violence —and that he wasn't quite right in the head. But he always seemed so—so meek and mild."

"That's often the way, Mr. Gascoigne-Chalmers. Perhaps you feel up to telling me now just what happened yesterday."

"I—I'll try, Inspector. I always used to chat for a minute or so to Willie every day, you know. I liked the boy. Yesterday morning I happened to mention that I'd had to get my own breakfast, as both my wife and our domestic were away. Later I chanced to see him again, and he said something like, 'I suppose you've got a lot of lovely things at your house—valuable, like—gold and silver.' I said, 'Not much gold, I'm afraid, but a bit of silver.' I was a fool. It honestly just didn't occur to me what he had in mind. I didn't think another thing about it until my wife phoned me at my office some time after four. She'd just arrived home from London, and she'd found Willie prowling about the garden. When she'd asked him what he wanted he'd become abusive. She'd hurried inside and slammed the door, but she could still see him hanging about. I told her to ring the police at once. Your man said she did do that?"

"That's right, sir—twice; the second time ten minutes later to say he'd actually broken in."

Edgar nodded. "Well, I told her I'd get home as soon as possible.

I wasn't unduly alarmed—just a little concerned—but I hurried home straight away. I was approaching my house when I saw my wife's Mini come tearing out and drive off very erratically. I was just going indoors when the police car arrived, and the constable told me she had phoned you, as I'd advised her to do. I went in and found . . ." Edgar's voice tailed off and he buried his head in his hands.

"A shocking experience, sir," the Inspector said quietly, "but I honestly don't think you can blame yourself for not anticipating what was in his head."

"But there was that study window, too. I must have left it open. It's so rarely I have to leave the house unoccupied that I just forgot about it."

"He could have easily smashed a window, sir."

"But he might not have bothered. If he hadn't actually seen an open window—who knows?"

"He went out to your place with the fixed intention of robbing it, sir. If he hadn't been determined to break in he'd have certainly cleared off as soon as your wife arrived home."

"Well, maybe you're right," Edgar said, in an unconvinced tone, "it would be some small comfort to think that you were." He hesitated. "I suppose there's absolutely no chance of his getting off, is there?"

"Oh, bless you, no, sir. There are his prints on the murder weapon, and on the mantelpiece and the window-sill in your study, clear footprints matching his shoes on the soft earth outside—and the other candlestick on the seat next to him, when he was picked up driving your wife's stolen car. All that is quite apart from your wife's own positive identification of him on the phone. He must have heard her ringing up and rushed out of the study to try and stop her getting through to us. Don't worry, it's the most cast-iron case I've ever had."

"Thank heavens for that, anyway. I'm not a vindictive man, but the thought that he might be walking around free again in a few months . . . ."

"Oh no, sir, it'll be Broadmoor for Willie Morgan for many years —perhaps for the rest of his life."

"What does he say about it, Inspector? Does he show any remorse?"

"Oh, he denies killing her, sir. He's living in a fantasy world. He tells some rambling, incoherent story about your having sent him to your house, and American millionaires and women burglars and your wife having red hair and goodness knows what. He seems to

think he's been arrested for driving without a licence and he keeps
insisting that you said it would be all right. Perhaps the psychiatrists
will be able to make some sense of it. And now you must try and get
some rest, sir. You've been through a tremendous tragedy. . . ."

Edgar stirred in his office chair and opened his eyes. Yes, that was
how it was going to be—that was how he was going to kill Sylvia. It
wouldn't be *exactly* like that, of course. Obviously, he couldn't an-
ticipate every detail correctly. But given any sort of luck, the
scenario he'd just run through in his mind couldn't be that far out.
And after the ghastly luck of the loosened wheel, he was surely due
for some good fortune.

Edgar looked at his watch. Four-fifteen. Sylvia should be home by
now—or very soon. At any moment he should get her call reporting
Willie's strange request—or perhaps Willie's call, reporting her re-
fusal to hand over the candlestick, would come first.

Then he heard a footstep in the outer office. Blast! Not a visitor
now. Why hadn't he locked the door? It would be tricky if Willie's
call came through while somebody was present. There came a hesi-
tant tap on the inner office door. Edgar got to his feet and opened it.

It was Willie.

For a moment Edgar just stared speechlessly. Then he gasped,
"Willie! What are you doing here?"

Willie grinned. "I just got back, Mr. Chalmers."

"But the candlestick . . ."

"I got it, sir." He held up a shapeless parcel wrapped in a comic,
tore back the paper and handed Edgar the second candlestick.

Edgar said weakly, "My wife . . . she gave it to you?"

"No, sir; I ain't seen Mrs. Chalmers. Fact is, sir, I took a Liberty.
I thought I was acting for the best and I hope you'll think so, too. O'
course, if you say as how I was wrong, I won't expect no payment."

"Liberty? I—I don't understand, Willie. What are you talking
about?"

"It's like this, sir. I rode out to your house, like you said, and
took me bike in. I was waiting for Mrs. Chalmers when I thought I'd
take a close look at them there red roses of yours. So I walked over
to 'em—and then I saw that the window there was open. Well, that
worried me a bit, the house being empty and all. I wondered as how
there might've been burglars. So I took a look in. And there was the
candlestick on the mantelpiece. Then I had my Idea, sir, and I sure
hope you're not angry. But it seemed, like, daft to hang about waiting for Mrs. Chalmers, and then her having to phone you, and me

taking the car, when the candlestick was there all the time. You'd said you wasn't leaving here till 'alf past five. I knew I could get back here 'fore you left and I thought as how then you could take 'em both with you. And that was when I took the Liberty."

Very quietly, through almost clenched teeth, Edgar said, "You climbed through the window and got the candlestick."

"Yes, sir. But you needn't worry. I didn't make no mess at all and o' course I didn't look at nothing, and I shut the window behind me and I wrapped the candlestick up in my comic and put it in my saddlebag, and it's not scratched nor nothing and here it is." And for the second time he held it out.

Edgar took it. Willie was never in his life to come closer to being beaten over the head than at that moment.

Edgar swayed. He literally saw red. He came within half a second of screaming out loud in sheer fury. Then years of training in self-control came to his rescue. He mustn't show his feelings. He mustn't. He mustn't even tick Willie off. If he did, Willie might talk. Besides, he might want to use the oaf again. He closed his eyes, breathed deeply and waited for the rage to pass.

After five seconds he opened his eyes again and smiled. "Well, Willie, you're certainly full of surprises. Yes, of course, you did quite the right thing. It was very careless of me to leave that window open, and smart of you to spot it. Thank you very much. Now I must let you get back to your work."

Willie coughed.

Edgar said, "Oh, yes, of course. I was nearly forgetting. Twenty pounds, wasn't it?"

"Well, er—" Willie blushed. "Actually, it were twenty-five you mentioned, Mr. Chalmers. But o' course, twenty will be fine if—"

"No, no. Twenty-five it shall be." Edgar went across to the cash box, extracted five five-pound notes and put them in Willie's hand. "There you are."

"Thank you very much, sir."

"That's all right. A bargain's a bargain. Now—I'm afraid I've got a lot to do, so . . ."

"Oh yes, sir." Willie turned and made for the door. Just inside it he stopped. "I suppose if you're going to Polchester, you won't be back by seven o'clock, will you sir?"

"No—why?"

"I was just thinking you'll have to miss *Columbo*. He's on then. That's a shame, sir. You ought to see it. It's smashing. The murderers are always wealthy folk, you know—big shots and really smart. But he always gets them. And do you know why, sir—where they go wrong?"

"No, I don't."

"They try to be too clever. There's a lot to be said for not being too clever," said Willie.

CHAPTER 11

For the next two days Sylvia was tense with nervous excitement. In her handbag was the notebook containing Nokes's phone number, and every so often she would take it out and stare at the illiterately scrawled figures. Sometimes it was almost the only thing that convinced her she'd ever seen Nokes at all.

So taken up was she with anticipation of what the phone call would bring that she only half noticed that Edgar was as preoccupied as ever, and at times almost irritable with it.

Thursday came. Throughout the long, hot morning the hands of the clock seemed to drag themselves around, and the temptation not to wait until the afternoon was very strong. But she was determined not to seem too eager, and she resisted. Afternoon she had said, and she held herself back until two-thirty. Then it was that with shaking and clammy hands she lifted the receiver and dialled.

A gruff male voice answered, "Yes?"

Sylvia said, "Is Nokes there?"

"Who?"

"Nokes—Duggie Nokes."

"Hang on."

There was the clatter of the receiver being put down on a hard surface, then silence apart from some indistinguishable voices faintly in the background. Sylvia waited, twisting the flex between her fingers, until she heard the receiver being lifted and a voice whisper, " 'Ullo?"

"Mr. Nokes?"

"Yus."

"This is Mary Smith. I'm ringing as arranged."

"Oh." There was a pause.

Sylvia said, "Any luck?"

"Luck?"

"Yes—you know, the—the specialist you were going to find for me."

"Well, it ain't easy."

"Does that mean you haven't?"

"Well, I ain't 'ad much time, 'ave I?"

"We agreed I'd ring at this time."

Nokes said nothing.

Sylvia said impatiently, "Well, what's the position now?"

"Ring me back in ten minutes." The line went dead.

Sylvia put the receiver down slowly. There was a chance, then. It didn't seem possible. She poured herself a gin and tonic, took her time drinking it, then went to the phone again. On this occasion it was Nokes himself who answered.

"Mary Smith," she said.

"When can you get up here again?"

"To London? Well—" She thought rapidly; she had no time to waste. "Tomorrow, I suppose—afternoon."

"OK. Be at the Zoo at two sharp. Wait outside the monkey-'ouse. Wear the same outfit as last week. Bring me two 'undred nicker wiv you."

And before she could say anything else, he'd rung off again.

Sylvia said, "Hullo?" twice, then hung up. This was ridiculous! He'd not given her a chance to ask any questions. Monkey-house? He was just playing with her. He obviously thought the whole thing was a put-on and she'd be left standing outside the monkey-house for hours.

On the other hand—he *had* told her to bring the two hundred pounds, which meant—which meant, perhaps, that she'd be set on and robbed of it. No, no—not in broad daylight—at London Zoo— not if she kept a tight hold of her handbag. . . . But perhaps on the way home her car would be forced off the road. . . . Absurd! He'd never go to all that trouble just for two hundred pounds. Although, he *was* hard-up—his wife had made that clear. . . .

She wouldn't go. Let them wait for hours by the monkey-house, and then see who had the last laugh. It was too risky, anyway, mixing with people of that sort. Anything might happen to her—anything at all. . . .

Regent's Park Zoo was a sweltering swarm of human and animal life. Sylvia was in position at ten to two, and stood waiting, feeling horribly conspicuous in her purple trouser suit and blonde wig. She was beginning to hate this get-up—especially as she knew she now looked a very odd and bulgy shape. This was because her pockets were stuffed with £190 in £1 notes. (She was carrying an old empty handbag; that would fool Nokes or his cronies if they tried a snatch.)

It really was revolting here. She had never been to a zoo in her life before, and certainly wouldn't come again. Children and ice-cream were everywhere, and from behind her came the incessant chatter and jibber of both inmates and visitors in the monkey-house.

Thank heaven Edgar would never know the indignities she was having to undergo in order to get rid of him. He believed she was at another sale. She had toyed with the idea of not telling him she was coming to London at all, but to say she was going to have a long day shopping in Polchester. But she had had to use the car, and it occurred to her that it would be just her luck if by fluke some acquaintance of theirs happened to spot it in London.

A very small child of indeterminate sex approached unsteadily, holding out a bag of unpleasantly coloured sweets, which it thrust in the general direction of Sylvia's knees, saying emphatically as it did so, "Dag."

Sylvia frowned and said sharply, "Go away." Then, as it showed no sign of doing so, moved away herself. Really, some mothers!

She took up another position twenty yards away. She looked at her watch. Ten past two. He wasn't coming.

A voice to her left said quietly, "Mary Smith?"

She turned quickly. The speaker was a shortish man of about forty-five, lean and tanned, with very close-cropped black hair and a hard lined face, a scar on the left cheek. His lips were thin and his eyes a cold light blue. He was dressed in grey trousers, an old tweed jacket and a black open-neck shirt, the collar inside his coat. His hands were in his pockets.

Sylvia gulped and said, "Yes. Who—who are you?"

His mouth twisted into a cynical grin. "My name's Smith, too. John Smith. Quite a coincidence, isn't it? Let's walk." And he started to stroll away.

She hurried after him and caught him up. She glanced sideways at him. He'd spoken like an educated man—which was a surprise, and a great relief. There was the trace of an accent there, though. Was it Scots? Sylvia thought so; but there was another element mixed in. Australian? South African? She couldn't tell. No doubt a man like this had been all over the place. There was somehow an exhilarating look about him. And while he wasn't exactly good-looking, he was in a way attractive. Sylvia began to feel the ripplings of excitement. This man was dangerous. The knowledge was strangely pleasant. She was glad she'd come.

Smith led her to a slightly less frequented part of the grounds, where there was a seat beneath some trees. Here he sat down. Sylvia sat next to him. He took out a packet of cigarettes, lit one and put the packet away.

Sylvia said, "Don't I get offered one?"

"You don't smoke."

"How do you know?"

"I can tell."

He didn't look at her, just leaned back, crossed his legs, stared up at the trees and inhaled deeply on his cigarette. There was silence.

She said, "I suppose Nokes did send you?"

"Nobody sends me anywhere, Mary. Let's get that straight for a start."

"Sorry. I'll change that. I suppose it was Nokes who told you about me."

"A bit."

"What bit?"

"That you've got five grand you want to dispose of, and you're looking for a bloke who can use it."

"He's got to earn it."

"Somehow I didn't think you were from Christian Aid."

"I told Nokes that the man I wanted had to be a villain."

"Not a pure white knight in shining armour? I'm disappointed."

"Are you a villain?"

"That depends who you ask."

"I'm asking you."

"Well, I've never slaughtered babies in their cots. But that's about all I haven't done."

"And why haven't you slaughtered babies in their cots?"

"No one's ever paid me to."

"I think you're the man I'm looking for," Sylvia said.

"That's what they all say. OK—who's the hit?"

She didn't answer immediately. Then she said, "How did you know what I—?"

"Oh, come on, Mary. Five grand! Has to be able to use a gun!"

"I thought you might think it was for a bank raid or something."

"I've never known anyone planning a bank job try to hire a gunman before anybody else."

"How do you know I haven't hired others already?"

"If you had any pros signed up you wouldn't have had to go to a runt like Nokes to get an intro to a marksman. So I repeat, who's the hit?"

Sylvia said nothing for a moment. This was the crunch. Once she answered, what had been until now merely a project within her mind would be out in the open. Suddenly she was frightened. But there could be no drawing back now. She thought of one hundred thousand pounds, and she thought of *The Elms* and *The Firs*.

"It's a man called Edgar Gascoigne-Chalmers," she said.

Smith gave a short hard laugh. "To name but three. All right, Mrs. Gascoigne-Chalmers, how soon does it have to be done?"

Sylvia's stomach gave a lurch. She started to babble out protestations. The man raised a hand. "OK—forget it. You're Mary Smith, and Gascoigne-Whatshisname ruined your husband in business, or seduced your daughter, or got your son on to drugs. It doesn't make a blind bit of difference to me, so shut up. Now where does he live?"

"Just outside Cornfield. Do you know it?"

"I've been there. Job?"

"He's an accountant—he has offices in Cornfield."

"What else does he do—hobbies and so on?"

"He plays golf—he's on the committee of the local club. And he's a magistrate and very active locally in all sorts of things. But I don't want it done when he's in Cornfield."

"Why not?"

"It's important I'm not suspected."

"Why should you be suspected?"

"Well, it's something like you said just now—I've got a grudge against him, and it's pretty well known locally."

"So you live in Cornfield, too."

"Well—near."

"So why can't you go out of town—come up to London again on the day it's done, and establish an alibi?"

"I could, but it's not that so much. My grudge against him is personal, and I thought it would be better if it was made to look as though the shooting was over a business matter."

"Look, a bullet's a bullet—if it's fired by a business enemy or a private one. It's no part of my contract to try and frame someone else for the hit."

"I don't want you to. But I was wondering if it could be made to look as though he was shot in mistake for someone else."

"Who, for instance?"

"Sir Hector Wainwright, perhaps."

"The financier? Why him?"

"Edgar—er, Gascoigne-Chalmers will be meeting him a week today in Birmingham. One of his clients—a farm machinery dealer —is thinking of selling out to one of the companies Wainwright controls—Amalgamated Farm Equipment. Gascoigne-Chalmers has to go up with him to AFE's head office, for a meeting with Wainwright and the whole Board. They'll be taking them out to lunch—I don't know where—but I thought if it could be done while they were together, people might think Wainwright was the intended target. You know how many enemies he must have."

"You make it sound so easy. It's not like shooting rabbits, you know."

"Oh, I realize that. It was just an idea."

"Would you still want it done—even if it would be obvious that Gascoigne-Chalmers *was* the intended victim?"

Sylvia gulped. Then, "Yes," she said.

He was silent. Nervously she asked, "Is there anything else you want to know?"

"No."

"Well, then, will you—"

"Shut up, woman, can't you?"

Sylvia went red, but she shut up. Three or four minutes passed in silence, before he took his cigarette from his mouth, dropped it on the ground and crushed it beneath his heel. He said, "If possible, I'll do it in Brum, in the way you suggest."

Sylvia felt a cold shiver shoot up her spine. She didn't look at him.

"But it'll depend on the geography," he went on, "—the situation of the company's office, of the restaurant, and how they travel from one to the other. If it doesn't work out, I'll have to do it where and when I can—but it *will* be outside Cornfield. Deal?"

She tried to speak, but nothing came out, so she just nodded.

"Half in advance," Smith said.

She swung towards him in surprise. "What—what do you mean?"

"What do you think I mean? I want half the fee in advance. That, if the arithmetic is beyond you, comes to two thousand five hundred pounds."

"But—I can't possibly . . ."

Smith got to his feet and started to walk away. "So long," he said casually.

"No—wait—please."

He stopped. "Why? Either I get two and a half grand before the job or there's no job. It's as simple as that."

"But I haven't got the money yet."

"When will you have it?"

"After he's dead."

"You mean you're mentioned in his will—this guy whom everybody knows you have a grudge against?"

"No, it's not that—" Sylvia stopped. "Oh, what's the use? I lied. You're right, of course. He is my husband. Until he's dead I can't get hold of that amount of money without his knowing."

"Poor little penniless waif! My heart bleeds for you."

"So if you could see your way clear . . ."

She hadn't said those words in that tone of voice to anyone for over twenty years. Then it had been their landlady in Paddington.

"Nothing doing, Mary. Half in advance it's got to be. If you think of any way to raise the cash, you can get in touch with me through Nokes."

Sylvia said, "Don't go away. I let *you* stop to think. You've got to let me, too. Now please just sit down. I'll see if I can work something out."

Smith gave a shrug, sat down beside her again, and lit another cigarette.

Sylvia's mind was working furiously. She daren't just draw the cash from the bank. Of course, if all went well Edgar would be dead before the withdrawal showed up in their statement; but the manager was a friend of theirs; he was a member of the golf club; suppose he just happened casually to mention the withdrawal to Edgar?

There was her own deposit account. Fortunately, that was in another bank. She had drawn lump sums from it at various times, to buy antiques and so on. But she had already taken £200 out today, to pay Nokes, and there was only £600 left in it. That would still leave her with nineteen hundred to find. Was there anything she could sell—anything that Edgar wouldn't miss?

The Begonzi. It was easily her most valuable painting. That little dealer in Polchester—Delgado—had offered her eight hundred for it a few years ago. It was sure to have gone up in value since then— perhaps to a thousand. And she had that copy of it in the attic. So she could replace the original. Edgar would never notice the difference. Anything else? Only her beaver coat. That wouldn't be missed during the summer. It might just fetch four hundred; it had a mink collar. That made a total of two thousand—with luck. And that was it. There was no way she could raise more. She made a quick decision and took a chance.

"Two thousand. I think I might be able to raise two thousand. But that's the absolute maximum. I should be able to let you have that by the middle of next week, and the balance later. If that's no good, we'll have to call it off. I'm sorry."

She waited for his answer, almost holding her breath. It was a long time coming, but at last, very quietly, he said, "All right."

Sylvia closed her eyes.

"Next Wednesday," he said. "That's your deadline."

"Very well. Where do we meet? Here again?"

"No: never meet twice in the same place. Indoors."

"Indoors?"

"You'll be handing money over. I'll be counting. You can never be sure you're not seen outside."

"All right. Where?"

"You'd better bring it to my hotel."

She was startled. "Is that safe?"

"Why not? Somehow I fancy you don't normally look like you do today, do you—so who's going to recognize you?"

"All right, then. Where is it?"

"It will be the Cogan in Islington by next week. Ask for John Smith. Any time between three and seven. And bring a photo of your husband—or several, if you can—different angles."

She nodded. "I ought to have thought of that."

"There was no need—I did. Wednesday, then. Stay here now while I leave."

She watched him walk away, glad that he'd left first, for she was shaking all over and knew that she wouldn't be able to walk steadily for a few minutes at least.

She leaned her head back, closed her eyes and tried to relax. Then she gave a start, as a low voice near at hand said: "Let's 'av it, then."

It was Nokes. He'd approached in complete silence and was sitting where Smith had been a moment before.

"You fool!" Sylvia said angrily. "Do you always do things like that?"

"Here, steady on, lidy. I set this up, didn' I? I got 'old've jus' the bloke you was looking for. So less of the fool, if you please. Now, I reckon you've done a deal wiv 'im, so I'll 'ave me money, if you don't mind. Two hundred."

Sylvia glanced round, waited for two or three people to walk past, then dipped into her pockets, and brought out the bundles of notes. She handed them to him. "Here, take it quickly, then clear off and leave me alone. And there's one hundred and ninety there. You had ten on account."

"Aw. I thought as 'ow you might think've that as a sort've expense accahnt—or as a bonus for a job well done."

"You'd be lucky," Sylvia said.

Nokes counted the money quickly, stuffed it into his pockets and stood up. "OK, lidy, that's it. Glad to do business wiv you. See you again sometime p'raps."

"Not if I can help it," said Sylvia.

The following Monday and Tuesday were for Sylvia both hectic and furtive. On Monday, while Edgar was at the office, she had to replace the Begonzi with her copy, and then take it to Delgado, the dealer in Polchester. On the way she stopped off at the bank where she had her deposit account. She found that, with interest, she had a balance of £620. She drew it all out. There had recently been a reduction in interest rates, and she made this her reason.

After some considerable haggling with Delgado, she managed to squeeze from him a highly satisfactory one thousand and fifty pounds. She asked to be paid in cash, and he complied without expressing surprise, obviously suspecting a tax dodge.

When she got home she spent half an hour with the classified phone book and the *Times* and *Telegraph* personal columns; and then quite a long time on the phone. She ended up with half a dozen names and addresses of people who bought second-hand furs, and a rough estimate from one of them that her coat might fetch around four hundred pounds. She set out with it on Tuesday morning. After a number of calls she had to settle eventually for £350. It was a little disappointing, but as it pushed up her total over the magic two thousand she was content.

That evening she again had to tell Edgar that she'd be out all day on Wednesday. The elusive guest-room dressing-table was really becoming a most useful object . . .

The Cogan Hotel in Islington was a dingy Victorian building, its windows badly in need of a clean. Sylvia drove on a couple of blocks before parking. It meant she had to walk some little way, carrying the two thousand, and although she was a trifle nervous about this, it had to be done, as she wasn't prepared to risk her car being seen outside the hotel.

She got out, locked it, and gripping the old zipped shopping bag containing the money, hurried back. It was just five past three when she entered the hotel. The interior was as seedy and shabby in appearance as the outside. A fat, bald man in shirt-sleeves and braces was sitting behind a tiny reception desk, filling in a pools coupon. Sylvia went across. He glanced up at her incuriously. As casually as she could manage it Sylvia said, "Mr. Smith?"

He gave a leer. "Which one?"

"Er, John Smith."

The leer became a chuckle. "Oh, *John* Smith. Of course, why didn't I guess? Twenty-nine. Second floor. There's no lift."

Sylvia said, "Thank you," coldly and made for the stairs. She was breathing heavily by the time she got to the second floor. She found herself walking on tiptoe along the ill-lit corridor. She came to room twenty-nine and tapped on the door.

Five seconds passed, then it opened. Smith stood in the gap. He was wearing the same shirt and trousers as on the Tuesday, but no jacket. He was unshaven. He raised his eyebrows and stood aside without speaking. Sylvia went in and he closed the door. He said, "I didn't expect you."

"Didn't you think I'd be able to raise the cash?"

"I didn't think you'd try. Thought you'd chicken out."

"I don't chicken out, Mr. Smith. I may be lots of things, but I'm not a coward, and when I make up my mind to do a thing, I always go through with it."

He looked at her closely and it seemed to her that there was a new respect in his eyes. For some reason this gave her a strange satisfaction.

"So you have got the money," he said.

For answer, she walked across the room, unzipped her bag and upended it over the bed. The five- and one-pound notes cascaded out into a heap.

He walked to the bed, picked up a five-pound note, put it down again and traced a path through the pile of money with his forefinger. Then he glanced at Sylvia once more. "Well done."

"Aren't you going to count it?" she asked.

He shook his head. "It looks about right, and you wouldn't be fool enough to try and cheat me. Finished with the bag?"

He took it from her, opened it wide, held it by the bed and swept the money back into it with his other arm. He closed the zip and chucked the bag casually under the bed.

She said, "About the balance—?"

"I'll be in touch in a couple of weeks. Got the photos?"

"Oh yes." Sylvia opened her handbag and took out a photographic shop's paper wallet, which she handed to him.

He glanced at the three photos inside. She said, "One's just a snap, but it's the only one I could find showing that particular angle, with—"

"They'll do." He put them down on the bedside table.

She said, "Then that's everything, I suppose."

"Yep. No changes in his plans?"

"No. Oh, and I've found out where they're having lunch. It's a place called Mario's in the Bull Ring."

"Yes, I know."

"You do? Oh, I see." She paused. "And you're going to do it on Friday?"

"That's what I said."

"Suppose something goes wrong?"

"Suppose it does?"

"Well"—she tried to smile—"do I get my money back?"

"Yes, Mary, you get your blood money back—every lousy penny of it. Providing I'm still alive and at large to get it back to you, that is, and you don't want me to have another go."

"How will I find you to let you know?"

Irritably he said, "I'll put an ad in *The Times* personal column, telling you how to contact me. Look for one to Mary, signed John."

"Very well."

"But get this straight, nothing's going to go wrong—I'm a pro and I do a pro job."

"How on earth," she said, "did a—"

He interrupted with a savage chuckle. "Did someone as nice as me get started in a job like this? Wrong, Mary: in rooms of this type its always the guy who asks that question."

Sylvia flushed. "Sorry."

"Oh, I don't mind laying it on the line for you. Prepare to weep buckets. Want a drink?"

"Yes—please."

He went to the dressing-table, on which there was a bottle of Scotch and a single whisky glass. He filled the glass and handed it to her, then went to the bed, sat on it and poured some more whisky into a tumbler on the bedside table. "Sit down," he said.

Sylvia sat down on the room's only chair.

He took a drink. "You want to know how I got started? Well, I was encouraged to take up the profession, almost begged, you might say, by some very kind gentlemen in the service of Her Majesty's Government."

Sylvia's eyes widened. "You were a secret agent?"

"Now that's a very melodramatic word. Let's just say I was trained at great trouble and expense to do one job—and do it quickly and efficiently. I learned fast. I was soon the best they had. I disposed of quite a few undesirable persons on behalf of my masters." He emptied the glass and put it down. "Plus one or two decent blokes, too, I shouldn't wonder. And then one day the kind gentlemen, having effectively made me fit for only one profession, decided they required my services no longer. Don't imagine it was because I'd sold my soul to the nasty reds or anything like that. All I did was just shoot one too many of the dear chaps—one that HMG happened to want unshot at that particular time. The fact that if I had left him unshot, I myself would have been very much shot was a defence that didn't impress them."

Sylvia drank some whisky. "What did you do?"

"What any highly trained but unemployed government assassin would do: went free-lance. I had a few contacts in blood-letting circles, and there's no shortage of commissions. One client tended to recommend me to another. It's been a real Cook's tour, I can tell you: Ireland, Cyprus, the Middle East. Then Africa for quite a long time. Great opportunities there, but it's not really a safe place for delicately nurtured white assassins any more. So then I made for the States. Did quite well for a time, but they're starting to operate a closed-shop there now, so it was back to dear old Blighty—where from now on I intend to concentrate on private jobs; no more political contracts, just people who want to get rid of their nearest and dearest. Right—that's it. Satisfied?"

He picked up a cigarette packet from the bedside table, shook it, stood up, went to the wardrobe and took a fresh pack from his coat hanging inside. Somewhat dazedly Sylvia said, "I can hardly believe it."

"Don't believe it, if it makes you feel more comfortable not to. Tell yourself it's all a tissue of lies. I don't give two hoots." He lit a cigarette.

"But—but do you intend to go on doing this—always?"

"Oh, I have the traditional numbered Swiss bank account. I should think another ten or a dozen commissions should see me through."

"Do you really think you'll get another twelve commissions—just like that?"

"Mary, Mary, you'd be surprised."

"But how will people find out about you?"

"Well, for a start, I'll naturally expect you to recommend me to all your girl friends. I'll give you some of my business cards to pass round."

In spite of the flip talk, she could sense a deep bitterness and disillusionment within him. Then he seemed to regret that he'd said so much, and abruptly, in a different tone of voice, said,

"By the way, I've been looking at pictures of Hector Wainwright, and now I've seen those photos of your Edgar it occurs to me that there is a superficial resemblance between them. So I think I'll try and wing Hector with a second bullet immediately after Edgar's shot. That should make it look as though he was the real hit."

Sylvia got to her feet excitedly. "But that's wonderful!"

"Not normally part of the service, but for you, no extra charge."

"Though why just wing him?" she asked. "Why not kill *him,* too? Then they'd be *sure* to think he was the real target."

"If I kill him, it'll cost you another five grand."

"I see. Well, I can't afford that. I can barely afford another three."

He stepped across to her. "I hope you have no ideas of reneging on our deal afterwards, Mary. Because I warn you, I wouldn't take at all kindly to that."

She looked him straight in the eye. "And just what would you do, Mr. Smith?"

His hand shot out, and almost before she could blink he had hold of her wrist in a grip like a steel trap. Then he pulled her against him, at the same instant pushing her arm behind her, twisting it and forcing it up her back. She cried out in pain. He increased the pressure further and she had to grit her teeth to avoid giving a scream. Watching her face intently all the time, he kept up the pressure for another ten seconds. Then he let her arm drop an inch or two and the pain eased.

His face was inches from her own. Very softly he said, "Scared, Mary?"

She nodded.

"*Very* scared?"

"No. Just medium scared."

"Scared enough not to think about trying to cheat me?"

"Do you really think I'd ever risk getting on the wrong side of you, Mr. Smith? I'd feel very much more comfortable if I thought you were my friend."

The next moment he'd released her wrist and both his arms were around her. Before she could speak, his lips were hard against her own. For a second or two she struggled and tried to fight him off. But only for a second or two.

CHAPTER 12

Sylvia spent Thursday in a whirl of conflicting emotions—self-disgust, elation, fear, excitement and (most of all) incredulity. If just three weeks ago anyone had told her . . .

It was fortunate that not only did Edgar lunch in Cornfield that day, but also that he had to work at his office most of the evening, preparing for Friday's meeting. Otherwise, he would surely have noticed something odd about her behaviour. She couldn't even face the prospect of seeing him when he eventually did come in, and she went to bed early, leaving a note saying that she had a headache.

He had to be off very early on Friday, and she got up earlier than usual, too, to prepare breakfast and see him off.

He'd put on his newest and most expensive suit, and she had to suppress a ridiculous pang of irritation when she saw it and thought how the bullet would ruin it. For a mad moment she almost found herself telling him to change into something older.

Somehow she got through the period in a relatively normal manner, and eventually kissed him goodbye, trying as she did so to force herself to realize that it was the last time she would ever have to do this.

"Goodbye, darling," he said. "Have a good day. I won't be later than eight."

"Take care of yourself, dear."

She waved him off, sat down for another cup of coffee and then went back upstairs to try and decide what she would wear at the inquest.

Afterwards she strolled outside and spoke to George. She intended to let him see her frequently throughout the day. She didn't for one moment think that anybody would suspect her of having shot Edgar. But it wouldn't do any harm at all to have an alibi. One couldn't be too careful.

She didn't know when John would do it. (She knew this wasn't his real name, but it was how she would always think of him.) Presumably it would be when they went out to lunch, though he hadn't been able to say that definitely. It might even be before that. She would listen to every news broadcast during the morning. Of course, the police would inform her, as next of kin, before it was announced publicly. But if an attempt was (apparently) made on the life of Sir Hector Wainwright, the BBC would certainly report it—plus the fact of another man being killed in the incident.

So she switched on every hour. But on none of the summaries was there any mention of Wainwright, or of any shooting in the Birmingham area. The same held true of the full-length bulletin at one o'clock. At two o'clock Sylvia could hardly bear to listen. But she forced herself. Again there was nothing. By three o'clock she was a wreck. This would be the one, surely: if John had pulled it off during the lunch period, they'd be bound to have it in by now. She stood by the radio, her eyes closed, her fists clenched, waiting for the previous programme to finish.

It seemed to take an age. Then there was music, followed by a trailer, and finally the time signal before at last the newsreader came on.

"Reports are just coming in of a fatal shooting incident" (Sylvia caught her breath) "a short time ago in the centre of" (Sylvia nearly fainted) "Belfast."

She made herself hear the summary out before switching off and dropping into a chair. Perhaps John hadn't been able to get a shot at Sir Hector after all. Perhaps for some reason Sir Hector hadn't even turned up at the meeting. They might not think it worth bothering to report the death of an unimportant country accountant. In that case, it was a visit from the police she had to be ready for. She was shaking and she knew her face was white. She must steady her nerves.

She fetched a bottle of gin and a glass and took them to a chair inside the drawing-room window, from which she could see a hundred yards of the road outside. Here she waited—and drank. And waited. And drank some more.

Four o'clock. Five. Six. The only things that passed along the lane were a farm lorry, a post office van, and two girls on bicycles. George trudged past the window a few times, casting slightly puzzled glances at Sylvia, as she sat, almost motionless. After he went home she was alone. She drank more gin than she'd ever drunk in her life before. But for some reason she didn't become drunk; she just passed into a kind of waking trance, in which time ceased to exist

At six-fifteen she gave a shake of her head, stood up and went to the telephone. She obtained Amalgamated Farm Equipment's number from directory inquiries and rang them. The call was answered by somebody who sounded as though he could have been a commissionaire. She asked if any of the executives were still present.

"No, I'm sorry, madam; everybody's left."

"Actually, I was trying to get hold of a Mr. Gascoigne-Chalmers. He should have been there earlier today with a Mr. Brownlow."

"Oh yes, madam. I showed them into Sir Hector myself this morning. They finally left about half an hour ago."

"I see. Thank you. There—er, hasn't been any trouble of any sort there today—or anywhere near?"

"Trouble, madam? Not to my knowledge. What sort of trouble were you thinking of?"

"It doesn't matter," Sylvia said. She rang off. It still wasn't too late. They'd hardly be clear of Birmingham yet. Probably John had found a better place for the hit. He'd know what to do. Perhaps Edgar and Brownlow would stop for a drink and he'd do it then.

Another half-hour passed and Sylvia's confidence began to wane. By quarter past seven she was in despair. She'd surely have heard by now if anything had happened. Something must have gone wrong. Which meant that after all Edgar would be coming home again. And she had to start preparing dinner . . .

Yet she couldn't. She couldn't do anything. She'd have to make some excuse. She just sat and waited.

Eight o'clock came. He had said he'd be home by eight. He was always punctual. He'd left the factory at quarter to six. Certainly the journey wouldn't normally take more than two hours or so. Therefore, even if he had stopped for a drink, he couldn't be very much longer.

At ten past eight faint hopes began to rise again in Sylvia's breast. By eight-twenty excitement was gripping her, and at eight-thirty her doubts had almost vanished. By twenty to nine she was telling herself that John hadn't let her down after all. He'd done it—the darling had done it!

Then, at eight-forty-five, she heard a car in the lane. She rushed to the window. No—it wasn't the Rover! It was a strange, large black car. The police . . . ? Yes—the driver was wearing a peaked cap. And the car was stopping outside!

Edgar was dead! They'd come to tell her.

Sylvia ran to the hall, threw open the front door, stumbled down the steps and started along the path.

Then she saw that the car was pulling away. It was a taxi. And Edgar—Edgar was just closing the front gate behind him.

Sylvia stopped. It couldn't be true. He was dead—he had to be. John . . .

Edgar turned from closing the gate and saw her. His expression changed. "Sylvia! What on earth's the matter?"

Sylvia burst into tears.

"Darling!" He hurried forward and took her by the arm. "What is it? What's wrong?"

"Oh, Edgar. You're so late. I thought that was a police car—that you'd been killed."

"Killed? No—I had a bit of car trouble on the way back, so I decided to leave it at Hillier's for them to repair first thing in the morning, and I took a taxi home. I'm sorry—I should have phoned. But it's not really very late."

Sylvia continued to cry.

He said, "I'm all right, darling. I'm not dead."

"I know," sobbed Sylvia. "I know."

Sylvia hardly slept that night, wondering what had gone wrong and if any harm had come to John. She was up waiting for the papers in the morning. She grabbed *The Times* as soon as it fell through the letter box, and ran her eyes down the personal column. But there was no message for Mary. She told herself that if the snag had arisen at the last moment, he wouldn't have had time to get it in yet.

However, no message appeared for her on Monday either, and as soon as Edgar had left for the office Sylvia phoned the Cogan Hotel.

She was told that John Smith had checked out the previous Thursday morning, and had left no forwarding address.

There was one channel of communication left. She fetched her notebook and called the number Nokes had given her. The same voice answered as when she'd rung first. She asked for Nokes, and a minute later heard a whispered: " 'Ullo?"

She said, "This is Mary Smith."

"Oh, wotcher, Mair. I been expecting you to call. I gotta message for you."

"From Jo—from your friend?"

"That's it."

She said eagerly, "Well, what is it? Tell me."

" 'Old on—'e wrote it dahn." There was the sound of the crumpling of paper, then Nokes said, "Ready?"

"Yes—yes."

"Right. 'Ere it is. 'Thanks.' "

"What?"

" 'Thanks.' That's the message."

"That can't be all!"

"It is."

"But—thanks for what?"

Nokes cackled. "Two grand, I reckon. Er, mostly."

"But he hasn't done the—the job I hired him for."

"No; 'e told me 'e couldn' make it Friday, arter all."

"Well, when's he going to?"

"That's 'ard to say."

"But he won't get the other three thousand until the job's done."

"Some'ow I fink 'e's gonna settle for two—less me five per cent, o' course."

"But if he's not doing the job he's got to let me have that back!"

This time Nokes gave a chortle that nearly shattered her eardrum. "Mair, in your own words, 'You'll be lucky.' "

Sylvia knew she'd gone white. She said weakly, "What . . . ?"

"You're awful slow to catch on, lidy. Let me spell it out, you've been taken—taken for two thousand nicker. But don't feel too bad abaht it. 'E's the best con artist in London. 'E's fooled smarter people'n you. 'E was on the stage once, but 'e makes a better living like this. Didn' 'e look the part? Didn' he look jus' like a killer? Marvellous when you think 'e's never 'urt a fly in 'is life. That tan—all aht of a bottle. And the scar! That was a master stroke. But 'e always takes so much trouble it's unbelievable. You should see 'im as a parson—great."

Sylvia gave vent to a shriek of pure rage. "You swine!"

"Now keep you 'air on. You enjoyed yourself, din' you? 'E said as 'ow you seemed to—and you was very affectionate."

"You lousy crooks!"

"Lidy, you *wanted* crooks. You come looking for crooks. You mustn' be surprised when they act like crooks."

"Listen," she hissed, "you're not going to get away with this. I'm going to get that money back, do you hear?"

"OK—if you want your money back, I'll tell you what to do."

"You'd better!"

"Sue us," said Nokes. Then the line went dead.

For an hour and a half Sylvia lay on her bed and sobbed in frustration and anguish. Two thousand pounds. Two thousand. Her Begonzi. And her fur coat. Why had she been such a fool?

Gradually, very gradually, she partially calmed down. It really wasn't her fault. It was Edgar's fault—all Edgar's. He'd forced her into this by being so beastly. He wasn't going to get away with it, though. She wasn't going to be beaten so easily. Edgar was going to die. She was going to get *The Firs*. But there'd be no more hit men. She was going to do it herself. And she was going to enjoy doing it.

CHAPTER 13

Edgar was stuck.

The Willie débâcle, following on his failure to engineer the car crash, had shaken him. Two attempts: one simple, the other complex; one rapidly thought out and executed, the second entailing much advance planning; one a completely solo affair, the other involving a third person. And both almighty flops.

Luckily, there'd been no disaster. But he was extremely wary of making another attempt until he could think of a plan that didn't involve as much reliance as the first two on chance or other people. But the days passed, and not one idea, of the many dozens he considered, withstood the test. He racked his brains harder and harder, becoming more and more absent-minded and making frequent mistakes in his work. The deadline was approaching inexorably. He grew first anxious, then seriously worried, and at last positively desperate. The only entry on the credit side was the fact Sylvia remained strangely unconcerned about *The Firs*. He'd been expecting an intensive campaign to persuade him to buy the place. But in fact she didn't seem even to want to talk about the subject at all. It was odd. He had noticed this ostrich-like attitude in her occasionally over the years—a tendency to ignore impending trouble, to take no action to avert it, in the apparent hope that it would just go away. There was the way she'd been just living on her tiny capital when he'd first met her.

However, since they'd been married he'd never known the trait to be quite so pronounced as it was now. The Horatio Dimsdale Trust might just not exist. Yes, it was very odd—but a great relief. For it suited him down to the ground, and left him time to think.

His main difficulty was that if one of only two people living in a house died of any but unquestionably natural causes, some suspicion was almost bound to fall on the other. Therefore, the only safe plan was to do the job when he and Sylvia were ostensibly apart. One way would be to go away himself, arrange some sort of alibi, slip home, do it, and go back again. But alibis depended so much on other people.

If only Sylvia would go away again. Because the exasperating thing was that, almost without trying, he had thought of a way he could have done it when she'd last stayed overnight in London, for the auctions. For he'd recently read of an outbreak of hotel thefts in the city, in one or two of which violence had been used. Suppose Sylvia, alone in her hotel room, had woken to find a thief ransacking her luggage? She would have started to scream. And of course would have had to be silenced . . .

Edgar knew the Alendale Hotel, had stayed there himself several times. It was in a quiet area, and was an easy place to enter or leave unobserved, the old night porter tending to spend his shift in the small office behind the reception desk. It would have been easy . . .

He would, of course, have been without an alibi. But in those circumstances it wouldn't matter; an alibi would, in itself, be suspicious. However, this was academic. He'd missed his chance. It would be unheard of for her to spend a second night away from *The Elms* so soon after the other. She hated being absent from the house and never stayed away a moment longer than was necessary. She wouldn't be going off again now. Pity.

It was on Monday afternoon she thought of it.

She'd spent the morning slowly simmering down, and forcing herself to put Smith and Nokes and all her problems out of her mind. It was this or go mad. She had to concentrate on normal, everyday matters for a while.

So after lunch she had gone into the garden to give George his instructions for the week.

"Heard about the water restrictions, mum?" he asked.

"I didn't get the details," Sylvia said. "What is it—no more sprinklers, watering of flowers, and so on?"

"Aye, that's about the size of it. And they're turning off at nights, too. Still, won't affect you so much, will it?"

"Not so long as our well doesn't let us down, and it's never done yet."

"They do say it hasn't dried up in near four hundred years. Mind you, mum, it's a bit of a hard job, having to wind them buckets up all the time. Pesky deep, that well." George rubbed the small of his back, ruminatively.

"Well, I'm sure my husband will help out with the hauling."

"I'd be obliged, mum. Perhaps he could get a bucket or two up ready last thing at nights, to give me a start in the mornings."

"I'll tell him," Sylvia said.

George wandered off and Sylvia strolled over to the well. She supposed there *was* still water in the bottom. She picked up a stone and dropped it in. She waited, listening. No, she thought—then there it was: that oddly satisfying plop. She never got used to the time it took things to reach the bottom. What a depth it was—

And then suddenly it was all there: the bones of a virtually foolproof plan, all wrapped up and presented to her—presented by Nature, some Council officials, and old George. All she had to do was use it.

The parapet round the well was low—not more than eighteen inches—too low for safety. Anyone approaching it at a brisk walk, who tripped when about four feet or so away, might easily fall in, especially as the old stonework was rather loose and crumbly and wouldn't provide a safe handhold. She and Edgar had discussed this years before, but as they hardly ever had occasion to use the well, and as there was nothing near it to trip over, hadn't taken any action; the well was very picturesque, and it would have been a pity to add a lot of ugly new brickwork.

However, during the next few days Edgar was going to *have* to use the well, and not—praise be—at her request, but at old George's. Three times a week at least he was going to have to go out to the well carrying a couple of pails. She knew he wouldn't object to doing this; he rather liked being called on to undertake the occasional heavyish manual job—so long as it was a clean one, and not beneath his dignity; it made him feel younger and fitter than he actually was. He always did such tasks with a show of speed and vigour. She knew he would stride out to the well, swinging a couple of empty pails—she could just see him. So easy—so tragically easy then to trip and fall. Particularly if it was dark or nearly dark at the time—he'd probably prefer to do it last thing, before locking up for the night. It would be cooler then.

She herself, of course, would be miles away at the time. That would have to be established beyond doubt. For one thing, he might not be killed by the actual fall—it was possible he would keep his head above water for some time before going under. There might be some way the pathologists could discover this had happened. And if she'd been on hand, the police would ask, why hadn't she sent for help straight away?

So, as far as everybody was concerned, she would be away at the time. No one would know she was really here, helping Edgar on his way down the well. Sylvia gave a giggle. Just like Pussy in the nursery rhyme. That's what she'd call it: Operation Ding Dong Bell.

With Edgar as Pussy and her as little Johnny Green. But no Tommy Stout around to do the pulling out.

"Darling, you're going to hate me," she said, applying cold cream daintily to her face that night.

Edgar, purple and grunting like a pig, was doing his press-ups. "Why's—that—darling?" he asked jerkily.

"Well, I'm thinking of having two more days in London. You won't mind too much, will you?"

His strength gave out at that moment. He went down on to his chest like a stricken hippo and remained there.

"Two days?" he said breathlessly.

"Yes; you see, there are these two auctions—one on Wednesday afternoon and the other Thursday." (This was true; she'd checked on it.) "I'd like to go to them both," she continued, "and I could come back in between, but it would mean rather a lot of unnecessary travelling."

His face contorted with effort, he forced his arms straight again. "So—you'll—go—on—Wednesday—morning?"

"Yes, and get back latish Thursday afternoon. So, you see, it won't be too long."

He got clumsily to his feet. "It always seems a long time when you go away, Sylvia. But I daresay I'll survive."

Not much longer you won't, she thought. Aloud she said, "Thank you, dear. I know I've been doing a lot of gadding about lately, but I promise you that after this trip I won't be going anywhere for a long time."

"Will you stay at the Alendale?"

"I think so. It's very comfortable and they know me there now." (*And it's a very easy place to leave in the middle of the night without being seen.*) "I really hate leaving you so often, but I expect you'll be able to occupy your time." (*What there'll be left of it.*)

He was doing his press-ups prior to going to bed when she said it. She was sitting at the dressing-table, smearing goo all over her face at the time.

"Darling, you're going to hate me."

Going to? he thought. "Why's that, darling?" he asked, not pausing in his exercises.

"Well, I'm thinking of having two more days in London. You won't mind too much, will you?"

The surprise was so great that he momentarily lost his rhythm and sank to the floor.

"Two days?" he said.

She started rambling on about times of different sales, but he couldn't be bothered to listen. It was providential! He remained on the floor for a few seconds, thankful that she couldn't see his face. Then he pressed up again. She'd mentioned something about Wednesday. "So you'll go on Wednesday morning?" he said, feigning breathlessness, so that the excitement in his voice wouldn't come through.

"Yes, and get back latish Thursday afternoon." Then she added simperingly, "So you see, it won't be too long."

He got lightly to his feet. "It always seems a long time" (*a delightfully long time!*) "when you go away, Sylvia. But I daresay I'll survive."

"Thank you, dear. I know I've been doing a lot of gadding about lately, but I promise you that after this trip I won't be going anywhere for a long time."

(*You don't need to promise, darling; I'll see to that.*) "Will you stay at the Alendale?" he asked. *Please, please,* he prayed, *let her say yes.*

"I think so. It's very comfortable and they know me there now. I really hate leaving you so often, but I expect you'll be able to occupy your time."

Oh, easily, my dear—very, very easily.

If the world was to believe that Edgar had tripped and fallen down the well there had to be something there that he could reasonably be supposed to have tripped over; something left on the grass near the well. At first Sylvia had imagined that finding a suitable object would be just a formality. But she soon discovered that it was nothing of the sort. After all, the "accident" would not occur, and would not be thought to have occurred, in total darkness. Even if she managed to convey the impression that he had left fetching the water until the last minute before locking up for the night, there would still be a moon, and in normal circumstances light from the kitchen. So she could not choose too large an object. It had to be something small enough to make the police believe that Edgar could have failed to see it. Something, then, that would lie low—a broom, say, or a rake.

Yet old George was famous for his tidiness, and would never leave things lying about—nor would Edgar himself.

For some time this was an irritating little problem. Then, wandering round the garden on Tuesday morning, Sylvia suddenly saw the clothes line. She stared at it. It ran at right angles between the back door and the well. But was the position right? She hurriedly moved behind the nearer line-post and followed the direction of the line with her eye. Yes—perfect. If it fell straight to the ground it would be just about four feet from the well.

Sylvia lowered the line and examined it. Unfortunately it was strong nylon cord and highly unlikely to break. She looked at the top of the post, where the line ran over a pulley. Then she went to the garden shed and fetched the step-ladder. (She was not observed, as on Tuesdays George didn't come until the afternoon.) She put the step-ladder by the post, climbed up, and examined the pulley. To her excitement she found that it was not all that firmly held. The wood was a little soft, and the screws shifted when she tugged at the pulley. All the same, there was no reason for it suddenly to fall.

She got down and considered. She hadn't done her own laundering for years; and as she owned a very expensive automatic washing machine, incorporating a dryer, for the use of Mrs. Thring, the line did not get a great deal of use. Quite possibly, therefore, a weakness could develop without anyone being aware of it. Certainly nobody had examined it as she had just done for a long time. Suppose, therefore, that the line was suddenly subjected to a considerable weight? The pulley could work loose, yet not actually fall—just remain held in position by a single twist of screw thread. No one could then forecast when it might finally come down.

What, however, could such a sudden weight be? Sylvia racked her brains. Curtains! That was it. Say she had decided to have the dining-room curtains cleaned. She'd needed temporary replacements for them and had fetched those old velvet ones from the box room. But they had smelt of mothballs, so she had decided to hang them out on the line to air for a couple of hours. There were four of them—thick, lined, and reaching to the floor when hanging. Very heavy.

Should she do it now? No; someone—other than Edgar—had to see them hanging there. And at this time nobody would. This afternoon. Then George would see her.

And tonight she had to get Edgar to fill a couple of pails of water to be ready for him. That would establish a pattern.

Really, she was beginning to know how generals felt when they planned their campaigns.

Sylvia lifted the final curtain on to the line and straightened it. Then she called, "George—will you come and help me pull the line up, please?"

He ambled across and lent his weight. "Heavy, aren't they?" he said.

She nodded. "I hope the line holds."

It was Tuesday afternoon. As soon as George left at about five she went out and got the curtains down again. Then once more she fetched the steps, erected them by the post, climbed up and went to work with a chisel. She carefully prised the plate of the pulley away from the wood. When she was satisfied that one strong tug would bring it down, and yet there was no danger of it coming loose before that, she left it.

Before putting the chisel away she took it to the well. The inside of the parapet and top of the shaft was composed of uneven and ir-regularly shaped stones, some of which jutted out a couple of inches. Without much difficulty she managed to gouge out one about the size of a grapefruit. It was no use relying on the fall killing him. Im-probable though it was, he might even remain conscious and able to keep afloat until help came. No—a good, sharp blow on the head was going to be called for. And this stone would be an ideal weapon; its removal left a very obvious gap inside the shaft; she could just drop it in after him; and if the pathologists found traces of similar stone in the wound on his head, the police would surely assume that he had struck his head as he fell and dislodged the stone.

She pushed it down into the long grass at the base of the well, from where she could snatch it up in a second.

There was now nothing more to be done.

Edgar realized over the next twenty-four hours how many snags there still were in the plan needing to be ironed out; how many things he hadn't decided. There were the matters of clothes, a possi-ble disguise—and the weapon to use. On the latter point he couldn't for a long time make up his mind. It would be very nice to let her see his face, just for a second or two, before the end—so that she'd know. And from that respect strangling would be best, and the weapon his own hands. But she might get out some screams or shouts before he could finish her off. So probably a knife would be better.

However, the problem that gave him the most trouble was simply how he was going to get to London. There were no trains at that time of night; and he daren't risk having somebody see his very well-known Rover out on the road at a time when he was supposed to be in bed. To hire a car would be almost as risky: he'd have to produce his licence; there were only two or three rental firms near enough to use, and in all of them, even if they didn't know his face, they'd cer-tainly be familiar with his name. Sylvia's death would undoubtedly be prominently reported in the local paper, and it surely wouldn't take the rental people long to put two and two together. Of course, he could probably steal a car . . .

The ease with which this idea slipped into his mind startled him. Absurd! He was really getting too carried away. And yet . . . Was the idea all that ridiculous? Car theft wasn't difficult. You just found one that was unlocked and then what they called "hot-wired" it—pulled out the wires from behind the dashboard and joined two of them together. That served instead of a key for turning on the ignition: it was the work of a few seconds. The only lengthy part of the job might be locating an unlocked car in the first place. But he could go out comparatively early—say around ten—and take his time in finding one. He knew from his experience on the Bench that there were some people—not many, but enough—who were chronically careless about locking their vehicles, even when leaving them overnight. There was a good chance that the theft of such a car wouldn't be discovered until the morning. In fact, if he could manage to put the car back on his return, the theft might never come to light. The main danger, of course, lay in being spotted actually trying a car door. But here in Cornfield, there was a good chance he would get away with such an action. He was a prominent, reputedly wealthy, and respected local citizen—a Councillor and JP. Nobody would suspect him of actually intending to steal a car. He could say he'd noticed the car door was not shut tightly and had merely stopped to close it—in case a potential thief spotted it. Something like that.

Of course the plan was not entirely without danger. However, he had to face the fact that he was never going to get rid of the creature unless he was ready to take *some* risk. Besides, he told himself, whatever else he was, he was no coward. He wasn't afraid of a little danger; it was something everybody needed in their lives now and again. A little excitement. A little fun.

CHAPTER 14

Sylvia checked in at the Alendale at twelve-thirty on Wednesday. She had lunch, then leaving her Mini in the hotel garage, went out to a large car rental firm and hired a Ford Escort. It was unfortunate that she had to give her true name and address. But there wasn't any real risk involved. The staff of a busy office in central London would be unlikely to remember her name. Even if they did, and Edgar's death made the national news—very doubtful in itself—there'd be no earthly reason for them to think it suspicious that his wife had hired a car from them the day prior to his death—and certainly no cause for them to report it to the police. And even if by some crazy chance the police did learn of it, she could always claim that the Mini had been giving her trouble; unless they could prove she'd actually driven the hired car home during the night, she'd still be in the clear. No, all in all the risk was far smaller than if she drove her own car home. If her Mini were spotted by anybody within miles of *The Elms* that night, or if she were seen driving it from the hotel garage, she could be in real trouble.

After leaving the rental firm she went to the auction—she had made up her mind to do everything she had said she was going to do —then returned to the Alendale, leaving the Escort in a car park about a quarter of a mile away. She had dinner at the hotel, watched television for a while in the lounge, talked to a couple of fellow guests, then, saying that she was very tired and intended to have an early night, went up to her room and lay down. Just as she did so, the phone went. It was Edgar.

"Darling," he said, "how are you?"

"Tired."

"Had a gruelling day?" His voice was sympathetic.

"I have rather. Traffic's terrible. I'm looking forward to bed."

"Er, which room number have you got?"

"Twenty-six. Why?"

"Oh, I just wondered whether you might have the one we liked so much when we were both there last year."

"Hardly, dear. That was a double; naturally I've got a single."

"Of course. Silly of me. That same old night porter still there?"

"Tommy? Yes, I just saw him coming on."

"What are you going to do now?"

"Have an early night. And you?"

"Same."

"That'll do you good. Oh, Edgar, did you remember to get the water up for George?"

"I did."

"Good. I'll see you tomorrow afternoon, then, darling."

"Right. Take care of yourself, dear."

"And you, Edgar. Good night."

"Good night, Sylvia."

She rang off. She had been going to phone him later, but now she needn't bother. She set her travelling alarm for 11:30 P.M., turned the light off and tried to sleep. She had a long night ahead. But sleep proved impossible. She lay in the dark, going over her plan again and again until at last the alarm went off. She got up, undressed and put on her purple trouser suit. She donned her blonde wig and dark glasses, took from her bag a few pounds of emergency money, a small but powerful torch, the key to the Escort and her house keys, and put them all in her pockets. As a final precaution, just in case, for some obscure reason, the porter or someone else used the pass key to look into the room, she rearranged the eiderdown in the bed to appear like a sleeping person.

She went to the door, took down the *Do Not Disturb* sign from the hook, turned off the light, opened the door and peered out. The corridor was empty. She slipped out, locked the door behind her and hung the sign over the knob. Then she went boldly downstairs. She was sure none of the staff who happened to see her would recognize her, and would assume she was someone who'd been visiting one of the guests. She went outside and walked quickly to the car park where she'd left the Escort.

Operation Ding Dong Bell was under way.

At 1:00 P.M. Edgar told Beryl that he was feeling a bit under the weather and wouldn't be coming back to the office that afternoon. He drove home, had a snack lunch, then went to the garage and spent two hours making up a set of false number plates. He'd bought the letters and figures in several different shops in Polchester the previous day, and for the plates themselves he flattened out a couple of old petrol cans. He cut them to size with a hacksaw, painted them and stuck the letters and figures on. They really looked quite professional. He wrapped them in a newspaper, put the Rover in the garage and locked up. He went indoors, had a cup of tea, lay down on the couch in the sitting-room and slept soundly for three hours.

He woke up at seven-thirty. She'd left some cold meat and salad in the fridge, and he had some, plus a glass of beer. Then he went upstairs and changed into some old clothes which he hadn't worn for years—comfortable brown shoes with crêpe soles, slacks, a polo sweater, sports coat, and a check cap. He also put on a pair of night driving glasses. He looked at himself in the wardrobe mirror. Yes—his appearance was completely changed. He was confident that nobody seeing him at night could recognize him unless they got very close. He took off the cap and glasses for the time being. Then he put in his pockets £20 in cash—for emergencies—some small change, a pocket torch, a roll of sellotape, a pair of white cotton gloves and one of Sylvia's old stockings.

There was now nothing more to do, and he went downstairs and watched television for a while. Then he telephoned Sylvia.

After this he went to the desk drawer in his study, unlocked it and took from it a sharp kitchen knife with a pointed six-inch blade, which he had purchased the previous day in the Polchester Woolworths. That was everything. He switched off all the lights, locked the house and set off on foot, carrying the number plates.

About a quarter of a mile short of Cornfield, Edgar turned off the road, down a dark lane, and pushed the number plates down into some thick grass at the side. Then he continued on to the town. He made his way to the older part, where there were several streets of large Victorian terraced houses, nearly all of which were now divided into flats. The houses, of course, had no garages, which meant that at night the streets were lined with cars. Edgar stopped in a shadow and looked round. They kept early hours in Cornfield and there were few people about. He put on his gloves and commenced his search.

It was nearly half an hour before at long last Edgar felt the near side handle of a car door give under his fingers. He could hardly believe it. He froze. Then he stared around. The nearest house, as well as every other one for forty or fifty yards on both sides of the street, was dark and silent. He bent down and hastily slipped into the passenger seat. He realized that the courtesy light had gone on, and he gingerly closed the passenger door behind him, giving a wince as its click seemed like a crash in the silent street.

Now for the wires. Edgar took his torch from his pocket and got right down on his side, his head beneath the steering column, and shone the light upwards.

And he'd thought it was going to be the job of a few seconds! In films it always looked so simple. In fact, it took him ten minutes— ten nerve-racking, groping, fumbling, sweating and swearing minutes —before at last the ignition light came on. Edgar gave a gasp of relief, sat up and slid across to the driving seat. After the Rover, this car seemed tiny. It was foreign—Japanese, he guessed—and the owner must have been a midget or something, for the seat was pushed right forward. Edgar's knees were against his chest. But there was no time for adjustments now. He shone his torch on the instruments, hesitated over whether to use the choke, decided against it, licked his lips and gingerly touched the starter.

The engine came immediately to life. Edgar gave a muted exclamation of joy, let off the handbrake, located what he hoped was bottom gear, and got the car moving. But the clutch was fierce, or his feet were too cramped to operate smoothly, and the car jerked forward. He heaved the wheel sharply to the right, avoided the vehicle parked in front by inches, and a second later was moving off down the road.

The thought that he'd actually done it—stolen a car, broken the law—filled Edgar's mind to the exclusion of all else for a time. He wanted to shout, blow the horn, flash the lights. It was as though this were an achievement for its own sake. But then remembrance of the danger that still lay ahead came over him, and he calmed down. He drove to the lane where he'd left the number plates. Here he got out, found them, and stuck them over the real plates with sellotape. By the light of his torch they looked pretty good. Next he checked that the oil and water levels were OK—the gauge had shown the petrol tank three-quarters full—shifted the driver's seat back to its furthest extent (must remember to restore it to its original position afterwards), started the engine, pushed the gear home, let in the clutch—and shot backwards at speed.

Edgar gasped and braked hard. As he did so he seemed to hear the faintest suggestion of some indefinable sound from behind the car. He peered over his shoulder out of the rear window. But all was darkness. He must have imagined it. He carefully engaged the correct gear and drove off.

It was nearly 2:00 A.M. when Sylvia, who'd parked the car in a field half a mile away, walked silently up to the front gate of *The Elms*.

All was quiet. She stopped. She wasn't nervous. On the contrary, she felt exhilarated—alert and alive. She stood still, mentally rehearsing for the fiftieth time each of the moves she had to make . . .

Up to the house, off with the wig, ring the bell, call out. Edgar coming to the window . . .

"Sylvia! What on earth are you doing here?"

"Oh, Edgar, thank heavens you're all right! I've been trying to phone you and couldn't get a reply. I had to come and see if anything was wrong."

"The phone hasn't rung. It must be out of order."

"Come down and let me in, Edgar. I've left my keys at the hotel. And Edgar, come to the back door, not the front—and put your dressing-gown on."

"Why?"

"I'll explain when you get down."

Edgar opening the door . . . "What's the matter?"

"Come to the well. I think there's a cat stuck down there. It was making an awful noise a couple of minutes ago."

Edgar grumbling, but coming. . . .

Shine her torch down. "Yes, you can see it—look."

Edgar leaning forward . . . "Where?"

Then snatch up the brick from the ground, raise it—and ding-dong.

Fetch the two pails, empty them and throw them down on the ground near the well. Get the step-ladder, take it to the line-post, climb up and loosen that last screw. Let the pulley, with line attached, fall to the ground. Put the steps away and finally make a kink in the clothes line just by the well, as though somebody had caught his foot in it.

That was all. Leave the door of the house open and the light on, and hurry back to the car. Return to London and into the hotel.

The only part that worried her was leaving the house open and unattended for the rest of the night. Just suppose a passing thief saw the light and decided to investigate? It was a frightful thought. But the risk was very small. Virtually no one ever passed *The Elms* at this time of night.

She forced the fear out of her mind, telling herself to think positively. In the morning old George would arrive. He'd find the door open, the light on, and the house deserted. Then he'd spot the two pails by the well. . . .

A few hours later in London she'd receive a visit from the police. "Mrs. Gascoigne-Chalmers? I'm afraid you must prepare yourself for a shock. There's been a terrible accident at your home."

Sylvia opened the gate and made her way towards the dark and silent house. She was about to go straight up to the front door to rouse Edgar when it occurred to her that she ought to check her weapon first. She went round to the back and down the garden to the well. Yes, here was the stone. It would be a good idea to move it back a little—then she could pick it up before she reached the well with Edgar and have it in her hand ready when he leaned over. She could fall a pace behind him and snatch it up without his noticing.

As she was returning to the house she nearly walked into the two pails full of water, standing a few yards from the back door. Might as well save time afterwards, she thought. She emptied them on to the grass, and went round to the front of the house again. Now she had to seem anxious and alarmed. She gave a long ring on the bell, then banged on the door half a dozen times with her fist, before running back from the porch, standing under the bedroom window and calling loudly, "Edgar! Edgar! Are you all right? It's me—Sylvia. Oh, Edgar, answer!"

She dashed back to the door, rang and banged several more times, then resumed her shouting beneath the window.

There was no reply.

It took two or three minutes for the impossible fact to sink in. He wasn't home.

But he must be. He had to be.

A thought struck her and she ran to the garage. She couldn't open the doors, but she shone her torch through a crack and clearly saw the light fall on the triangular badge on the front of the Rover.

So he *was* home. Then why didn't he answer? Suddenly Sylvia gave a gasp. Perhaps he was dead. A real accident. Or natural causes. What an incredible coincidence, if so. Sylvia scampered back to the front door and with trembling fingers let herself in.

However, only two minutes later her hopes had been dashed. There was no Edgar—dead or alive—anywhere in the house. And the bed had not been slept in.

Her mind numb with anticlimax of it, Sylvia went slowly back downstairs and slumped into a chair in the sitting-room. Where on earth was he? Why would he leave the house for the night, having told her he was going to bed. Why?

Then the truth hit her. Fool! Fool that she was! The obvious explanation just hadn't occurred to her.

A woman. Edgar was visiting another woman.

The pig! The loathsome, two-faced pig! All these years, pretending to be madly in love with her, and all the time . . .

But why hadn't he taken the car? Of course—obviously because he didn't want it seen outside the Woman's place. Then why hadn't he brought the slut here? And how had he got to her house? He certainly wouldn't have taken a taxi—or walked. Presumably the Woman had collected him in the car and taken him home. Ye gods, what ghastly sort of creature could she be? She'd kill her. She'd kill them both. When they were together. She'd watch them die.

For several minutes, Sylvia was so infused with rage that she gave no thought to her immediate moves. When at last she did so, her first reaction was to wait and confront Edgar on his return. But no. This would be bound to lead to a huge row. He'd probably leave home. She wouldn't get another chance to kill him. He might—horror of horrors—even remove her as the beneficiary under his life insurance. She couldn't let him know what she'd discovered. She had to behave normally. Which meant returning to the Alendale.

Sylvia pummelled the arms of the chair in sheer frustration. Her beautiful, beautiful plan . . . All her thought and work for nothing —just because of that lying, unfaithful creep. He'd *promised* her he was staying in. Oh, he was going to suffer for this! It would be no easy death for him now.

Eventually she pulled herself together and looked at the time. Quarter to three. She'd have to hurry. She went rapidly through the house again, making sure that all doors were closed and lights off, just as she'd found it. Then she let herself out of the front door and closed it after her.

She was half-way down the path when she remembered the pails of water. She'd emptied them. Sylvia swore out loud. She'd have to refill them. She darted round to the rear again, picked up the two pails, opened the back door with her key and hurried to the sink. She turned on the tap. Nothing happened.

The water was being turned off at night.

That was why the pails had to be filled.

From the well.

Sylvia uttered a word she had never before said out loud, went outside again, locked the door behind her and ran to the well.

She was about four or five feet from it when her foot caught on some hard object. She gave a sharp cry, staggered forward, dropping the pails, and toppled head first into the well shaft.

CHAPTER 15

It was just gone one when Edgar parked the car a couple of blocks from the Alendale Hotel. He picked up the knife from under the seat where he'd put it, wiped it carefully with his gloved hands, pulled up his trouser leg and slid the knife down inside his sock. He got out of the car and started walking.

He approached the hotel cautiously, keeping in shadow. There was a dim light in the porch, but no sign of movement. The lights were on in only one or two bedrooms. The Alendale was a hotel of the "quiet," "respectable" kind, its clientele tending towards the elderly middle-class—early-to-bed types.

Edgar looked around, then went quickly and quietly along the pavement, slipped swiftly in through the swing doors, his eyes darting round the foyer, and stood quite still and silent. There was no sound or sign of movement anywhere. And there was nobody behind the reception desk. It seemed old Tommy had not changed his habits during the past year. Barely breathing, Edgar sidled across to the desk. The office behind was lighted, and in an armchair was Tommy, fast asleep.

Edgar crept round behind the desk and groped for a hook up under the counter. His gloved hands touched metal, which moved and made a tiny click—the pass key. His fingers closed over it and lifted it off the hook. He blessed the lucky chance which had led him to be in the lobby late one evening when staying here the previous year, and an anxious guest had arrived to inform Tommy of a smell of burning from a locked bedroom. It had turned out to be a cigarette end in a waste-basket, but it had shown Edgar exactly where the pass key was kept.

Gripping it tightly in his hand, Edgar crept across the lobby and upstairs. He rounded the bend and relaxed fractionally, letting out his breath. Stage one completed. He went up to the second floor, walking normally and making no attempt at concealment. There was little probability now of meeting staff—who might conceivably recognize him—but only guests; and they were far less likely to remember him later if he behaved naturally. He just kept himself ready to snatch off his gloves at the first sign of life. They would draw attention to him for sure.

He reached the second floor and quickly located Room 26. There was a *Do Not Disturb* sign hanging from the knob. Edgar grinned to himself. Sorry, Sylvia. Strange, though, that she should hang it out tonight. She had gone to bed early and had an auction to attend (or so she thought) in the morning. Surely she wouldn't want to sleep late. But then, the idiot woman's actions were frequently hard to follow.

Her room was the second along from the head of the main stairs —which was convenient. Convenient, because Edgar had no intention of just barging into Sylvia's room and killing her. To all appearances, she was going to be murdered by a hotel thief; she was going to wake up, see him in her room, and he was going to stab her to keep her quiet. That was what the police were going to think.

But Edgar knew that they would find it hard to believe in a thief who chose to enter initially the second room in a corridor, and who killed his very first victim. No. If he was going to establish this as a killing by a burglar, there had to *be* thefts—from at least two other rooms—first. That would then present the police with a logical case.

Edgar walked quietly back to the first room, No. 24. This was the crunch—the riskiest thing he'd ever had to do. If he were caught it meant ruin and disgrace. Yet he felt quite calm. He told himself he wasn't going to be caught.

He took the stocking out of his pocket and pulled it over his head, first removing his cap. It was itchy and uncomfortable, but he had practised with it a few times in recent days and had become accustomed to it. The mask in place, he reached out, turned the door knob and pushed.

The door was locked, but that didn't matter. He gently inserted the pass key and turned it. The tumblers slid easily back, with just the faintest of clicks. Edgar withdrew the key, put it in his pocket and stood quite still for a whole minute, just to be sure he hadn't woken anybody. Then he opened the door, slipped inside as quickly as possible and closed the door behind him. He stood motionless again, his back against the door, waiting for his eyes to grow accustomed to the dark. Gradually he became aware that there were two people soundly asleep in the bed. He quietly crossed the room to the dressing-table. He wasn't going to spend a lot of time on this. The first things he laid his hand on would do—let the police think they were looking for an inexperienced, easily panicked thief.

It was hard to stand with his back to the bed, but he had no choice. He took his torch out and, shielding it with his body, flashed it quickly on to the dressing-table. Yes: a necklace—pearls—and a brooch and a man's wallet. More than adequate. He picked them up, crammed them into his pocket and turned back for the door. A few seconds later he was outside in the still-deserted corridor.

Well, that couldn't have been much easier. There was really nothing in this burglary business. He rather wished he'd taken it up as a career. Now for the next room. He waited a minute or so to become completely calm—for he was breathing just a little quickly—then moved along to No. 25, which was on the other side of the corridor, between 24 and 26.

This time the door was unlocked. He went in. It was a single room, and it didn't take him long to discern that the person in the bed was male.

Like a ghost Edgar moved to the dressing-table. The room being smaller, this was closer to the bed than in 24, and he felt tension mounting within him. He flashed the torch. Nothing. Blast! He glanced over his shoulder at the figure in the bed. On the bedside locker the faintest gleam of silver caught his eye. He peered closer. It was a lighter. That would do. But did he dare go so close to the bed? He hesitated, then made up his mind. He had planned this expedition with extreme care—and he was going to stick to his plan: thefts from at least two other rooms.

His eyes fixed on the figure in the bed, Edgar inched with infinite caution towards the locker. Three feet from it he stopped and reached forward. He grasped the lighter, picked it up and slipped it into his pocket.

As he did so, the man in the bed stirred.

Edgar froze. But the man made no further movement, and he started to back away. However, he was just a little too hasty. His foot caught the leg of the bed. It made the smallest of noises, but in that silent room it sounded almost like a gun shot.

The man in the bed said sleepily, "What?"

Without hesitating Edgar took one step to the bottom of the bed and sank silently to his knees. He lowered his head and made himself as small as he possibly could.

"Somebody there?" The voice from the bed sounded a little more alert. Edgar held his breath. Then, to his horror, the bedside light went on.

There were five seconds of nerve-rending silence. Would the man notice the missing lighter? Would he get out of bed?

The voice gave a slightly puzzled "Hmm," and the light went out again.

For what seemed like several hours, but in fact couldn't have been more than fifteen minutes, Edgar remained where he was, while the man in the bed turned over, sniffed, coughed and shifted his position in a dozen tiny ways. Then gradually the movements grew less frequent and eventually stopped, and the man's breathing took on a more regular sound.

Edgar gave it a further five minutes, then unwound, eased himself to his feet and, making not another sound, left the room.

In the corridor he leaned against the wall, shaking. To think that people did this sort of thing for a living—year after year! Surely any job on earth had to be better. He silently cursed Sylvia for putting him through it. If only she was a decent sort of woman, he would never have had to do this.

But he'd come through it! Stage two had been successfully accomplished. What remained was going to be sheer pleasure.

Outside Sylvia's door he took off his stocking mask. He would be better without it now. For if she woke before he had a chance to kill her, and she saw a masked man in her room, she would undoubtedly scream. If she merely saw her dear Edgar, she'd be amazed—but she wouldn't be frightened.

He tried the door. Locked, as he'd expected. She always kept her door fastened when sleeping in a hotel. He took the pass key out again, inserted it in the keyhole and turned it very, very slowly. It made practically no noise. He put his hand on the knob, twisted, pushed open the door and slid into the room. He closed the door behind him and locked it again. She was a heavy sleeper and from now on he didn't need to keep quite so silent.

He peered into the darkness. The curtains were tightly drawn, but he could just distinguish the outline of her body in the bed. He reached into his pocket, took out the jewellery, the wallet and the lighter and put them quietly down on the floor. The police would think that after the murder the burglar had panicked and immediately discarded his loot.

Edgar bent down, pulled up his trouser leg and took the knife from his sock. He gripped the handle tightly and approached the bed. He stood looking down at the inert figure. He was greatly tempted to awaken her. It would be marvellous to see her face when she realized the truth. But it would be too much of a risk. She might cry out before he was able to stop her, and that could wake the people in the next room.

She might even cry out *after* the blow was struck. He had never stabbed anybody before and couldn't guarantee a first time kill. He'd better put his hand over her mouth.

He raised the dagger and braced himself. Now. Goodbye, Sylvia.

He bent down and clapped his left hand over where her face had to be. At the same instant he started the downward sweep with the dagger.

Then he could barely hold back a cry of disbelief as his left hand met nothing but a soft and cushiony mass. Checking his knife blow, he made frantic grabs right across the top of the bed. Where was her head?

It took him seconds to realize that it wasn't there. None of her was. The bed was empty.

Edgar's knees turned to water and he fell right down on to the bed dropping the knife. It was impossible. It didn't make sense. Unless —oh, no!

Could he have come to the wrong room?

He scrambled up, fumbled for the light switch and turned it on. His eyes darted round the room. It was all right. There was her handbag on the chair. And there were other things of hers too.

All right? What was he thinking of? It would be infinitely better if he'd come to the wrong room. At least then he could find the right one. Whereas now . . . What on earth could he do? And where could she have conceivably got to?

The scheming, lying minx! She had assured him she was going to turn in early—and then she'd gone sneaking off into the night—and ruined his superb plan. Why should she have lied to him like that? If she'd been meaning to go to a late show or something, or had met somebody she knew and been invited to a party, why not say so? Why should a wife lie to her own husband about where she was going to spend the night—?

Oh, never!

Not that!

Sylvia? Sylvia—who was so crazy about him? She had never looked at another man in that way. She'd just not been interested.

Had she?

She'd certainly been going off on her own a lot lately. She'd said she'd been going to sales. But she hadn't bought anything.

The two-faced little tramp! Pretending to be so affectionate, so loving, crying with relief when she'd learnt he was safe the other week. And all the time, behind his back . . . In fury and frustration, Edgar ground his knuckles into the palm of his left hand.

Eventually he got a grip on himself. Never mind where she was now: the important question was what his next move was to be. For one thing there was the stolen stuff. What should he do with it? He'd leave it here. Why not? Let her find it when she got back. That would shake her. Or, better still, perhaps someone else would find it before she returned—which might at least give her a few embarrassing moments. Apart from that, the only thing to do was scrap the whole plan: get away from here as quickly as possible and go home. It was so infuriating that he felt if he went on thinking about it his head would burst. So he'd better stop thinking and start acting.

Edgar put the knife back in his sock and rearranged the eiderdown in the bed as Sylvia had left it. He looked carefully round the room, extinguished the light and went out to the corridor, locking the door behind him again. He crept downstairs, crossed the lobby for a second time without being seen, replaced the pass key, returned to the car and started for home.

His fury had passed. Instead, he felt like weeping. It had been such a lovely murder plan, and had all gone so superbly well. The only thing lacking had been the victim. It wasn't fair.

CHAPTER 16

Sylvia clung by her fingertips to the rim of the violently swaying well bucket. First her right hip came in sharp and painful contact with the side of the shaft, then, as she swung across the shaft, her left. Three, four, five more times it happened. But it wasn't the pain that worried her; it was the fact that each blow threatened to shake free her precarious grip. She knew that she couldn't hold on much longer. She prayed just for the swaying to stop. Then at the end of the next swing her body didn't strike the side. Slowly the arcs of the bizarre pendulum grew shorter, until eventually she hung suspended but virtually motionless in the centre of the shaft.

Not that her position was much better now, for the tunnel still gaped blackly beneath her, and her remaining strength was rapidly giving out. Her shoulder muscles were cramping with the strain and so were her fingers.

What had happened was that after filling the two pails for George, Edgar had left the bucket hanging a couple of feet below the winder, simply slipping the handle lock into position to prevent the bucket falling back down the shaft. It was fortunate for the state of his mental health he didn't know that in doing this he had undoubtedly saved Sylvia's life. Her blindly clawing hands had caught the rim of the bucket by pure chance.

Her weight had tilted the bucket over at a steep angle and every second she was having greater difficulty in keeping her grip. She knew she had to get a firmer hold, and she fixed her eyes on the spot where the base of the bucket handle joined the rim. She was terrified of loosening her grip even momentarily, but it had to be done. She relaxed her right fingers fractionally and slid her hand three inches to the side. Then she brought her left hand to join it. The bucket swayed terrifyingly for a moment, the rope vibrating. She waited for it to become still again and then repeated the manoeuvre. A third time—then her two hands were clasped together round the handle, and she was able to take a brief rest.

But it was a rest only in comparative terms, for although the pain in her fingers had eased, her shoulder and arm muscles were screaming for relief.

Her only chance, she knew, lay in getting into, or at least on top of, the bucket. She would never be able to pull herself up by brute force. The only way was to bring a leg up sideways, rather like someone trying to mount a very large horse, holding only on to the pommel, without the aid of stirrups. Though her task was more difficult than that, as she had no solid ground beneath her feet to push against.

With her first attempt her foot didn't come up higher than the bottom of the bucket—which began swaying jerkily on the rope again. Her second try was no better, and if she hadn't been already sobbing from fear and pain, she would have cried with frustration. She had a third effort, but made no progress.

At that point she nearly gave up. It would have been so easy just to let go. To relax would be so beautiful. She felt her head starting to swim. Then she thought of Edgar—and his Woman—living in her house, using her things, sleeping in her bed, and she found reserves of strength she'd never known she possessed. She strained up a fourth time and got her leg half-way up the side of the bucket. She waited thirty seconds, gritted her teeth and closed her eyes. Up—up—up—and then her left shoe was over the rim. To bring her right leg up too was comparatively simple, and she knew that—so long as the rope held—she wasn't going to fall. She had been so worried about her own ability to cling on, that this latter possibility hadn't occurred to her before, but now it had done, she couldn't allow herself any respite.

She faced several more minutes of awkward manoeuvring, but at last, after what seemed like hours, she pulled herself on to the parapet of the well and stepped down from it on to the grass. She stood panting and swaying on her feet in the moonlight, then collapsed in a dead faint on to the ground.

It was the pain in her arms and shoulders that brought her round. She lay flat for a few seconds, trying to collect her thoughts, then sat up. Her pocket torch was lying beside her and she picked it up, switched it on and squinted at her watch. It showed only five past three. She thought it must have stopped, but then she saw the second hand was moving. She could hardly believe it. If she had been unconscious for five minutes, it meant that she had been in the well for not much more than four. It had seemed like hours. But the important thing was she still had time to get far away from the area before daylight.

Her body groaned in protest at the prospect of a nearly two-hour

drive—let alone the brisk walk that had to come first. But she had
no choice. She got slowly to her feet. She shone her torch round.
The first thing she saw was the object she had tripped over. It was
the stone she had prised from inside the shaft. Next she saw the two
empty pails.

Sylvia nearly screamed.

Bringing up a full bucket of water from the well was undoubtedly
the hardest thing she'd ever had to do in her life. On the very few
occasions she had done it in the past she had found it a back-break-
ing task. Now, coming on top of everything else, it was almost too
much for her. Every muscle in her body throbbed and cramped as
she strained at the handle; she had to take repeated rests, and by the
time she had finished the job she was covered in sweat. All she
wanted to do was rest, and the temptation to go indoors, throw herself on the bed and sleep was enormous. But she had to go to London. Sylvia moaned. It wasn't fair.

Edgar's chief worry during his journey home was that someone
would spot the stolen car. True, he had false plates. But if the theft
had been reported, the police might look extra closely at any cars of
this model, and those plates wouldn't stand up to close scrutiny. As
long as he was in or near London, the risk was small: the Metro-
politan Police had too many stolen cars to concern themselves with
to be likely to note this one. But when he got to the country district
around Polchester and Cornfield, things might be different. It would
be better therefore to keep to quiet roads as much as possible. This
would entail leaving the motorway much earlier than usual and taking a cross-country route home. It would take longer, but it would
be safer.

By the time Sylvia reached the Escort and started for London she
was nearly dead with tiredness. She decided one thing almost immediately: she wasn't driving back along the motorway—she was far
too likely to fall asleep at the wheel; the concentration needed on
twisting side roads would help to stop her dropping off.

She did manage to stay awake. But only just. And she drove
badly. Her head kept nodding and twice in the first twenty minutes
she found she'd wandered over to the wrong side of the road and
had to jerk the wheel violently to get back. She gritted her teeth and
determined, whatever happened, to stay well into the left. And it
was this resolve which, only a few minutes later, caused the incident.

She had just joined one of the few stretches of straight and lighted
road on her route. She was fighting to keep her eyes open and at the

same time concentrating on not straying to the right. She blinked,
blinked again, longer—and opened her eyes to see she was about
two feet away from, and heading straight for, the rear wheel of a
motor-cycle. A split second later she realized that the rider was a
policeman.

Sylvia gave a gasp of horror and yanked the wheel to the right,
just as the policeman looked over his shoulder and took evasive action. The Escort swerved wildly across the road. Sylvia swung round
and gazed out of the rear window. Had she hit him? She thought
not. She had felt nothing. But, more important, could he have got
her number? Then she saw that he had come off the bike. But he
was picking himself up. He probably hadn't had time to see her rear
plate.

So concerned was Sylvia with what was going on behind her that
she virtually forgot she was still moving forward—and on the wrong
side of the road. The next second she heard the mad hooting of a
car horn. She jerked round to face front—and gave a scream. A
small car was coming straight towards her at what seemed an enormous speed.

Sylvia stood on the brake and closed her eyes. She heard a sort of
rushing noise and the Escort rocked. Then blessedly all was still and
quiet. Sylvia opened her eyes, turned, and again stared over her
shoulder. The small car had veered to its right, missing her by what
could only have been inches, and was now stationary some yards
behind her on the other side of the road.

For a few seconds Sylvia sat unmoving. Then abruptly she came
to her senses. She slammed the Escort into bottom gear and accelerated off at top speed. She was shaking all over. But at least she now
felt wide awake.

Desperately tired by now, Edgar started on the last quarter of his
journey with his mind still on the problem of the car. He decided to
scrap the idea of taking it back to where he had found it. It would
be too risky—and besides, unless he spent heaven knew how long
restoring the wires behind the dashboard to normal, the tiny owner
would know the car had been tampered with anyway. Moreover, it
would mean another long trek home on foot, and he couldn't face
that. So it would be better just to abandon it half a mile or so from
The Elms and let it be assumed it had been taken by joy riders.
Then—

That moment Edgar was brought back to the present with a jerk.
He was on one of the occasional main roads which it had been impossible to avoid, and he suddenly saw that there was a car—a Ford

Escort—approaching him on the wrong side. It was coming straight at him.

Edgar was so tired that his reflexes had slowed and for a moment he didn't react at all, just waited for the Escort to swing back to its correct side. But it didn't. A split second later the fact dawned on him that it wasn't going to.

He put his hand on the horn, but his wits had come back enough now for him to realize that at the speed they were closing, braking was going to be useless. There was no way he could get past it on the left. Edgar did the only thing possible. Praying that the other driver didn't go the same direction, he held off until the last possible moment and heaved his wheel to the right.

Somehow he avoided the car. As he flashed past he caught a glimpse of the driver, a woman with long blonde hair. Then she was behind him. Edgar came to a halt on the other side of the road and sat, his heart pounding like a steam hammer. He heard the roar of the Escort's engine and in his mirror saw it disappearing along the road. He swore after it and looked ahead again. Then his eyes bulged.

Fifty yards away, standing by a motor-cycle lying on its side, was a policeman.

Edgar's stomach gave a lurch. Ye gods! He had to get away quickly. Reverse? No, that would look suspicious. Just drive sedately by, perhaps, raising a hand in polite salute? He started the car moving forward. The next moment he nearly passed out. The policeman had stepped right into the middle of the road and raised his hand.

Instinctively Edgar stopped again. The policeman began a measured tread along the road towards him. Edgar sat in the driving seat, his mind a maelstrom of fear and indecision. He was driving a stolen car, which might already have been reported missing. Perhaps this policeman was actually watching out for it. There were false number plates on it, which wouldn't stand up to a moment's close examination. He didn't have his licence with him, or anything with which to prove his identity.

This could finish him. Edgar Gascoigne-Chalmers, JP, FCA, County Councillor, found guilty of car theft. Ruined. And what possible explanation could he give? What conceivable reason could a sane man have for acting in this way?

He couldn't allow it to happen. He had to do something—save himself from disgrace, humiliation, financial disaster. Yet merely driving away was no good. The policeman would chase him on his motor-bike. No—something more drastic was needed.

These thoughts flashed through Edgar's mind in a couple of seconds. The policeman had still taken only five or six steps. Edgar had often read of a person having a sudden rush of blood to the head. He had never quite understood what it meant. Now it happened to him. His engine was still running. Edgar trod on the clutch, rammed the gear into bottom, stood on the throttle—and let out the clutch. At full speed he drove straight at the approaching policeman.

He saw the man's expression change, first to one of amazement, then of fear. He turned and started to run. Then at the last second he leapt desperately to one side. Edgar missed him by a foot and skidded to a halt. He looked back—becoming dimly aware that yet another car had appeared from somewhere and had pulled level with him on the far side of the road. But he couldn't concern himself with that. He was committed to fighting now and he had to go on.

The policeman was sprawling in the road behind him. He was gripping his knee, as though he'd hurt it. The instinct of the hunter had now been roused in Edgar and he felt a thrill of satisfaction. A sitting target. He engaged reverse gear, then he backed at full speed towards the prone figure.

His rear wheels could have been only six feet from the policeman when with a most almighty bang something struck Edgar's car from the near side. It was hurled sideways and with a horrible crunch came in contact with the fallen motor-cycle.

Edgar's head was nearly jerked from his body by the impact, and he sat in the driving seat gasping and trying to discover if he was injured. He wasn't in any pain, but he knew that meant little. He turned his head to the left, dazedly trying to make out what had happened. Then he understood. It was the car that had stopped across the road. Seeing what Edgar was trying to do, the driver must have decided to intervene. He had pulled across and rammed Edgar's car, shunting it sideways—and certainly saving the constable's life.

The newcomer's car was an old Daimler and looked to Edgar to have fared as badly as his own. There were two occupants and they made no attempt to get out. They were certainly as shaken as he was.

Edgar suddenly realized that he just might, even now, have a slim chance of getting away. If only the car wasn't too badly damaged . . .

Again he thrust it into gear and accelerated. With a horrible grinding sound the car moved forward. Edgar pushed the accelerator down further. The engine howled—but the car went hardly any faster. It crawled away, screaming and grating as it did so. Edgar jammed the pedal hard down on to the floorboard—and the car did at last increase its speed. At about ten miles an hour it shuddered off along the road, Edgar gripping the wheel and trying to urge the car forward, as though it were a horse.

It must have been the slowest getaway in the annals of crime. Edgar peered fearfully into the mirror. If either of the people in the Daimler decided to come after him—on foot—they'd stand a good chance of catching him. However, either they had concluded they'd already played their part, or were too shaken up to start running, and they stayed in their seats.

Edgar kept his foot hard down, though he was fearful that at any moment the car was going to disintegrate, so fierce was its protesting. Fortunately, the road was free of any other traffic; all the same something might come along any second—and any second, too, that policeman, surely, would be radioing for help. At his present speed, the police who responded would find their suspect still in sight.

Edgar kept going for another two hundred yards, until he'd rounded a bend in the road. But he couldn't carry on like this. He had to try and do something. He stopped. The cessation of sound was in itself a blessed relief. He got out and examined the damage. The rear near-side bodywork had been smashed in and was pressing against the wheel. Edgar bent down and gave it a tug. But it was jammed fast. Hopeless. He had no choice: he was going to have to abandon the car.

Thirty yards ahead was a crossroads, with two minor roads branching off each side. Edgar left the car where it was and ran up to the junction. Which way to go? Left ought to take him in the rough direction of home. But he had to get off the road. That policeman would certainly have radioed by now.

Edgar ran along until he came to a gate into a field. He climbed it and started walking.

Then began the nightmare. With only the light of his torch to guide him, Edgar trudged on. He crossed field after field—ploughed fields, fields of grain, fields of vegetables, fields of sheep that fled from him in terror, fields of cattle, who stood threateningly until he was almost on them, constantly making him wonder if perhaps he was approaching not a cow but a bull. He climbed gates, forced his way through hedges, wriggled under barbed-wire fences, tumbled down steep banks. He crashed his way through an endless wood, tripping over tree roots, feeling thorny fronds plucking at him, hearing strange unnerving scamperings and rustlings all around him, once nearly jumping out of his skin when an owl screeched horribly about a foot from his ear.

An hour, an hour and a half, passed and it was already light when Edgar at last came from yet another field on to a stretch of road he recognized and knew that he was only a quarter of a mile from home. When he eventually tottered through the front door of *The Elms,* he was more exhausted than he'd ever been in his life. Like a drunken man he reeled into the sitting-room and across to the drinks cabinet. He poured himself a treble whisky, downed it in one go, fell on to the sofa, kicked off his shoes and was asleep in sixty seconds.

Edgar awoke feeling ghastly. His head was throbbing, his legs hurting horribly and every joint was stiff. He uttered a groan and somehow pulled himself to his feet. The mantelpiece clock showed that it was gone nine. Beryl would have arrived at the office. She would soon start wondering what had happened to him, and it was vital he led a normal day.

He made his way painfully upstairs, took a long hot bath and shaved. Then he phoned Beryl to tell her he'd been delayed, but would be in shortly. He had three cups of coffee and a few slices of toast and then left for the office. It was just ten-thirty when he arrived. To get there by that time after the night he'd had was quite an achievement. He certainly had a right to feel proud of himself.

Sylvia got back to the Alendale at five-thirty. She staggered up to her room, heedless now who saw or recognized her. Let them think she'd had a night on the tiles. What did it matter?

Fully dressed, she dropped on to the bed and fell into blessed slumber.

She was dredged slowly up from deep, deep levels of sleep by an irritating, persistent knocking. For what seemed like hours her half-conscious brain resisted the knocking's demands, but at long last she was forced to open her eyes.

Someone was tapping repeatedly on her door, and now they were calling, too. "Mrs. Gascoigne-Chalmers? Madam? Are you all right?"

Sylvia croaked thickly, "All right. Coming," and the noise blessedly stopped.

By a prodigious effort of will she forced herself to sit up. She winced from an acute shooting pain in her back. She sat on the edge of the bed for a few seconds, trying to collect herself. She felt as though she'd died and just been dug up again. Only worse. Her head was ramping, she was aching in every joint and muscle. She peered, slit-eyed at her travelling clock. It was only six-thirty.

Six-thirty. . . . It couldn't be true. Why did the fools want to call her at this hour? She'd put the *Do Not Disturb* sign out. Hadn't she?

Sylvia lurched to her feet and zig-zagged towards the door. Half-way she realized that she was still dressed in her trouser suit and wearing her wig, so she snatched off the latter, grabbed up her dressing-gown and wrapped it round her. Then she opened the door. It was the manager. She stood swaying slightly, her mouth open, not speaking.

"I'm terribly sorry to disturb you, madam," he said, "especially as you hung out the placard, but one of the guests has just reported seeing a strange-looking blonde woman, very dirty and bedraggled, entering your room about an hour ago. As there have been a number of hotel thefts lately I thought I ought to check that everything was in order. Madam? Are you all right? Mrs. Gascoigne-Chalmers, you don't look at all well."

When Edgar got home at lunchtime he found to his disgust that She was already back. Blast! He'd wanted some time alone, to think, before speaking to her. But he had to make the best of it.

"Darling!" he said, kissing her. "What a lovely surprise! I didn't expect you home for hours."

"I know, but I decided to skip the second auction. When I woke up this morning, all I wanted to do was get home to you as soon as possible."

"So you didn't have a very good time?"

"Oh, it was all right. Routine, you know. How have things been here?"

"Er, quite uneventful." He paused. "Sleep well at the Alendale? You don't always, in hotels."

"I was like a log last night. Eight hours' solid."

"Oh, good. So there was, er, no trouble of any kind?"

"Trouble?" She looked at him sharply. "What do you mean—trouble?"

"Oh, nothing, only I was reading there've been a lot of hotel thefts in London recently. But as long as nobody got into your room . . ."

"No, no, nothing like that." She stopped. "I see you've made the bed."

"What? Oh yes."

"Thank you, darling. You've done it very well. Just like I do it. It almost looks as if it hadn't been slept in."

"Well, I should know your way of doing things by now."

"It was very thoughtful of you, dear. I'm beginning to feel quite guilty, leaving you on your own so much. I must try and make it up to you."

So the creep *did* have a girl friend. There couldn't be any doubt now. Sylvia clenched her fists in rage, imagining him last night, hanging up the phone after speaking to her, and straight away going off with some slut. Then she calmed down. Nothing was really altered—except that she had more justification than ever for executing him. It simply meant that she had to kill two people instead of one.

But first she had to find out who the woman was.

So chaotic were Edgar's thoughts, coming as they did on top of a ghastly tiredness, that he never knew how he got through the rest of that day's work. Firstly, he was filled with incredulity and fury at Sylvia's betrayal of their marriage vows. Of this he now had complete certainty, following the tissue of lies she'd told him. Eight hours solid! The lousy little hypocrite. The maddening thing was that he couldn't let her know he knew—nor punish her for her behaviour. Of course, he *was* going to kill her. But he'd been going to kill her anyway, and he couldn't kill her twice. He would have liked to give her a particularly painful death, but he could foresee great difficulty in arranging that. However, of one thing he was now determined. Before he killed her he was going to make quite sure she knew the truth—that he'd found her out, had hated her for years—and after she was dead was going to sell *The Elms*. If she died knowing all that, even though only for a minute, then he would be happy.

Another frustration, though a comparatively minor one, was not knowing what had happened about the stolen property he had left in her hotel room. What had she thought, how had she got round it?

But time and time again throughout the day all these thoughts were banished from his mind by the constantly recurring cold dread that the police might yet trace him as the driver of the stolen car. Could they? Had he left a trail—or any kind of clue? If only he knew.

Somehow he struggled through to five-thirty, miraculously maintaining an outward veneer of normality. He left the office and immediately bought the local paper. He scanned it feverishly for any report of the incident. Yes—there it was.

The police are anxious to trace a car thief, who attempted to run down a constable near Cornfield last night. The officer was saved by the intervention of a passing motorist, the Rt. Rev.

Denis Mowbray, the Suffragan Bishop of Polchester, who, with his wife, witnessed the incident and rammed the stolen car as the driver was making a second attempt to run over the constable.

PC Brian Davidson, 27, said, "I had waved the car down and was walking back towards it when the driver suddenly drove straight towards me at speed. I leapt aside, but fell. The driver then began reversing fast at me, and if it hadn't been for the action of the Bishop, who deliberately ran into the car with his own, I should not be alive today."

The Bishop said, "My wife and I witnessed the whole incident and I acted on the spur of the moment."

The car, to which home-made false number plates had been attached, was later found abandoned. It transpired that it had been stolen from outside a house in Queen's Road, Cornfield, earlier in the evening.

PC Davidson added, "The ironic thing is that I did not at the time know that the car had been stolen, nor was I intending to book the driver for any offence. I simply wished to ask him if he had noticed the number of another car which had nearly killed us both a few seconds before."

The police would like to hear from anyone who saw a man on foot near the scene of the incident, which took place at—

Edgar screwed the paper into a ball and threw it on to the ground.

CHAPTER 17

By the beginning of the following week Edgar had relaxed a little. If the police were going to catch him, they'd surely have done so by now. All the same, he felt spent—physically and mentally. Doing all the normal weekend things had been a terrific effort. His mind was constantly on the Trust's deadline, now just three weeks away, but he remained sunk in lassitude and bereft of ideas.

On Monday he dragged himself to the office and went through his work mechanically. His memory kept letting him down and Beryl had repeatedly to remind him of jobs to be done and appointments to be kept. Just as she was leaving for lunch, she said, "You haven't forgotten Miss Eversleigh this evening, have you?"

Edgar groaned. He *had* forgotten. It was the last job he felt like doing. He only hoped he could force himself to concentrate on the wretched woman's financial affairs.

At lunch he said to Sylvia, "Oh, by the way, I'll be going out this evening. I have an appointment at the Mill."

She said sharply, "With Madge Eversleigh?"

"That's right."

"But why? Do you have to go?"

He was surprised. She never normally took the slightest interest in his professional life. She sounded rather put out, too. Did the idiot woman consider he was neglecting her or something? He felt a wave of intense irritation. However, he could not afford to let even the slightest hint of trouble arise between them at this stage. He hastened to explain.

"Well, I don't *have* to, but it will be convenient. You see, she's got into an almighty muddle with her tax. The commissioners are writing extremely stiff letters. I've promised to try and sort everything out. Now, it seems she's got no sort of filing system and keeps the most casual accounts. She has hundreds of bills and receipts and bank statements all over the place, and to ascertain which are relevant I'm going to have to go through them all. Either she gathers the stuff together, brings it to the office and stays with me while I go through it, or I go out to the Mill. Firstly, I don't want her rubbish cluttering up the place; and secondly Madge is behind with a very important commission and can't spare the time. So we agreed I should go out there this evening and sort through everything, while she carries on working. Then she'll be on hand to explain the papers to me when necessary. All clear?"

Sylvia smiled. "My, what a long explanation."

"It's a confused situation, requiring a long explanation."

"I see. Well, I suppose if you've got to go, you've got to. I'm the last person to want you to let down a client."

"I can't say it won't happen again, because I've a feeling I'm going to need a number of sessions out there."

After he'd gone back to the office, Sylvia sat down. Madge Eversleigh? *Madge?* Surely not! She was the type of person Edgar usually despised—vague, untidy, casual, absurdly free and easy, and with a quite warped sense of humour. No, it couldn't be Madge. Surely . . .

Edgar's fears were justified. He got through barely half the work at the Mill that evening, and when he returned home he had to tell Sylvia that he'd made another appointment for the following night.

So it *was* Madge. It had to be. Edgar hardly ever went to his clients' homes, and for him to visit the same one two nights running was unheard of. Moreover, that rigmarole of an explanation he'd come up with earlier had been thoroughly unconvincing.

In addition, Sylvia had to admit that Madge was, in a bohemian, neglected sort of way, quite attractive. So he *might* be stupid enough to become infatuated with her. But even if he had, could it conceivably be mutual? Could Madge have been attracted by such a dull, stuffy, stick-in-the-mud as Edgar?

Well, nothing, Sylvia supposed, that Madge did could ever surprise one who knew her. There *was* such a thing as attraction of opposites. Or Madge might think it a great lark to hook a man as ultra-conventional as a JP-County Councillor-Chartered Accountant. One could even imagine her being vastly amused at the idea of picking him up in her own car to take him home with her.

Sylvia actually knew nothing at all about Madge's love life, had never even heard a rumour about it; but as she disapproved generally of Madge's life-style she was prepared to believe anything bad about her that she could. Madge Eversleigh was a moderately successful artist, who had moved to the area seven or eight years previously, and had purchased a disused and derelict windmill on the opposite side of Cornfield to *The Elms*. She had gradually converted this into an unusual though comfortable home, where she lived alone apart from a constantly changing assortment of animals. She was both a painter and sculptress, whose style varied, as necessity or whim dictated, from the wildest avant-garde to an almost photographic representationalism. But in every style she was, if not brilliant, at least extremely able, and she made a comfortable living. She entered fully into Cornfield's social life, though many people, Sylvia included, were always made somewhat uneasy by her air of mocking amusement, and couldn't avoid the belief that Madge attended functions for the sole purpose of observing the natives at play.

After the initial shock of learning about Edgar's unfaithfulness had worn off, Sylvia had found, somewhat to her surprise, that she didn't feel very much anguish at the knowledge. Her only real emotion had been a mild annoyance that she wasn't able to find it in her to hate him more intensely. But she'd hated him so much before that she didn't have any extra hatred available.

Over the weekend she had decided that, after all, she was going to have to forego the pleasure of a double murder. For, if she did kill them both, the love affair would almost certainly come to light. She would then very likely find herself in the dock and probably convicted; and although, as a wronged wife, she would undoubtedly receive a lot of sympathy and a comparatively light sentence, she wouldn't then get the insurance money.

So the Woman must wait her turn. For, of course, later on, when Edgar was safely disposed of and she'd bought *The Firs* and had plenty of leisure, *then* she could turn her attention to the trollop. That would be something to look forward to; though, of course, it wouldn't be quite so satisfying as a double murder.

On Monday, however, having learnt about Edgar's second appointment at the Mill, and knowing who his Woman was, Sylvia began to get stirrings of excitement. Perhaps a wonderful opportunity had presented itself and she would be able to have her double murder after all. For there were several factors which tended to neutralize the risk involved. Firstly, Edgar would be there openly, ostensibly on business . . . So the affair could remain undiscovered—and with it Sylvia's motive.

Secondly, this visit did represent a break from Edgar's usual routine. His life followed such a regular pattern—office, golf club, council offices, etc.—in which for a great proportion of time he was surrounded by people. This had been the major obstacle to a dozen schemes Sylvia had been forced to abandon. The Mill, on the other hand, *was* isolated. Tomorrow evening there would be nobody but Edgar and Madge present. He would be off his guard, relaxed. In addition, the Mill was undoubtedly the kind of unusual dwelling where a stranger (as Edgar supposedly was) would be more prone to an accident than in a conventional building.

In the couple of hours before going to bed on Monday night Sylvia thought fiercely and the next morning, immediately after Edgar had left for the office, she got her car out and drove in the direction of the Mill. She wanted to take another look at the place—remind herself just what it was like.

The Mill was about two miles from the centre of Cornfield. It was set forty yards back from a lonely, narrow road, and was separated from the fields each side by a ring of shrubs and trees, within which was a small garden. A straight concrete driveway, also shrub-lined, led from the road, widened to make a forecourt, and then branched to form a level path right round the base of the building.

Apart from the fact that the vanes had long since been taken away—as an actual working mill the building had had a short and unsuccessful life—its original function was still very obvious. It was round, built almost entirely of wood, and was four storeys high tapering towards the top. From her rare visits, Sylvia knew that the ground floor consisted solely of a garage-cum-storeroom. Madge's studio was on the first floor, with her living quarters above it, and her bedroom at the top.

Sylvia surveyed the building from the road for about five minutes. Wood. Dry as tinder after this long hot spell. The living quarters upstairs. No fire escape. And solid concrete round the base. She got back in her car and drove home, thinking furiously all the way.

On arriving, the first thing she did was kneel down on the ground and look up underneath the rear of her car, paying particular attention to the underside of the petrol tank and the surrounding chassis work.

She went indoors, made herself some coffee and drank it, her mind still intensely active. Five minutes later she stood up. Her heart was beating a little faster and her cheeks were flushed.

She'd do it.

Sylvia went outside again, took an old gallon can from the garage (funny; surely the other day there'd been several of them around; now there seemed to be only the one) and put it in the boot of her car. Then she drove to Polchester.

In Polchester she called at a petrol station she had never patronized before and filled the can at a self-service pump. Then she went to a tobacconist's and bought a tin of liquid lighter fuel. While she was there she also purchased a box of matches. *The Elms* being all-electric and centrally heated, and both she and Edgar non-smokers, these were things she rarely had to buy, and she was unsure whether there were any in the house.

She drove home again, went indoors and sat down with the lighter fuel, a screwdriver, a roll of sellotape, and a small hook. First she sellotaped the hook to the side of the fuel tin, at the bottom, so that the tin could be suspended upside down. She removed the stopper and enlarged the hole at the top so that the liquid would flow out more freely than normal. She replaced the stopper and put the tin away in her handbag. The preparations were complete.

Just after five o'clock that afternoon Sylvia drove up the driveway leading to the Mill and stopped on the forecourt. She got out and, carrying her handbag, walked up to what was nominally the front door. It was next to the double doors of the garage, where stood Madge's battered old Bedford van. The front door was closed, but as both entrances gave access to the same area, it might just as well have been standing as wide open as were the double doors. However, there was a bell-push set into it, which Sylvia dutifully pressed.

The bell sounded from on high, and a few seconds later a female voice, also from above, yelled, "Who is it?"

Sylvia walked a few feet to her right and stepped inside through the double doors. On the right was a single window, on the left a flight of wooden steps climbed steeply upwards to an open trapdoor in the wooden plank ceiling.

Sylvia cleared her throat and called out, "It's Sylvia Gascoigne-Chalmers."

"Can't hear you. Hang on."

There was a patter of footsteps on the bare boards overhead and then Madge Eversleigh appeared, on her knees, peering down through the trap.

Sylvia said, "Good afternoon, Madge."

"'Struth! What you doing here?"

"Well—"

"Don't tell me—I know. Eddie can't come tonight and he's sent you to cook me books for me instead. Really, that perishing man. He ought to be boiled in oil. I bet you've often wanted to, haven't you?"

"It's nothing like that," Sylvia said a little coldly. "As far as I know, Edgar is coming tonight, as planned."

"Bully for him, then. Well, what can I do for you, Sylv?"

"It's a little awkward to explain—from down here."

"OK, toddle on up. But don't expect any tea."

Sylvia mounted the stairs and emerged into Madge's studio. This, naturally, was circular and appeared utterly chaotic. Half-finished paintings were everywhere—on easels, hanging round the walls and stacked in piles. There were also two uncompleted sculptures: a huge bulgy abstract, next to a large pile of clay, and a life-size portrait bust of a man's head; as well as a number of finished works. A long table covered with paints and other artist's equipment was in the centre of the room, two cats asleep on it. From the ceiling hung a cage occupied by a moth-eaten and malevolent-looking parrot. Ashtrays, overflowing with cigarette ends, were everywhere and there was little of the room not liberally spattered with paint.

Madge said, "Well, this is unexpected. I won't say an unexpected pleasure, because frankly it's not. Now that's not personal, because the Director of the Tate, offering me a one-woman exhibition, wouldn't be welcome today. I'm way behind with a portrait and some beastly children's book illustrations, and I just can't stop work. So excuse me if I carry on."

She was in her early thirties, red-haired, snub-nosed, with freckles and a wide mouth. She was wearing a man's shirt (and whose, Sylvia wondered, had *that* been?), with the tail hanging outside blue jeans. Her hair was tied back in a scarlet square. There was a cigarette in her mouth.

She turned and hurried across the room, going behind a canvas, which was standing on an easel with its back to Sylvia.

"I'm sorry if I've called at an inconvenient time," Sylvia said.

"Don't be—though you have. You couldn't know, and I'm being an ill-mannered slob. But this really is frightfully important. By the way, forget what I said about tea. You're welcome to some, if you like to go upstairs, make it and bring me a cup, too. I'll come over to your place and make you some one day when your maid's out."

"We don't have a maid, unfortunately. Just Mrs. Thring, who's been away for over a month."

"Life's 'ard, ain't it, Sylv?" She said this in broadest Cockney, then immediately reverting to her normal accent, asked, "What do you think of the state of my studio?"

Sylvia hesitated, "Well, I'm sure—"

"Foul, isn't it? I keep it like this deliberately. Makes me work faster—so I don't have to stay in here so long. At least, that's the theory."

Sylvia found herself getting a little puzzled. There was nothing remotely embarrassed or guilty in Madge's manner. And surely if the wife of a man with whom one was having an affair turned up unannounced, one would be bound to feel some apprehension. Yet Madge didn't seem to. Surely, Sylvia thought, I can't have been wrong about her. No—this was undoubtedly all an act. She *was* embarrassed, and this irrelevant chatter was her way of disguising it. That—and going the other side of the easel so that she could hide her face behind the canvas whenever she wanted to. Yes, that was it.

Madge's face now reappeared round the side of the canvas. "Oh, you're still here. You were so quiet I thought you'd gone. Why don't you sit down."

Sylvia glanced round, then perched herself gingerly on a rickety-looking high stool by the table.

Madge gave a chuckle. "This isn't really your scene is it, Sylvia? You look like a fish out of water. To which you ought to reply that I look like one in water. But do tell me why you're here."

"I wanted to talk to you, Madge."

"You know, I thought perhaps you might want to talk to me the moment I saw you. In fact, even before I saw you, the very second I heard the bell, I said to myself, Madge, I said, I bet that's someone who wants to talk to you. Do you think I'm telepathic?"

Sylvia flushed slightly. "I mean I wanted to talk to you alone."

"Oh, Sylvia, this is so sudden!"

"I wish you'd take me seriously, Madge."

"I'm sorry. Yes, I agree you should be taken seriously, Sylvia. You are a most take seriousable person, and I'm sure you almost invariably are. Trouble is, I always talk like this when I'm working— usually to the animals. It helps me concentrate. What about?"

"What do I want to talk to you about?"

"Yes."

Sylvia waited until Madge's face came in view again, then said deliberately, "About Edgar." She kept her eyes fixed on Madge.

Madge took a step back, squinting at her painting, then reached out and seemed to make a tiny addition to it with a precise little dab of her brush. Her voice completely casual, she said, "Then fire away. Talk about him to your heart's content."

Sylvia gave an inward sigh of exasperation. The woman was an infuriatingly good actress, there was no doubt about that. She wasn't going to be able to surprise her into giving the truth away. Oh well, it had been worth a try.

She said, "I wondered how much you'd charge to do his portrait."

"Just head and shoulders? Life size? Oil?"

"Yes, I suppose so."

"About two hundred quid. Oh well, say one eighty to you."

"That seems very reasonable."

"It's ridiculously reasonable. Don't you know that I'm the greatest portrait painter for at least two hundred yards in any direction?"

Sylvia ignored this. "The difficulty is I wanted to surprise him with it—and anyway I don't think he'd agree to sit for you. I'm wondering if you could do it without his knowing."

"You mean perch up a tree outside your bedroom window, with all my gear and a pair of binoculars? That'll cost you an extra fifty danger money."

"No, of course not. Will you work from photographs?"

"Well, I will if really necessary, but I much prefer not to. And I don't guarantee such good results."

"But he will be coming here tonight, and perhaps again. I thought perhaps you could study him as he works and make your preliminary sketches. I'm sure he wouldn't realize you were drawing him."

Madge put down her brush and came round the easel, wiping her hands on a piece of rag. "I couldn't do that tonight," she said. "I'll be taking my equipment upstairs and working like a mad thing in the living-room while Edgar goes through my papers, so as to be handy if he wants me. If he comes in a week or so, I could try then, and I could make a start on the actual portrait. But to do it justice I would need a couple of sittings later on."

"I see. Well, that's clear enough." Sylvia stood up. "I'll have to think it over, try and gauge Edgar's reactions and let you know. I'll phone you one day next week."

"Fine. I'll be able to concentrate more on the problem then. Sorry I can't give it more time now, but I really am terribly rushed. Thanks for thinking of me, anyway. I'd enjoy painting him. He's an attractive cove, your old man."

Before Sylvia could reply to this, the doorbell rang. Madge crossed to the trapdoor, got on to her knees and peered down through it. "Who is it?" she shouted. "Show yourself."

Sylvia heard a man's voice. "Miss Eversleigh?"

"None other."

"I wanted to speak to you about a commission."

"Must be my day," Madge remarked to Sylvia. Then, dropping her voice a little, added, "If I ask him up, will you stay a couple of minutes, just until I'm quite sure he's OK?"

"Yes, of course." Sylvia gladly sat down again. It would be a pity for Madge to be strangled by a homicidal maniac now. It would spoil her plan completely.

"Come on up," Madge shouted. She got to her feet.

There were footsteps on the stairs and a few seconds later a young man appeared at the top. He looked from one to the other. "Good afternoon." He was squarely built, with dark curly hair and a cheerful face.

Madge said, "Hi. This is my friend, Mrs. Gascoigne-Chalmers."

"My name's Warburton. How do you do?" He shook hands with both of them, and then went on to explain that he worked for a firm which would be moving into new premises in three months' time, and which was considering having a series of murals painted in the entrance hall and waiting-rooms. They discussed the matter for a minute or two, Madge expressing her willingness to consider the commission and Warburton saying he would be in touch with her again later.

Then he said, "Before I leave, might I look round at some of your work?" He made a gesture, embracing the whole room.

"Sure."

"Thank you. Oh—but first, I'm sorry to trouble you, but I wonder if I could look at your phone book for a moment? I have another visit to make in Cornfield, and stupidly I've forgotten the address."

"Of course. It's upstairs. I'll fetch it." Madge went to the stairs that led to her living quarters and disappeared up them.

Warburton took out a packet of cigarettes and a lighter. He indicated one of the ashtrays. "Miss Eversleigh plainly doesn't object to smoking in her studio." He offered the packet to Sylvia.

"No thank you. I don't."

He took one himself and tried to light it. But the lighter produced no flame. He gave a tut of irritation. "I forgot to fill this. As a non-smoker, you don't happen to have a match by any chance?"

"No, I—oh yes, I have." Sylvia opened her bag, took out the matches she had purchased that morning and handed them to him.

"Thank you." He turned away and began looking at the paintings on the walls. "Her work is excellent, isn't it?"

"It's considered very competent, I believe."

Warburton lit his cigarette and continued to study the pictures for a few more seconds, until Madge reappeared. Then he turned back, said, "Your matches," to Sylvia, and took the phone book which Madge handed to him. "Many thanks."

Sylvia stood up, putting the matches in her bag. "If you don't want me any longer, Madge . . ." She gave the slightest jerk of the head towards Warburton, who was bending over the directory on the table, flicking over the pages.

"Oh no, I don't think I do," Madge said. "Quite all right, I'd say, wouldn't you?"

"I would think so. I'll phone you next week, then." She moved to the stairs. Madge followed her. "Don't bother to come down," Sylvia added.

"I wasn't going to. I never do. What's the point? Thanks for calling, Sylvia. Sorry it's been a bit hectic."

"You won't tell Edgar I've been, will you—or what we talked about?"

"Of course not. And I'll try not to keep him too late tonight. So long."

"Goodbye, Madge." Sylvia went down the stairs. At the bottom she paused and glanced up. Madge had disappeared from the top of the stairs. Sylvia looked round. The doors were still open. A car—Warburton's—was parked next to her own. It was unoccupied. Nor was there any sign of life in the field or in the road.

Sylvia hurried to the far side of Madge's van and got down on her knees by the rear wheel. She reached into her bag and took out the tin of lighter fuel and her torch. Then grimacing slightly, for the floor wasn't very clean, she got right down on her side and shone her torch up under the car. Yes—the general layout was very similar to the Mini. And there was a conveniently placed piece of metal jutting out right next to the tank. Sylvia turned the tin of lighter fuel upside down and hung it up by the hook she had taped on to it. Then she removed the stopper. Fuel started to run from the tin on to the floor, rapidly forming a little pool.

Sylvia got to her feet, made sure that the tin was not visible, brushed herself down hurriedly and replaced the torch in her handbag. Then she went back to the foot of the stairs and called out in urgent voice, "Madge!"

Madge appeared again at the top, looking surprised.

Sylvia said, "You've got some trouble down here, Madge."

Madge's expression became a little alarmed. "What do you mean?"

"Your van. Petrol leak, I think."

"Oh no!" Madge gave a howl of dismay and came hurrying down the stairs. Before she had reached the bottom, Sylvia had fallen on her knees again beside the rear wheel. Madge threw her cigarette down and ground it into the floor with her heel at the foot of the stairs, then came across to the van, uttering a groan when she saw the fuel trickling out from under it. "Better get the beastly thing outside, I suppose," she said.

"Wait just a moment," Sylvia took out her torch again, lowered herself and peered up at the fuel tin. "I can see the hole." She reached out and put her finger over the opening in the tin, blocking the flow. "Yes, I can stop it. I wonder if I could plug it somehow for you. Could you get something?"

"What sort of thing?"

"How about some modelling clay?"

"Oh, what a super idea. I've got heaps of that. Hang on." She ran back up the stairs, and her voice could be heard, breathlessly explaining the situation to Warburton.

Like lightning Sylvia unhooked the nearly empty tin of lighter fuel and put it back in her bag. When Madge reappeared a few seconds later, she was still kneeling down, one arm under the rear of the car.

"Here." Madge thrust a handful of damp clay at her. Sylvia took a piece and, getting right down again, pushed it firmly against the underside of the tank. She took her hand away, remained kneeling, shining the torch upwards for a few seconds, then said, "That seems to have done the trick—at least for the moment." She got to her feet.

Madge was gazing at her in surprise and admiration. "Thank you very much. My word, aren't you efficient? I would never have thought of that."

Sylvia looked modest. "It was lucky I spotted it. I was outside, hunting in my bag for my car keys, and I couldn't find them. I thought perhaps I'd left them upstairs and I started to come back. That's when I saw the puddle. And now I remember I left the keys in the ignition all the time."

"Lucky for me you didn't remember before. I wonder how on earth it happened."

Sylvia gave a shrug. "Probably a nail flew up from your wheel sometime and punctured it."

"But why should it only start to leak through now? I haven't had the thing out today."

"I daresay the hole was blocked by grit or dried mud, and the petrol only just started to seep through."

"How weird. I wouldn't have thought it possible. Still, everything to do with cars and things is a mystery to me. Point is, what do I do now?"

"Well, if I were you, I'd ring up Hillier's straight away." She looked at her watch. "You'll probably just catch them. Tell them you've got a leaking petrol tank and ask them to send somebody out first thing tomorrow. They won't come tonight now. I certainly wouldn't drive it as it is. It's doubtful if that clay would hold once the van started to move, and you might lose your petrol before you got to the garage. Besides, it might be dangerous. It could splash on to the hot exhaust pipe."

" 'Struth, yes. I hadn't thought of that. I'll go and ring Jack Hillier now."

She strode to the stairs, just as Warburton appeared at the top. He made to step back, but Madge beckoned to him to come down. He did so, saying, "Anything I can do?"

"Thank you, no. My mechanical friend here has performed a temporary miracle and stopped the leak. I've got to go and phone the garage. Excuse me?"

"Of course. I must be off. My firm will be in touch, Miss Eversleigh."

"Fine," said Madge, half-way up the stairs. "Look forward to it. So long." She disappeared.

"Nice to have met you, Mrs. Gascoigne-Chalmers," Warburton said.

"Goodbye," Sylvia said.

She watched him walk to his car and drive off. She breathed a slight sigh of relief as he did so. His presence could have been a complication. Her plan had been dependent on Madge's well-known ignorance of mechanical things. Had Warburton shown an interest, and Madge told him Sylvia's diagnosis of the cause of the trouble, he might well have realized the extreme unlikelihood of a nail puncturing the petrol tank—and, in the event, the even greater unlikelihood of dirt preventing a leakage of petrol until the van had been standing still for what must have been nearly twenty-four hours. However, no harm had been done.

Everything hung now on Madge not giving Hillier too detailed an account of the trouble. As long as she said no more than that she had a fuel leak, all well and good. Sylvia waited for her to return and a few minutes later Madge reappeared on the stairs. "Hillier's are coming tomorrow morning."

"What did you tell them?"

"Just that my petrol tank was leaking."

"You didn't mention about it suddenly starting after the van had been at rest for hours?"

"No—why? Should I have?"

"No, no. I just wondered if they had any explanation other than my guess."

"I'll ask them tomorrow. Thanks for your help."

"Don't mention it."

"All right, I won't next time. S'long." And Madge vanished again.

"There won't be a next time, you insolent cat," Sylvia muttered to herself as she returned to her car. "There won't be any next times for you."

CHAPTER 18

Edgar put down his coffee cup and glanced at his watch. "Well, I'll have to be getting along to the Mill. Mustn't keep Madge waiting."

"All right, dear. What time will you be back?"

"About ten, I expect. I've promised Beryl I won't keep her there after nine-thirty. She wants to get home in time to tuck the children in."

Sylvia sat up suddenly. "Beryl! She's not going with you?"

"No, I'm meeting her there. Why?"

"I—I didn't realize. You didn't say."

"I only decided this afternoon to have her along. Actually I don't really think I'll need her, but it occurred to me it might be advisable to have a chaperon present—as this will be my second visit in two days. I can't be too careful in my position. Of course, a woman like Madge has no reputation to worry about. But I do. Well, 'bye, dear. Hope you won't be bored." He went out.

Sylvia sat very still for a long time. This really was most unfortunate. Beryl was a pleasant person—quiet and respectful. Sylvia had no desire to kill her. But really she couldn't see any way to avoid it. The set-up was altogether too good to abandon the project at this stage. There would never be another chance just like this.

Eventually she reluctantly decided that Beryl would have to go too. A pity. It would mean that those children of hers would be left orphans. Still, there was the grandmother, and if she couldn't care for them, orphanages were supposed to be very nice these days. And perhaps it would be possible to do something for them financially, later on—if she had any money to spare. She would think about it, anyway, and do what she could. Nobody had a right to expect more than that of her. Her conscience could be clear. And there was the further advantage, that if Beryl was killed, too, the incident would look to the authorities even less like a possible *crime passionnel* than it would if Edgar and Madge were the only fatalities—another point that would keep Sylvia herself in the clear. So perhaps it was for the best.

Sylvia put Beryl from her mind. She wanted to think about Madge for a bit. She wondered uncomfortably if, after all, she was wrong about her and Edgar. It certainly seemed that tonight at least there was going to be no funny business between them. He must really be going to do the woman's tax. What a sell! All the same, she couldn't think she was mistaken—in spite of the way Edgar had talked about Madge. No—she'd be willing to bet he went there at other times for the other reason. That disparaging talk—taking Beryl with him—all that was just camouflage.

But even if she were wrong, she couldn't really feel regretful about killing Madge—not like she did about Beryl. No one would miss Madge. She had referred to herself as a slob, and that was exactly what she was. Imagine living like that! And so utterly insulting in her speech and manner. Yes, the world would be a better place with Madge Eversleigh gone.

Sylvia went upstairs and changed into a pair of dark slacks, a black polo sweater, and flat soft-soled shoes. This was a much more workmanlike outfit than that trouser suit. She looked rather good in it—like some girl detective or secret agent in a TV series. She took out her blonde wig, but didn't put it on; she would wear it as a precaution in the vicinity of the Mill, just in case she was seen. She transferred the matches from her bag to her pocket, went downstairs and out to her car, and set off.

She made a detour around Cornfield and approached the Mill from the opposite direction. About a mile from it she pulled up on to the verge in a quiet lane and stopped. She got out. Although the lane was quite deserted, there was the possibility that someone who knew her would pass, recognize her car and just happen to remember the fact later. Unfortunately, this was an unavoidable risk. There had been no alternative to using the Mini. Luckily, the grass on the verge was long, and by pulling it up around the front and rear plates she was at least able to obscure the number. So, as there was nothing distinctive about the car, there was no reason for anyone just passing by to recognize it as hers.

Sylvia placed the wig on her head yet again, took the can of petrol from the boot and set off on foot. If anyone saw her now she'd pass as a motorist, out of petrol, en route to the nearest filling station. She hoped nobody offered her a lift.

Sylvia stood motionless behind a tree and peered along the driveway leading to the Mill. This was the crunch moment. She had to walk up to the building—in full view of Edgar or Madge or Beryl if one of them happened to look out of a window. On her side was the fact that they would all be working busily, and probably wouldn't have time to gaze from windows.

She took a deep breath, left the cover of the tree and started briskly up the driveway. As far as possible she kept the shrubs that lined the drive between her and the Mill, but made no exaggerated darts from cover to cover. She watched the windows closely, but saw no sign of life. If it hadn't been for the two cars—the Rover and Beryl's old VW—the place might have been empty.

At first the two cars obscured her view of the garage, but then she saw that the double doors were open—and the lights on inside, almost spotlighting Madge's van. Why? she wondered. Just typical carelessness on Madge's part, presumably.

Keeping her eyes fixed on the second-storey windows, Sylvia darted across the forecourt and into the Mill. Her eyes hunted for the light switch. Daylight was beginning to give way to dusk, and with that bright electric bulb immediately above her head she now felt uncomfortably illuminated. Not that there was anyone about outside. But there might be at any time. So she had to get the light out before anything else. Then she saw that there were two switches side by side at the foot of the stairs. Obviously one controlled the lights in the studio. But she didn't know which one. Suppose she turned the wrong one? At the moment there was complete silence from the first floor—Madge had said she was going to work in her living-room—but if the light suddenly went on in the studio, Madge or Beryl or Edgar would almost certainly notice the glow coming up the stairs—especially as Sylvia had seen from outside that they didn't yet have their own light on. And Madge would be bound to come down and investigate.

So she couldn't risk the switch. She considered removing the bulb, but to do that she would have to stand on the bonnet of the van, and she might make a noise. Or she could close the doors. But if they scraped the floor or the hinges squeaked, that too would alert Madge.

No—she was going to have to work with the light on and the doors open. After all, it would only take a minute or so, and the two cars parked outside would provide a fairly effective screen if anybody should happen to pass along the road.

Sylvia closed her eyes and concentrated. Was there anything she had forgotten? Any loophole? She was sure there wasn't. The windows would be the only way out for them. There were absolutely no footholds outside. And this would mean a straight drop from the second storey on to that concrete path. It would be a hundred to one against surviving that. If by some miracle the fall didn't kill them, it would certainly knock them out, and the flames blazing just a couple of feet away would do the rest.

However, before that, before anyone tried to leap to safety, as soon as the flames had really taken hold and Edgar and the women rushed to the windows, Sylvia—and this was the part she was really looking forward to—was going to walk into the open, where Edgar could see her, blow him a kiss, turn and walk slowly away. A crazy, foolhardy gesture, maybe. But she had always been a romantic. And she was still determined that at the very end he was going to know the truth.

There would be no doubt about the cause of the fire. Madge herself had reported a petrol leak to Hillier. She had a reputation locally both as a heavy smoker and a careless person. A match or cigarette end carelessly thrown down, falling through the trap, landing in a trickle of petrol from the leaky tank, a sheet of flame along the floor—and the van would go up.

All was still silent aloft. Sylvia uncapped the can of petrol, crossed to the van and poured a pint or so on to the ground immediately beneath the petrol tank. Then she got down and splashed some up on to the underside of the tank and on the wheel. (The lump of clay was still there, and she pulled it off and dropped it on the ground.) From the small pool that formed she made little rivulets of petrol to every wall, taking particular trouble to saturate as much as possible of the ground inside the doors. Then she ran another rivulet to the stairs. With extreme caution she started to mount them.

To be on the safe side, she had to ensure that the first floor started to blaze within seconds of the ground floor. It was hard to estimate how long it would take for the flames to break through the ground floor ceiling. It would surely be no more than a minute—two at the most. But if their minds worked quickly enough upstairs, they might just think to rush down, towards the fire, and try to get out through a studio window. Even from there the fall would be highly dangerous—but there would be a chance of surviving. Therefore, she had to cut off that exit. Some petrol on the floor of the studio, especially near the windows, would do the trick.

She reached the top and peered through the trapdoor. It was empty, though from here she could just hear a murmur of voices from the living-room above. She went up the last few steps and silently darted round the room, pouring petrol from the can. It took her only about thirty seconds. Then she went backwards down the stairs again, pouring fuel over every step as she descended. She reached the bottom and looked around. Everything was satisfactory. And it wasn't more than two minutes since she'd started pouring. It was still all clear outside. She scurried back to the far side of the van and added a little more petrol to the pool underneath it, then, still pouring, walked away backwards. She went through the open doorway and keeping low, backed half-way across the forecourt. Here she stopped and looked up. There was nobody at any of the windows. Not that it would really matter if they did see her now. Before the truth sank in it would be too late for them.

She backed a few more yards, still pouring, until the can was empty. She'd judged it to a nicety. The little dark deadly path of petrol stretched invitingly away from her, across the light grey concrete, straight into the open doors of the Mill. She reached into her pocket for the matches, knelt down, opened the box, took one out and, hands shaking, tried to strike it against the side of the box. The head broke off. She swore quietly, took another out and tried again. But nothing happened. The match wouldn't ignite. Desperately she fumbled for a third, scraping it viciously along the side of the box. Still there was no trace of a spark. She grabbed a fourth, dropped it, snatched it up and tried striking it on the concrete. It was to no avail.

By now Sylvia was sobbing. No—no—it couldn't be possible. She tried a fifth—a sixth—a seventh match. Not one of them ignited. Nearly hysterical with frustration, she straightened up.

The cars! Perhaps. . . .

She ran to the Rover. Every door was locked. That pig! Why here of all places did he have to lock it? She threw herself across to the VW. This was unlocked. Dear, dear, trusting Beryl. Sylvia groped frantically in the glove pocket. No matches.

That left only Madge's van. Throwing caution to the winds, she sprinted into the Mill and tore open the Bedford's door.

The sight of the box of Swan on the passenger seat almost brought a crow of delight to Sylvia's lips. She snatched it up and turned to run outside. Then the feel of the box caused her to pause, shake it, and despairingly jab it open. It was empty. She looked outside. The petrol trail had quite dried up.

Sobbing quietly to herself all the way, Sylvia walked back to her car and drove home.

CHAPTER 19

"Darling," Edgar said, "I think I may have found a solution to our problem."

Sylvia blinked. Problem? What was he talking about? *They* had no problem. *She* had a problem: how to kill a man around whom the fates seemed to have built an impregnable wall. And he talked about having a problem!

It was the morning following the débâcle at the Mill. He'd come home unexpectedly early from the office and seemed in obnoxiously high spirits. Sylvia for once made no attempt at a show of responding. She was cast down in a pit of frustration. Desperation at the ever-approaching deadline was having superimposed on it a growing, hopeless conviction that she was not going to succeed. She was very close to dropping the whole project. It would be so easy just to give in, not to have to rack brain or body any more.

Her mood had not been helped, a few minutes before Edgar had come in, by a rambling and bewildered phone call from Madge. That leak had started again last night. Well, it must have done, because the whole place reeked of petrol. Yet when she'd investigated she'd found the outside of the tank quite dry and no hole in it at all. Now everything seemed to be all right and she had told Hillier's not to come. What could have been the trouble?

On the verge of shouting out the whole truth and having done with everything, Sylvia had forced herself to explain that she had never actually seen a *hole* in the tank, only a spot from which the fuel had been flowing. It could have been running down the outside of the tank. Making use again of Madge's mechanical ignorance, she blithely suggested the trouble might have been an intermittent overflow caused by an air blockage.

Madge seemed only partly satisfied, but Sylvia rang off, confident that she would puzzle over the incident a bit longer and then consign it to the limbo of life's unsolved mysteries and forget all about it.

But this knowledge gave her no satisfaction. How could it when the Creep still breathed—and beamed and babbled all round her morning, noon and night?

She realized he was looking at her quizzically, waiting for some reaction to his remark.

She made a huge effort, smiled, and said, "I'm sorry, darling, I was miles away then. What were you saying?"

"An answer, darling, to the problem of next door—the Trust."

Her eyes widened. "An answer? Edgar, what *do* you mean?"

"Well, I've been giving the matter a considerable amount of thought."

"Have you?"

"Naturally. I said I would. Surely you have been, too, haven't you?"

"Oh, of course."

"I was sure you had—you've been a little *distrait*. We haven't talked about the problem as much as I anticipated we would. Several times I've been going to, but as I had no ideas, there didn't seem to be any point."

"I felt the same."

"But now I really believe I have got one."

"Got one what, darling?"

"An idea, darling."

"Oh, I see. Then tell me."

"Well, since we don't want either to sell this house, or buy *The Firs,* I've been trying to work out a way to stop these fools coming here at all—to make them withdraw their offer for the house."

"You mean legal action—an injunction to prevent Charles selling to them?"

"No, that's not on; he can do what he likes with the place. I mean a way to put them off wanting to buy. What I'm thinking of is not legal action—but illegal."

For the first time she really gave him her attention. "What *are* you talking about?"

"I'll explain. But let's get one thing straight first: you don't like Charles, do you?"

"You know I don't."

"No more do I. But how deep does your dislike go? Would you be willing to see him hurt?"

"Physically?"

"No, no—just in the pocket."

"More than willing. I'd be delighted. He has far too much money. And I think it's disgusting the way he's intending to saddle us with these freaks."

"Good. We're agreed. Now, would you be prepared to do something—something a little bit sharp perhaps? Nothing really dishonest, of course, but technically illegal. In addition you'd have to tell a few white lies. I mean, would you be willing if, as a result, the Trust were to withdraw their offer to Charles and go right away?"

"Of course I'd be willing. I'd do almost anything to stop those weirdos coming next door."

"Charles would probably never speak to you again."

"That wouldn't keep me awake at nights."

"He might accuse us publicly of being liars and thieves."

"Could he prove it?"

"No."

"Then we could sue him, couldn't we?"

Edgar smiled, "You know, I hadn't thought of that."

"Edgar, I'm getting terribly worked up. I wish you'd tell me what's in your mind."

"Well." Edgar paused to marshal his thoughts. "The Trust only want *The Firs* because it's the place old Dimsdale was staying at when he formulated this tomfool theory. Right?"

"Right."

"Now: how do they *know* that he was staying there at the time?"

Sylvia frowned. "It's a well-known fact, isn't it?"

"Not at all. Nothing about Dimsdale is really well-known. He's a very minor sort of figure on the cultural scene. I've been making some inquiries at the public library. There are really only two sources of information about his life: his published Journal; and a biography written in the 1930s. The author of that is long dead."

"Presumably then the Trust know about his visit from one of those sources."

"Of course they do. I've been reading both those books myself— or, at least, the relevant sections."

"Oh? What do they say?"

"Well, on the subject of the visit, the biography is nothing more than a re-hash of the Journal. The author obviously had no other source material for it except the Journal. All he did was simply re-write Dimsdale's words in the third person."

"Then what does Dimsdale himself say?"

"Not a great deal. The actual visit plainly wasn't an important episode in his life. He was much less interested in his surroundings than in the theory he was working on. As a matter of fact I copied the entry from his Journal in the library." Edgar took a piece of paper from his pocket and unfolded it. "Now this is the whole basis for the Trust's interest in *The Firs*. Ready?"

Sylvia nodded.

Edgar read, " 'Jun 17th. In response to gracious invitation of Mr. and Mrs. S. Inchcape, today travelled to Cornfield by rail. The weather continued delightful. Inchcape himself greeted me at the railway station, and we enjoyed an extremely pleasant drive in open carriage to his home. Upon arrival I was made most welcome by his charming lady. The house is a fine and spacious residence, with an atmosphere most conducive to creative work. Have felt intense mental stimulation ever since my arrival.' " Edgar folded up the paper.

Sylvia said, "That's all?"

"That is all. For the rest of his time here he concentrates exclusively on the development of his theory. One June 23rd he simply writes something like: 'Bade farewell to my kind host and hostess and returned to London by noon train.' "

"Well, I agree that isn't a lot. But it's quite specific, isn't it? He *did* stay there, and he *did* feel stimulated."

"Where did he stay?"

She looked puzzled. "At *The Firs*."

"Prove it."

"What do you mean?"

Edgar handed her the sheet of paper. "Show me a single reference there to *The Firs*."

"Well, he says the home of Mr. and Mrs.—" Sylvia broke off.

Edgar said triumphantly, "Precisely, darling: 'Mr. and Mrs. S. Inchcape.' S.—only S."

Sylvia's face cleared. "You mean it could just as well have been *Sidney* he was staying with—in this house."

"From the written evidence—yes, certainly. And if that was the case, the Trust wouldn't have any interest in *The Firs*."

"Well, *did* he stay here?"

"I don't think so for a moment."

"Why?"

"Because Charles says it was *The Firs*. And he heard it from his grandfather. But the point is this: how can he prove it was *The Firs?*"

Sylvia considered, "Has he got to?"

"As things stand, no. The Trust people have taken his word for it. All Dimsdale's followers are obviously familiar with his Journal, and they no doubt made inquiries about any houses in the Cornfield area once owned by a family called Inchcape. And that would naturally lead them straight to Charles. They'd assume automatically that it was at his house that Dimsdale stayed. That solicitor's letter

Charles had, asking if he was in fact the owner of the house where Dimsdale stayed, couldn't have been more than a formality. The Trust probably knew nothing about Sidney at all. Charles may have casually mentioned to them since that *The Elms* was built by Silas's brother, and that you're Silas's great-niece, but I'd be very surprised if it's occurred to any of them that it might have been this house in which Dimsdale stayed."

"But there's no way we could convince them that was the case."

"Not unless we could cast a real doubt on Charles's word."

"Call him a liar?"

"Not necessarily—and not in the first instance: just claim he's mistaken."

"But won't they be more likely to accept his word than ours? After all, he's got a bit of a reputation as a scholar. And if he says that he remembers his grandfather telling him that *his* father—Silas —was host to Dimsdale, I'm sure that would satisfy them."

"He could have got his grandfather's stories confused. After all, it must be forty years since he heard them."

"But we'd have to back up a suggestion like that."

"I think we could."

"How?"

"You've forgotten something. There *is* evidence of Dimsdale's visit, apart from his Journal. You and Charles talked about it that Sunday night when all this started."

"Of course—the photo! Of Silas and Dimsdale together. But that doesn't do us any good. It merely proves Charles is telling the truth."

"Listen—who did you think that photo was of, when you first saw it in your aunt's collection? Dimsdale and who?"

"Sidney. Oh, you mean . . . ?"

"Yes, dear—identical twins. If you claimed that the man in the photo is Sidney, I doubt if there's anybody in the world, except Charles, who could argue with you."

"Perhaps not. But there *is* Charles, and he *will,* and he's got the photograph."

"He's got the photograph *now*. But why should he keep it?"

Sylvia gave a gasp. "You mean we should *steal* it?"

"That's not a very nice word, darling. Take possession of it would be more accurate. We'd be acting from the highest motives: trying to prevent a very wealthy man ruining our lives simply in order to add a few more thousand pounds to his bank balance. And I mean, who's to say that the photo is not really of Sidney? He and Silas always gave each other photos of themselves with their important guests. Your Aunt Maude had a copy of that photo—the one you threw away. Charles says the photo is of Silas and a copy was given to Sidney. It could just have easily been the other way round, and the photo in Charles's attic at *High Tors* was given *to* Silas *by* Sidney."

Sylvia's mind was working fast. "All right: assuming for a moment that we could get hold of it, what are you suggesting we should do then?"

"Go along to the next meeting of the Trust and show it to them. Tell them you think they've made a serious mistake—that Dimsdale never stayed at *The Firs* at all, but at your house—*The Elms*."

"But how would we explain not having said anything before—as soon as Charles told us about the Trust?"

Edgar shrugged. "Your aunt told you years ago about Dimsdale, but you'd forgotten. There were so many guests here in the old days that you couldn't keep track of them all. Charles's story struck a chord in your mind, and the more you thought about it, the more sure you became that you'd been told Dimsdale stayed at *The Elms*. You remembered a photo of Dimsdale standing with your great grandfather. You thought you'd thrown it away, but you made a search and luckily found it. And so you feel it is your duty to produce it."

"But what will Charles do then?"

"He'll be furious. He'll tell them that the photo is of Silas and that he's got a print too. He'll try and find it. But he won't be able to— because we've got it. He'll have to come back and tell the Trust that he hasn't got it after all. Now that's when they'll begin to doubt his reliability. Next, he might accuse us of having stolen the photo from him. But don't forget, Charles may have a reputation as a scholar, but we have our reputation, too—as honourable, upright citizens. In addition, we'll have first-class alibis. And finally, we'll also have a perfect counter-attack."

"What's that?"

"We can ask why Charles persuaded the Trust not to approach us themselves—why he offered to act as a go-between. Did he know from the beginning that the Trust had got hold of the wrong house —that it was ours which they should be after? Did he see a chance of making sixty-five thousand pounds and deliberately go on deceiving them? Of course, he didn't know that they'd be making an offer for *both* houses. But having started the deception he was stuck with it."

Sylvia gave a giggle. "I say, wouldn't that be one in the eye for Charles?"

"I thought that might appeal to you. Of course, we'd only suggest any of that if he started, er, impugning our honesty."

"It almost makes me wish he would. There's still a strong chance they will believe him, though, isn't there?"

"I expect some of them will. But not all of them, I'm sure. And that's the important thing—to cast doubt. We don't want to convince them Dimsdale stayed in this house—we're not interested in selling—but to question that he stayed at *The Firs*. And that will be another point in our favour. Charles stands to make a small fortune if they believe Dimsdale stayed at his house. We make nothing if they believe he stayed at ours. We could do—but we refuse to. So what motive could we have for bringing this up—other than a pure desire to prevent the Trust wasting their money?"

"I'm sorry, but I can't quite follow that."

"Well, given the belief of these people that certain buildings are conducive to his Conductorism thing, before they fork out sixty-five thousand, they're going to have to be absolutely sure they've got the right house. Granted, they'll buy both houses if they can. But if you state categorically, as you did to me, that you will never, under any circumstances, sell *The Elms*—not for five hundred thousand pounds—then they're not going to have any alternative to dropping the idea of coming to Cornfield altogether, and going after one of those other places that Charles mentioned."

"Darling, it's most ingenious." Sylvia's voice was full of admiration.

"There may be factors I've overlooked or don't know about, of course. It's possible, for instance, that Charles has already found the photo himself. He can't have shown it to the Trust yet, but he may have put it in a safe place."

"Oh, I wouldn't think so. He won't have had much time at *High Tors* yet, and he's a terrible procrastinator. I'm sure that photo is still in the box in his attic."

"So—what do you think? Is it worth the risk of trying to get hold of it?"

"It depends how great a risk, Edgar. You're not suggesting we should break into the house, I suppose?"

Edgar smiled. "Hardly. Though actually it did briefly occur to me to hire a burglar to do it for us. Quite a few have come before me on the Bench over the years."

"Now that's a good idea!"

"No, I discarded the idea immediately. It's just not on. Firstly, as soon as we approach any crook and ask him to steal something for us, we leave ourselves wide open to blackmail by him. Secondly,

High Tors is virtually burglar-proof. I'm not saying a master thief might not break in, but all the burglars I know are by definition unsuccessful burglars. However, even if the man pulled it off, he'd be bound to leave traces of the break-in behind. And that wouldn't suit us. Charles must not know there's been a thief in his house. Once he does know that, he'll be immediately alerted to the possibility of something having been taken. He'd be sure to report it to the police. Then later, when he couldn't find the photo to produce to the Trust, he'd have a very good excuse: he could tell them it had been stolen."

"But couldn't he do that anyway?"

"Not if he's never reported a burglary. Think how phony it would sound: a pitiful excuse for not having it. But if he already knew there'd been a break-in, and had officially reported it—then immediately he's got an explanation for the missing photo—and two very obvious suspects: the only people who knew of and could have wanted that picture. No, Sylvia, we've got to handle this ourselves."

CHAPTER 20

Sylvia pursed her lips. "I must admit I don't like it, Edgar."

"Darling, there's another factor that makes it unavoidable. Think of that box containing the photos. According to Charles, there are hundreds of them in it. They're old and most of them are probably faded. Silas or the almost-identical Sidney will be in nearly all of them. You thought there was another person or persons in the Dimsdale photo, in addition to one of the Inchcape brothers. Charles wasn't sure. Even *you* weren't certain if it was a man or men or women or what. Remember we only want that one photo removed from the box. Now, how on earth is anyone we might hire going to pick out the right one?"

She frowned. "There's Dimsdale himself for identification."

"But he's not exactly a familiar face to the average burglar, is he? There are some photos of him in that biography I mentioned. He's extremely ordinary-looking. In some of the pictures he has a moustache, in others he's clean-shaven. Sometimes he wears glasses. In the outdoor ones he's mostly wearing a hat. Now imagine: we'd have to get a copy of that book, show our burglar the illustrations and tell him to pick out, from a box containing hundreds of photos, one picture of that particular man, standing alongside another man, who will appear to be in almost all of them, together with a third or possibly even a fourth person, both of unknown age and sex. Darling, he'd have to examine every photo minutely. It would take hours!"

Sylvia looked thoughtful. "That's true. It hadn't occurred to me before. It does look as if we're going to have to do it ourselves."

"Not *we,* darling. You."

"*Me?* Alone?"

"I'll be there—in the house. But you're going to have to be the one actually to find and take the photo. Because don't forget, I haven't seen it. I couldn't pick it out any more quickly than our hypothetical crook could. But you *have* seen it. You may not remember much detail about it now, but the moment you see it again, you'll recognize it."

"Do you really think so?"

"I'm positive of it."

"Perhaps you're right. But Edgar, I—"

He raised his hand to interrupt her. "Just hear me out—one more minute, darling, please. The decision, of course, has to be entirely your own. But remember why we're doing this: to keep *The Elms*. After a great deal of thought I cannot think of any other way this might be done. If I could do the whole job on my own, I gladly would. But I can't. That's the position. Now—do you want me to go on and tell you exactly what you'd have to do?"

"Yes, of course, I do."

"Good girl. Well, it's really very simple. I ring up Charles and arrange to call and see him at *High Tors* on Saturday."

"Why Saturday?"

"Because that's the Bruntons' day off and he'll probably be there alone. He usually is."

"Suppose he isn't? Suppose for once he has guests?"

Repressing with iron control an almost overwhelming desire to follow Willie Morgan's example, pick her up and hurl her through the nearest window, Edgar smiled gently. "Well, darling, in that case, we'll have to try and arrange it another day. Let's meet that problem when we come to it, shall we?"

"All right. Sorry."

"I'll make up some story about wanting to speak to him with reference to our buying *The Firs* and that I'll be driving down alone. In fact, you come in the car with me. However, as soon as we get into the grounds of *High Tors,* and before we're in sight of the house, we stop. I then break a window of the gardener's cottage."

Sylvia's eyes widened, but she didn't say anything.

Edgar went on, "I let you in and you wait there while I drive on up to the house. I take my brief-case with me and leave it in the hall. You give me, say, half an hour and then phone *High Tors* from the cottage. You tell Charles that you're speaking from here. After you've rung off I go out to the hall, ostensibly to fetch something from my brief-case, and put the front-door latch back. I then keep Charles talking for half an hour. You come up to the house, slip quietly in, go up to the attic, find the photo, leave again, just as quietly, go back to the cottage and ring up a second time. That is my signal that the mission has been successfully accomplished and I can leave. I pick you up and we come home—leaving behind no evidence except a broken window in the cottage."

"But, darling, suppose you can't keep him talking for half an hour? Suppose he comes out into the hall and runs right into me?"

"That's all right. Surprise, surprise! Practical joke. You were here all the time."

"He'll think it very odd."

"Of course he will. But he'll never in a hundred years suspect the real reason."

"Suppose I've already got the photo and I'm on my way out when Charles finds me?"

"That'll be up to you, darling. If, when he does later discover the loss of the photo, you don't mind him suspecting you personally of the theft—not being able to prove it, just suspecting you—then you hang on to it. If you don't want to risk that, then you just make the usual excuse to go upstairs, and replace the photo. You needn't make up your mind on that yet."

Sylvia was silent, thinking. "What if the phone in the cottage has been disconnected?"

"It hasn't. I got the number from Inquiries today and dialled it. It rang. If it had been disconnected I would have just got the unobtainable signal."

"If we do pull it off, he'll suspect *you.*"

"No, because I'll make certain I'm not out of his presence long enough to have done it."

She nodded thoughtfully, then said, "It's extremely well thought out, darling. Except for one thing: there's only going to be my word to say that I actually am here at home."

Edgar grinned. "Wrong, dear. You can provide very strong evidence that you're here."

"What?"

"Being able to tell him about something that you can—quote—'see' happening next door, at *The Firs,* from your very window."

She looked blank. "What sort of thing?"

"Well, let's say two young men poking around in a rather furtive manner, examining the windows and so on."

"But that wouldn't prove anything."

"It would if they actually were there at that time, wouldn't it, if somebody else saw them as well—and that if necessary they were later willing to admit the fact quite freely?"

There was no gleam of understanding on Sylvia's face and he said slowly, "Listen, darling: there are two young men in Cornfield, brothers called Joe and Jerry Atkins. They've recently set up together as builders and decorators, and they're very eager to get business—almost desperately so. Now Joe is on the thick side. I intend to ring up at a time when Jerry's not there and ask Joe if they can come out to my house on Saturday at five-thirty, say, to give me a quotation for painting the outside, fitting new windows, and so on. I'll tell him they must be there exactly on time, as I want to speak to them about the job and I have a very busy schedule. I'll warn him that I may be called away at the last minute, anyway, but that if I'm not there when they arrive they're to have a look round and I'll get in touch with them later. Then I'll give him the name of the house." Edgar paused. *"The Firs.* I'll add that it's next door to *The Elms."*

"I see." She nodded slowly, with the air of a great light dawning. "They actually will be poking around the house at five-thirty, so if I phone Charles and tell him I can see them, it will apparently be proof later on that I actually was here, three hours' drive away from *High Tors.* That's brilliant."

"Thank you, darling. Anyway, you describe them to Charles over the phone—I'll have to see that you get a good but surreptitious look at them and their van beforehand—and he, of course will say he knows nothing about them. You promise to keep an eye on them and ring the police if they don't go away. You say you'll phone him back and let him know developments. Then after you ring off, I'll say to Charles, 'Oh, I expect those were the Atkins brothers— painters that I asked to call. The fools must have gone to the wrong house.'"

"You'd better tell Charles that you forgot all about sending for them—and forgot to mention it to me."

"Yes—good idea."

"You said something about another person seeing them as well."

"Oh yes. Well, we've got to be absolutely certain they really are there at five-thirty. I mean, I'm sure they will go if it's humanly possible. But we've got to allow for hold-ups. So we'll need confirmation that the plan has worked. We can get that from Miss Killigrew."

Sylvia said, "Wait: let me work this out for myself. They'll have to pass her cottage on their way here. She works in her garden every day during the summer from four until seven. You've made quite a joke about her always being there to give you a wave when you come home in the evening. We also know that she keeps her living-room window open and has her telephone on the window-ledge just inside, so that she can answer it without going indoors. But I don't see how we can just ring her up out of the blue and ask if two young men have driven past her house lately."

"Of course not. But could you think of a legitimate reason for ringing her?"

"Well, I could ask her to write out one of her recipes for me, and tell her I'll pick it up the next day. I have done that once or twice."

"Fine. Then you do that, at about half past five from the gardener's cottage, letting her think you're speaking from home. Then you behave as though your attention has been momentarily distracted, and say, 'Did you see a van with two young men in it pass your place a few minutes ago?' If all's gone well, she'll say yes. At which you reply, 'They've just pulled up next door. I wonder what they want.' After that you ring Charles, as arranged, come up to the house, find the photo, return to the cottage, ring him again, ostensibly to tell him the young men have gone away, actually as a code to me that the job's over. Then just wait for me to pick you up. That's it. The next day I phone Jerry Atkins and say I think he and his brother went to the wrong house; that I said *The Elms* next to *The Firs,* but that my wife saw them looking around next door. I'll tell him I'll see them later about the painting work."

"Suppose Miss Killigrew says she hasn't seen the boys go past. Do we abandon the plan?"

"Not necessarily. They live with their mother. If you get no joy from Killigrew, I suggest you ring the mother and ask her where they are."

"What reason do I give?"

Edgar felt waves of irritation starting to rise within him. He controlled them manfully. "Well, I don't know, dear. You could say you were trying to get hold of somebody to do an urgent repair job. If she says they're out on another job, say you wonder if it's near your house, because if so you could go and see them there. Should she say they've gone to *The Firs,* you'll know everything's OK, and that Killigrew just happened to miss them driving past. Tell Ma Atkins that's too far away—you live the other side of the town, ring off quickly and carry on as planned."

"Suppose Mrs. Atkins doesn't know where they are, or says they've had a breakdown or an accident or something—what then?"

Edgar felt a pulse beating violently in the side of his head. He closed his eyes and took several deep breaths, pretending to be giving intense thought to her question. Then he said, "In that case, darling, we'll have to scrap the plan, won't we—at least temporarily?"

"But by then you'd actually be with Charles. I'd need to have some way of telling you I wasn't going through with it."

"That's all right, we'll think up some code word or phrase. Just ask Charles to let you speak to me."

Sylvia said, "I do congratulate you, darling. It's a beautifully worked-out plan. I just wish my alibi was going to be a little more cast-iron."

"You can't have a false alibi that's cast-iron. You can bribe witnesses to say you were with them—but they can go back on their word and you're in the soup. This is a circumstantial sort of alibi, but—it cannot be disproved. And it'll have the ring of truth. It's the sort of unforced, normal alibi that an innocent person would be likely to have—not too airtight. Do you follow?"

"Yes, perfectly. It's simply that it's my alibi—it'll be me who'll be in trouble if it goes wrong, so I absolutely must examine it as closely as I can. For instance, suppose someone calls here or rings up on Saturday afternoon. If Charles did bring charges against us later that person might come forward and say that I wasn't here."

"Well, as for a phone call, we'll leave the receiver off—which will make it look as though you were here. Nobody's likely to visit. There are never any deliveries made then. You've always discouraged friends from dropping in uninvited. And we've never been bothered by salesmen. But even if it did happen, you could always say you heard the door bell but didn't answer because you were alone in the house and were nervous about the two men you'd seen. I agree, this isn't one hundred per cent foolproof—*no* plan can be. But it's as *near* it as any plan can be. And let's not get pathological about the risk. I mean, you won't be stealing government secrets. It's quite on the cards Charles will just think he's lost the photo. I don't think the possibility of our having stolen it will occur to him. He'll assume the photo we'll produce was your aunt's. So taking it all in all, the risk of either of us ever being prosecuted is minute. I thought that perhaps, to keep *The Elms* as we've always loved it, you would consider that risk a worthwhile one. So—how about it? Will you do it?"

"Oh yes, Edgar! Of course I will."

She'd bought it! The gullible little nincompoop had bought it! Edgar could hardly believe it. But how he'd had to work! They seemed to have been talking for hours. He'd played her beautifully, though. Manipulation—that's what it had been: a superior mind making an inferior one do its will.

She asked, "Who will you phone first, to fix the appointments—Charles or the Atkins brothers?"

"Oh, Charles, I think."

"When?"

"No time like the present." He went to the phone and rang *High Tors*. However, it was Brunton who answered, and told him that Charles was out walking. Edgar said he'd phone again. But within fifteen minutes Charles had rung him back. Five minutes after that it was all arranged. And in addition Edgar had learned that Charles expected to be spending Saturday completely alone. He rang off and told Sylvia.

"Good," she said. "It seems to be working out. Are you going to ring the Atkins boys now?"

"Not just yet. When I ring I want to speak to Joe. Anyone could believe in his having got a message wrong. But if Jerry answered, it would seem very queer if I *asked* for Joe. Now, Jerry has a girl friend, and he likes a good time. Joe, on the other hand, tends apparently to be the stay-at-home type. So it would be best to ring this evening."

"I see. By the way, I've just thought of something else. You're quite well-known round here: suppose these boys know you live at *The Elms,* not *The Firs.* Or suppose Jerry looks up Gascoigne-Chalmers in the phone book, just to be sure his brother has got it right?"

"I won't give my name, just the address. If Joe should ask, I'll pretend not to hear him and ring off quickly."

"You've thought of everything, haven't you, darling?"

"I think so," said Edgar.

He had to choose his moment for ringing the Atkins house very carefully. It was true that he did want Joe to be alone. But what Edgar hadn't told Sylvia was that he wanted to be alone himself, too. For she couldn't be allowed to hear all the conversation.

She seemed to hang about within earshot of the phone for hours and several times reminded him of the call he had to make. He was rapidly running out of excuses for delaying it longer when fortunately she suddenly decided to shampoo her hair. He waited until she'd gone to the bathroom, then immediately rang the Atkins' number.

A rather gruff man's voice answered.

Edgar said, "Who am I speaking to?"

"Joe Atkins here."

"Oh, hullo, Mr. Atkins. I'm told you and your brother have recently set up as builders and decorators."

"Aye, that's right."

"Looking for business?"

"You bet."

"Good. Well, I want the outside of my house painted. It's a large house, so it's quite a big job. And it could lead to a lot more work, as I'll probably want the whole interior of the house done before long. Would you and your brother like to come out and have a look at it?"

"Yes—great."

"How about next Saturday—at five-thirty?"

"I'm sure that'll be all right, sir."

"I must warn you I'm going away immediately now, but I hope to get back home just for a short time then. However, if I can't manage it, you can still have a look round and see what needs to be done. Oh, and have a look at the window frames, will you. I think they need renewing."

"Will do, sir. It's in Cornfield, is it?"

"Oh, didn't I tell you the address? Sorry. It's a little way outside Cornfield, actually. You may know it. Do you know two houses next door to each other called *The Firs* and *The Elms?* They're on the road—"

"I know 'em, sir."

"Good. Well, my house is *The Firs*—next door to *The Elms*. Got that? *The Firs.*"

"Got it, sir."

"Now, try and get there exactly at five-thirty, will you? I can't guarantee it, but I'm most likely to be there then, and I'd like to speak to you if it's possible."

"Bang on, sir. You can rely on us."

"That's five-thirty next Saturday, *The Firs*. Oh, and the lane's a bit narrow just there, so you'd better run your van right up the drive to the house. And if I should happen to be out, make a thorough survey so that you can give me an accurate quotation."

"Will do, sir."

"Thank you. You sound like a reliable man, Mr. Atkins. I own several other properties and I've been looking for a really first-rate decorating firm for some time, so this could be a big thing for you."

"I realize that, sir."

"Good man. I look forward to meeting you both."

"Same here, sir."

Edgar glanced at the door and automatically lowered his voice a little. This was the part She hadn't got to hear. "Oh, by the way, I forgot to give you my name. It's Inchcape—Charles Inchcape. Good-bye."

"G'bye, Mr. Inchcape."

Edgar rang off. He was breathing heavily. With those last words he felt that he'd somehow burnt his boats.

There was one other thing, apart from that final sentence on the phone that Sylvia didn't know about. Jerry Atkins had done time for housebreaking, and was going to make a great fall guy.

Edgar suddenly grinned to himself at the words which seemed to come so naturally to his mind: *done time, fall guy*. He was starting to sound a real professional.

CHAPTER 21

"Right," Edgar said, "let's go through it again one last time."

"Oh, Edgar, this is becoming more and more like living out a thriller. First that surreptitious surveillance of the Atkins boys yesterday. Next having to lie down on the seat for the first twenty minutes of the journey today. Then learning code words—and now this constant repetition of the plan."

"I know it's boring, darling. But it doesn't do any harm, and it'll be ten minutes or so before we reach *High Tors*. So go on—just for me."

"Oh, very well." She did so, ending up, "If I can get no indication from either Miss Killigrew or Mrs. Atkins that the boys have actually gone to *The Firs,* I ring Charles, ask to speak to you, and then use the phrase 'take care of yourself.' You'll know then that the plan is off and I'm staying at the cottage."

"Yes, and if I use the phrase, it means something's gone wrong at my end—visitors or something—and in that case you also remain where you are for me to pick you up."

"I know."

"Sorry to be such a fuss-pot, dear. But this is entirely my plan, I more or less talked you into it, and I want to be quite sure nothing goes wrong."

"It won't Edgar."

It was just after a quarter to five. They'd been travelling since two. They had long since left the main road and were winding along a narrow lane. Occasionally they caught glimpses, through trees and behind hedges, of the Bristol Channel. The country here was wilder, more rugged than around Cornfield, and Sylvia didn't like it so much. She felt exposed, not protected as she was near her own home. There were no buildings anywhere in sight.

Suddenly Edgar said, "There it is," and pointed ahead to the right. Sylvia looked and saw a flash of white on a prominence overlooking the sea. *High Tors.* The next moment it was obscured by trees.

"Better get down again," Edgar said. "We don't want to spoil things at this stage by having you seen."

Sylvia obediently lowered herself below the level of the window. Edgar drove the last few hundred yards, then saw the familiar brick wall on the right, fringed on the far side by trees, and with wrought-iron gates standing open. He turned the Rover in through them.

High Tors had extensive grounds, but the house itself was not large or grand enough ever to have run to a gatehouse. However, it had been the conceit of the original owner to have his gardener's cottage erected just inside the gates, on the left, so that small though it was, it could be taken for a lodge. Edgar stopped outside it. His memory had not been at fault. The house was quite invisible from here. There was nobody in sight. He looked at the cottage—and received a shock.

Sylvia said, "All right?"

"I—I'm not sure. The downstairs windows have been boarded up."

She sat up quickly. "You mean we can't get in?"

"Perhaps it's just at the front." He took out a pair of gloves, put them on (Sylvia was already wearing hers), got out and hurried round to the rear of the cottage. There was one downstairs window this side, next to the back door. It was not boarded up. Edgar called, "It's OK," and smashed it with his elbow. He reached in, drew back the catch, got the window open and climbed through. He was in a tiny kitchen. He opened the door that led off it and found himself in the living-room. The kitchen door swung to as he crossed the room, plunging it in darkness, and he had to grope for the light switch. He went out to a minute hallway and opened the front door. Sylvia slipped in. She was carrying the bulging hold-all, which she'd surprised him by bringing with her.

"Books," she had said, "plus knitting, radio and thermos. I've got to have something to keep me occupied, or I'll be worrying about my part of the job and getting my nerves on edge."

"You'll only have half an hour to wait," he had told her. But he hadn't argued. Anything to keep the idiot female happy.

Edgar closed the front door. Sylvia put down her bag and pointed to the telephone, standing on a ledge near the door. "Check that quickly," she said.

"I dialled it again this morning—it rang then." But he picked up the receiver and put it to his ear. "It's all right." He held it out for her to hear the tone before replacing it.

She looked relieved. "Good."

"Now I'd better go. Good luck, darling."

"You too, Edgar."

"Oh, my part's easy. 'Bye."

He went outside, got into the car and drove off in the direction of the house.

High Tors was a squarely built house, two storeys high, with white walls. It gave an impression of spaciousness and solidity. It was much exposed to the elements and even on a sunny summer's day in the middle of a heat wave such as this one there was a strong breeze blowing.

Edgar drew up outside the front door. As he did so it opened. Charles emerged and walked up to the car. He grinned. "Hullo, Ed."

"Good afternoon, Charles." He got out. His brief-case was lying on the back seat, but he left it where it was.

"Come on in. Good trip?"

"Yes, pretty clear run, thanks."

They went indoors. "All alone today—as expected?" Edgar asked.

"That's right—until about ten when the Bruntons get back." He opened a door on the right. "Come on in here."

It was a large, pleasant, airy room, looking out over the drive. A table was laid for tea, with sandwiches and a fruit cake.

"Feel like a spot of tea?" Charles said. "Mrs. B always leaves me quite a spread, and I have just brewed up."

"Thanks very much."

"Have something stronger to drink if you like."

"Never touch a drop if I'm going to be driving. Tea'll be fine, thanks."

They sat chatting generally over their tea for twenty minutes. Then Charles said, "Well, I don't know exactly what it is you want to say to me, but it must be important, so let's get along to my study. That'll put me in a business-like frame of mind. I always find it quite impossible to talk seriously in a room in which I've just eaten a meal."

The study was at the back of the house. There was a big flat-topped desk, covered with papers, books everywhere and several deep and shabby-looking leather easy chairs. Charles dropped into one of them, put his feet on a pouffe, saying, "Sit down." He pointed to another chair.

Edgar did so, glancing at his watch at the same time. It was just coming up to five-thirty.

Charles lit a cigarette. "Well, all you told me on the phone is that you've come to a decision about the house."

"Yes. We'd like, if possible, to buy *The Firs* from you."

Charles's eyebrows went up. "Well, well, well." He looked thoughtful. "I won't insult you by asking if you've really gone into this thoroughly, but I must admit to being fairly flabbergasted. I mean, sixty thousand pounds—"

"Now that's one of the things I wanted to talk to you about. We both realize you've already been extremely generous in dropping five thousand. I hate to ask this, but could you possibly consider dropping a little more—another five thousand, say?"

Charles pursed his lips. "Oh dear."

"I know we've got an awful cheek to ask."

"It's not that. But I've been basing all my plans on the assumption of getting at the very least sixty thousand, and most probably sixty-five, and I—"

The phone rang.

Charles said, "Oh, excuse me." He stood up, crossed to his desk and answered.

Edgar could just hear the voice on the other end, "Charles?"

"Yes."

"It's Sylvia."

"Oh, hullo, my dear, what a nice surprise. Edgar tells me you're well."

She seemed to lower her voice and from that point Edgar could pick out only odd words. But this didn't matter as he knew very well the gist of what she'd be saying.

Charles said, "You want to speak to Edgar, I expect." He paused, then said, "Oh, I'm honoured." He put his hand over the mouthpiece and turned his head. "She doesn't want to speak to you, old boy. What have you been doing to annoy her?" He removed his hand. "Yes, Sylvia, I'm still here—just gassing with your old man. What can I do for you?"

Sylvia said something else, and Charles replied, "What exactly do you mean—'poking around'?"

This time she spoke at slightly greater length, before Charles said, "Oh? How odd. No, I know nothing about them. I suppose the Trust might have sent them, but it seems rather ill-mannered, if so. I haven't sold them the place yet."

This time there was a period of about ten seconds, during which Edgar could hear her prattling on like a distant chipmunk. At last she stopped and Charles asked, "They haven't done any damage?" Sylvia replied, then he said, "Well, yes, if you could find out who they are, I would be grateful. Perhaps you could call out of the window to them? If they can't give a satisfactory explanation, I suggest you threaten them with the police."

Edgar put an alarmed note to his voice. "I say, what's happening?"

Charles covered the receiver again. "Sylvia says there are two young men—rather rough-looking types—messing around *The Firs*. She can see them from the window. Wanted to know what she ought to do about it."

Edgar stood up. "Can I speak to her a minute, Charles?"

Charles said, "Sylvia, here's your better half." He handed Edgar the receiver.

Edgar said, "Darling? Look, it's probably nothing at all to worry about, but don't do anything silly, will you?" He paused. "Take care of yourself."

Sylvia said sharply, "What did you say?"

"Just take care of yourself, darling."

There was silence before she spoke again. "Do I understand you properly, Edgar?"

"I hope so."

She lowered her voice. "You think I ought to stay indoors?"

"That's right."

"I see. All right, Edgar, if you say so. I'll ring off now."

"All right, my dear, you do that." He quickly replaced the receiver and sat down again. He said, "She's going to ring again as soon as she's found out something."

"Fine. As you said to her, probably nothing to make a song and dance about, but as well to make sure. *You* have had no ideas about them obviously?"

"Did she describe them?"

"Yes; she said they were fair: one short and plumpish with long hair, the other a little taller and slimmer. Looked rather alike— could be brothers. Driving an old blue pick-up, registration letters ROT—which caught her attention—she didn't get the figures."

Edgar frowned. "Ring a bell?" Charles asked.

"I'm not sure. There *are* a couple of brothers in Cornfield who answer vaguely to that description. Name of Atkins. One—the elder, I believe—has got a criminal record."

"Really? What for?"

"Breaking and entering."

Charles looked a little alarmed. "Oh dear."

"Yes, it is rather disturbing, isn't it?"

"Well, no doubt if it is them, they'll scarper soon enough when Sylvia calls to them."

Edgar nodded. "Yes; if they are up to no good, they probably believe both houses are empty. Sylvia was thinking at one time of coming with me today, and you know what small towns are like: she'd only have to mention it casually in a shop and it could reach their ears in no time."

"Oh well, not to worry. We'll hear from her again any moment. Now—to revert."

They talked inconclusively for ten minutes or so. During this time Edgar kept glancing at his watch and eventually said, "It's strange Sylvia hasn't rung again. Do you mind if I call her, Charles?"

"No, of course not."

Edgar stood up, went to the phone and dialled the number of *The Elms*. He waited until he heard the expected engaged signal, then told Charles, holding the receiver out for him to hear.

Charles said, "I expect she's trying to ring us."

"Yes, that must be it. I'll just wait." He hung up, then stood by the phone, eyeing it. Two minutes passed.

Charles said, "You know, I bet she's been doing exactly the same as you. She's standing by the phone now, waiting for it to ring, just as you are."

"Yes—possibly." Edgar lifted the receiver once more and dialled. Then he said, "Still engaged." He rang off.

Charles chuckled. "The same thing's happened again. You could go on like this all night, old boy. Look, why not come and sit down and leave her to ring us—as she arranged to do?"

"Yes, you're right, of course. Sorry." Edgar returned to his chair.

Charles said, "Where were we? Oh yes. Well, frankly, I'm really awfully sorry, but I don't honestly see—"

He broke off as Edgar again looked at his watch, then with an obvious effort gave his attention to the discussion.

"That's all right, Charles, forget it, please. I shouldn't have asked."

"You were quite within your rights. But I'll tell you what: suppose we settled on an immediate payment of fifty-five thousand and you let me have the balance later—say in a year or two. How does that grab you?"

"What? Oh—sorry. You were saying?"

Charles repeated the question. Edgar looked confused. "I—er—I really don't know. We'd have to discuss it." He glanced at his watch yet again.

Charles said, "Tell me, Edgar, why are you so worried?"

"Well, something's just occurred to me, Charles. I think I did a rather silly thing just now."

"What's that?"

"Well, Sylvia said something like, 'I'll go and speak to them now and then come back and let you know what they say.' I assumed she meant that she'd call us again, so I rang off."

"But now you think she may have meant you to hold on?"

"Well, if you think about it, the words do bear that interpretation more than the other, don't they?"

"I suppose they do. And if she just put the receiver down on the table that would explain why you've been getting an engaged signal."

"Exactly. But it doesn't explain why she hasn't replaced it by now. She can't be talking to them all this time. Do you think anything could . . . ?" He tailed off.

"Oh, nothing could have happened to her. Burglars hardly ever use violence unless they're caught red-handed, and not often then. If these fellows were casing the joint, as they call it, they'd clear off as quickly as possible once they knew they'd been spotted."

"Perhaps." Edgar sounded unconvinced.

"But even if they were violent types, they'd have to break into your house to get to her. She'd have time to dial 999—and once she'd told them she'd done that, they'd be out of their minds to try and harm her. There'd be no point."

"Everything you say is perfectly logical, Charles. I'm sure that if she did stay indoors she's safe."

"If? You mean she might not have?"

"Quite probably. She's very plucky, you know—foolhardy sometimes. She'll tackle anybody. If, when she went back to the window, she found they'd disappeared round the far side of *The Firs,* I can just imagine her going to investigate."

"But you warned her—"

"I know. That was a mistake. Being told to take care might be just enough to spur her into doing something particularly rash."

Charles lit another cigarette. "Well, rather than go on worrying, the only thing you can do is ring the police in Cornfield, explain what's happened and ask them to go out and investigate."

Edgar shook his head. "No. I couldn't do that. As you say, I'm probably worrying about nothing, and she'd be terribly upset if the police suddenly turned up. She hates any sort of fuss, or being the centre of attraction. But I'm afraid I must go home, Charles—at once. I'm sorry, but I won't relax until I know she's all right. Do you understand?" He stood up.

"Yes, of course." Charles also got to his feet.

"Thanks for being so nice about the other business. I feel a fool that after coming all this way to raise the matter I've got to break off in the middle."

"Oh, don't worry about that. Just get home and reassure yourself."

They went out to the hall. Edgar looked at the big grandfather clock that stood there. "Five to six. I should be home by about quarter to nine."

Charles said, "It's a long time. Are you sure you wouldn't like me to ring the police for you?"

"Yes, quite sure. I'll give it a bit longer, and then phone home from a call box en route. If our number's still engaged I'll ring one of our friends and ask them to slip round to *The Elms* and check up."

"Just as you wish. And ring and let me know as soon as you get home, won't you?"

"Yes, of course."

They shook hands. Edgar hurried out to the Rover, jumped in, raised a hand in farewell to Charles and shot off down the drive. His mouth was dry and his heart was racing. This was it. He drew up outside the cottage, put his right hand glove on again, and then reached under the driver's seat and lifted out a smooth round pebble about the size of a large orange. He jumped out of the car and holding the pebble behind him hurried up to the front door of the cottage. As he reached it, it was opened from the inside. Sylvia stood in the doorway.

"What on earth went wrong?" She hissed the question. "Why did you tell me not to come?"

"It's infuriating, I know. Especially as I suppose Miss Killigrew *did* see the Atkins boys?"

"Yes—very clearly. She was actually suspicious of them herself! Everything was right—and then . . ."

"I know. Go into the living-room and I'll explain."

"Does Charles know I'm here or something?"

"No, of course not—he thinks you're at home."

"Thank heaven for that, anyway." She at last turned away and walked through the doorway into the living-room.

Edgar tightened his grip on the stone and went over in his mind once more the few choice words with which he was going to explain the true situation to her—after he'd got his left arm round her neck, with his hand over her mouth, and before he brought the stone smashing down on her head. Then he stepped through the doorway, left arm outstretched ready to grab, right drawn back.

Instead he stopped dead. She was facing him. And held high, gripped in both hands was a pointed, long-bladed knife.

As he froze, so did she. And he knew that it was the sight of the stone in his hand, and the instant realization of its meaning, which had distracted her from her intention of plunging the knife into his chest.

In a sudden blazing flash of revelation total understanding came to him—as he could see it come to her. Instantly everything slotted into place. Questions he'd never asked even of himself were now answered.

CHAPTER 22

For both Sylvia and Edgar the moment came with a strange lack of shock, or even of surprise. It was as though somehow, subconsciously, they had both known the truth all along. For seconds they stood, like figures in a tableau. Then Edgar let his breath out slowly.

He said, "So." Without turning, he closed the door behind him.

Sylvia just said, "Yes."

"Congratulations. You fooled me completely."

"And you me, Edgar. I understand a lot of things now."

"Such as?"

"Such as this trip—the whole plan. You never intended me to steal that photo, did you? It was just a ruse to get me here, in secret, and to persuade me to co-operate in convincing Charles that I was still at home. You planned for your victim actually to give you an alibi."

"That's right. You understand so well that you must have been planning to do the same thing yourself."

"I was. But it was your plan for stealing the photo—which I did really think you were serious about—that gave me the idea."

He asked, "Do you hate me?"

"Intensely."

"For how long?"

"I don't know exactly. Years now. And you?"

"Years."

"Any particular reason?"

"No. Just your whole personality."

"Same here. I know about your lady friend."

"There's no lady friend."

"Oh, don't play with—"

"There's no one, I tell you. There have been girls, in the past, but there's nobody now."

She said, "I believe you're telling the truth."

"I am. And what about you: is there a man?"

"No. There was once. But not now."

"So it's just . . . ?"

"Money, yes. Your insurance. I'm going to buy *The Firs*."

"Correction, you *were* going to buy *The Firs*. In fact, I'm going to sell *The Elms*."

"We shall see."

He asked, "Could you really have killed me—with that thing? Driven it into my heart?"

"I wasn't going to drive it into your heart. That would have killed you outright—which wouldn't have suited me. I wanted to talk to you before you died. I was going to stab you in a spot that meant you stayed alive for five minutes. I've been reading up on anatomy to be sure of getting it right."

"You really would have done it, wouldn't you?"

"Why are you surprised?"

"I don't know. I've always known you were as hard as nails. I suppose I'm old-fashioned; when I think of murderesses I think of poison. I can imagine a woman using a knife in a fit of temper, but I don't expect her to plan the cold-blooded stabbing of another person."

"You mean that's more the action of a gentleman than a lady?"

"It's certainly true what they say about adversity bringing out the best in the British. That's the first mildly witty thing you've said for ten years."

"I thought it would be nice for you to die laughing."

"I'm not going to die, Sylvia—you are. I've got it all very carefully worked out."

"You may not find it too easy to kill me. I do have this." She waggled the knife.

"I'm confident I can handle you, Sylvia."

"Just what have you got planned?"

"I'm glad you asked. I've been wanting to tell someone. I'm going to put your body in the boot, drive home at full speed, take you around the far side of *The Firs* and put you down on the ground. Then I'm going to force a window—as though somebody had been trying to get in. I'm going to drop this stone beside you—it's actually from that little rockery there—go back to *The Elms* and call the police."

"And the Atkins brothers get the blame?"

"That's it. They've almost certainly left their fingerprints in various places there, including the windows. Miss Killigrew saw them passing her house. You yourself actually gave a description of them and their van, with the registration letters, to Charles. Jerry Atkins has been in prison for housebreaking. The police will have them inside in no time. The only defence they'll have is that Mr. Charles Inchcape instructed them to go to the house. You see, I gave that as my name. Charles will deny that he sent for them. The case will be that they knew the house was empty and went to rob it. You saw them, went to see what they were up to and caught them at it. One of them panicked, snatched up a heavy stone and hit you. They remembered to wipe their prints off the stone, but not off anything else. And that'll be it. However, even if they should get off, I won't be unduly worried. I'll be in the clear."

"You're relying on the medical evidence for that, of course."

"My, my, your brain is working quickly. Yes. You phoned Charles at five-thirty. You were then at home. There will be no doubt about that: you said you were at home; and anyway you couldn't have seen the Atkins boys if you hadn't been. I reckon the police doctor will examine your body at around ten o'clock tonight. He'll say you've been dead about four hours. I don't know just how precisely he'll be able to determine it, but he'll certainly put your death at a time much earlier than I could conceivably have reached home—having left Charles at about six o'clock."

Sylvia nodded. Her manner was quite calm—though Edgar was so taken up with the cleverness of his own plan that this fact hadn't struck home to him yet.

"Oh, by the way," he said, "I'd be interested to know just what your little scheme was."

"Not 'was,' Edgar—'is.' "

"I don't think so, Sylvia."

"I do." Before he could move she had dropped the knife and taken two steps backwards. In one swift movement she bent down and made a grab behind a nearby armchair. Edgar took a quick step towards her. She straightened up. In her hands was a double-barrelled, twelve-bore shot-gun. She pointed it straight at his chest. He stopped dead, his face going suddenly white. It was his own gun.

"It's loaded," Sylvia said, "both barrels. And cocked."

He whispered, "Where did you get that?"

"From its usual place, Edgar—the cupboard under the stairs."

"But—but—how did you get it here?"

"On the floor in the back of the car, under a rug. I got it out quickly and hid it temporarily behind a bush while you were climbing in the back here earlier. I *had* been hoping to kill you with the knife—it would look slightly more natural, but now I'm terribly glad I decided to play safe. You wanted to know my little scheme? Well, I'll tell you. Of course, I never meant to steal that photo. I thought the whole plan was crazy—full of loopholes—though I did believe you were quite genuine about it. But don't you think my acting was exceptionally good just now—considering I never had the least intention of coming up to the house? You see, when you said 'take care of yourself' to me, I'd just been going to say it to you."

Edgar didn't speak. His eyes were fixed on the twin muzzles of the shot-gun.

"However, to revert," Sylvia said in a conversational tone, "as soon as you outlined your method for giving me an alibi for the theft of the photo, I saw that it would work just as well for a murder. So what I'm going to do now is shoot you dead—no one will hear the shot. Then, to put Charles's mind at rest about the prowlers, I ring him up again—still apparently speaking from *The Elms*—tell him I've been trying to get through for ages and that there must have been something wrong with the line, and that the two men drove off again without doing any harm before I had a chance to speak to them. He then tells me that you left him about fifteen minutes ago, and I say I'll expect you about nine. Then I take your wallet, your watch and your fountain pen. I put on my dark glasses and your cap —tucking my hair up underneath it. I cover the lower half of my face with a scarf. Then, leaving your body here, I drive the Rover back in the direction of home. Later, though, instead of turning off for Cornfield, I carry on along the motorway towards London. By then I'll be getting low on petrol. But I won't stop to get any. I'll continue until the tank is practically empty. Then I'll turn off the motorway and stop in some lonely lane or field. Oh, incidentally, in that capacious bag of mine, there's a can containing a gallon of petrol—just to make sure I don't run out at some awkward spot. If necessary, I can pour in a pint or two at a time until I find a suitable place where the car's not likely to be seen until the morning. I abandon it, with the engine running—so that when it's found the tank will be completely dry—and with this gun, together with your wallet, watch and pen, and a little ornamental clock, which I just took from the bedroom upstairs, inside it. Then I discard the cap and scarf, put on a blonde wig, at present also in that bag of mine, and start walking."

Sylvia paused. It was clear to Edgar that she was thoroughly enjoying herself. She continued, "I walk perhaps to Hungerford or Swindon or Newbury. From any of those places I can get a bus or a train to Polchester—I have all the timetables—in time to catch the last bus to Cornfield, which leaves at ten. I get off at the crossroads and as you know it's about forty minutes' walk home. I should be there by about eleven-thirty. I immediately phone Charles. 'Oh, Charles, I'm getting terribly worried. Edgar isn't home yet. I've been expecting him for over two hours. I just thought perhaps he's been trying to ring me, but couldn't get through—you remember how the phone was playing up earlier? He hasn't rung *you,* has he?' Charles will be very sympathetic. He'll no doubt suggest I ring the police. He might even offer to do it for me. But of course he'll discover there hasn't been any road accident. I needn't go on, need I? I don't know which they'll discover first—the Rover or your body, but it doesn't make any difference. The medical examination will prove that you died just about the time I was phoning Charles from home to report that the prowlers had left. What happened will be obvious to everybody. Some crook decided to burgle *High Tors.* But as he had to pass the cottage, and it was empty, he thought he might as well try his luck here first. Perhaps he had ideas of hiding here until dark. But he was just a little careless, and as you drove past on your way home you saw a movement inside through the upstairs window. You knew nobody should be in here, so you stopped to investigate. You took your shot-gun and surprised him. Who can say exactly what happened then? Presumably he 'jumped you,' as they say. There was a struggle and the gun went off. You were killed. He took the gun, your valuables and the clock and escaped in the Rover. He made for London. But he didn't dare stop for petrol and eventually ran out. He decided that after all it was too risky to keep the stolen property, and went on by foot. And no one will ever find him."

Edgar swallowed. "What about the gun?"

"What about it?"

"People will never believe I brought it with me today. Why should I?"

"I shall say that as you hadn't used it for so long, you decided several weeks ago to sell it. You were meaning to take it back to the shop in Polchester where you bought it, and you'd been carrying it in the boot ever since, trying to find time."

"You expect them to believe I'd been carrying it around *loaded?*"

"No; I have your box of cartridges in my bag. I shall leave them in the car. Naturally, like a good citizen, you intended to hand them in when you parted with the gun."

"You think you've thought of everything, don't you?"

"Yes."

"Well, you haven't. Do you imagine for one moment that Charles would believe, after the way I left here—worried to death about you and only interested in getting home as quickly as possible—that I would actually stop to investigate—with a shot-gun—a movement in his gardener's cottage?"

For a moment she looked shaken, then she said, "He'll have to believe it. There won't be any other explanation."

"And what about the coincidence?"

"Coincidence?"

"Yes; hurrying home because I think you've been attacked by burglars, I'm attacked by one myself. Who'd swallow that?"

"Coincidences happen."

"Yes—and people talk about them."

"Then they'll have to talk." Her voice was suddenly high-pitched and charged with tension. "I'm not being frightened out of this now. I've got to have that money—don't you understand? I've got to save *The Firs*. And this is the only way. I don't care how dangerous it is. I'll risk something going wrong. It's all or nothing. Goodbye Edgar."

Her finger tightened and whitened on the trigger. Edgar gave a despairing cry and twisted away, raising his arms to protect his face and head.

Sylvia squeezed the trigger.

The gun gave a loud click.

Edgar nearly fainted. Sylvia uttered a gasp of horrified dismay. She stared stupidly down at the weapon and started fiddling with it. Like one hypnotized, Edgar gazed at the muzzle as it wavered in the air. He tried to brace himself to jump her. He knew it was his only real chance. But he couldn't move.

The next instant there was an ear-shattering report and the room was plunged into darkness.

For seconds Edgar stood, motionless. His ears were ringing and he couldn't think. But he knew he must have been hit. Any moment his legs would go and he'd collapse to the floor. Then he realized that immediately following the report, something had landed on his head. He raised a trembling hand and in his hair felt small pieces of stuff—hard and jagged and sharp. Yes, and hot. Bits of a broken light bulb. She'd shot it out. She'd missed him.

But she still had one barrel left.

The real reason Edgar fell to his knees was that his legs gave way under him. But as his hands landed on the floor he realized that it was the best thing he could have done. The door. He had to get to the door. He started crawling.

For a split second after the report, Sylvia thought that her gun had misfired. Then she realized that there had been not the slightest kick from it—and that anyway the bang had come from some feet away.

He'd had a gun all the time. A revolver. He must have drawn it while she'd been looking down at the rifle. He'd shot the bulb out.

He'd probably got another five bullets in it. She had—*had* to make her own gun work.

Desperately fumbling, she managed to break it open at the breech. She pushed a finger in. Sick horror swept over her. There were no cartridges in it. The gun was not loaded.

Sylvia panicked. She had to get out of the room. She turned and lumbered blindly towards where the door ought to be.

Then she tripped over something and fell flat on her face. She lay on the floor, half winded. Partially dazed, she just had enough wits left to grasp the fact that the thing she had fallen over had been something that moved—something alive—and on all fours. Some sort of animal had got in.

She started to scream.

Edgar felt Sylvia's legs come in contact with his ribs, and his heart almost stopped beating. But then he heard her fall and begin screaming and he realized that she was momentarily out of action. So he still had a chance. He scrambled to his feet and staggered in what he prayed was the direction of the door. His groping fingers came in contact with the wall. Desperately he threw himself sideways—and felt glass.

Oh no! The window! He gave a sob.

Which way was the door—either door? He just couldn't remember.

He realized he was still sobbing. He was telling her his precise position.

Any second she'd fire again.

In blind terror, Edgar turned and blundered across the room. Then he tripped over something—something soft that gave before his shin, something that moved. He went sprawling.

He'd fallen over her. Which meant she now knew exactly where he was. He had to stop her firing the second barrel—get her hands.

He scrambled backwards and grabbed at her. His fingers caught her hair and then he felt her nails on his cheek. The next moment they were wrestling, rolling over and over on the floor. Edgar got hold of one of Sylvia's wrists and groped for the other. Instead, she caught his and jerked it to the side. Before he could resist she bit his thumb hard. He gave a yell and pulled away from her. They both lay still, panting.

Then, through the darkness, a voice boomed.

"I'm not going to die, Sylvia. You are. I've got it very carefully worked out."

Sylvia had no breath left for screaming or she certainly would have done so. For it seemed that Edgar had suddenly developed a voice three times as loud as usual—and still believed himself in charge of the situation. Too bewildered and exhausted to do any more, she just stayed where she was.

Edgar didn't recognize the voice as his own, and his first momentary reaction was a tremendous relief at this miraculous intervention by an unknown ally. In sudden hope he gazed blindly round. Then he nearly jumped out of his skin. For, in the voice of a giantess, he heard Sylvia bellow, "So what I'm going to do now is shoot you dead. No one will hear the shot."

Edgar gave a cry of terror and threw himself flat again—realizing only as his back hit the floor that the voice was coming out of the opposite direction from where she was lying.

The next moment the room was flooded with light.

Sylvia and Edgar blinked dazedly round. The light came not from the ceiling, but from a lamp on the mantelpiece. Then, from the kitchen doorway, another voice spoke.

"Yes, quite a good quality recording, I think."

They jerked their heads towards the door. It was Charles. In his hand was a revolver.

CHAPTER 23

It was Edgar who recovered his senses first. Scrambling to his feet, he stepped towards Charles, saying in a hoarse gasp, "Charles! Thank heavens! She's been having a kind of brainstorm. She's got some sort of idea I've been trying to kill her. She followed me down here. We must get her to a doctor. She's terribly sick—not responsible—"

"Be quiet, Edgar," said Charles.

Edgar stuttered into silence. Charles stepped right into the room. He looked down at his cousin. "Get up, Sylvia. You're far too old to lie around on the floor like that. You look thoroughly undignified."

Too shattered to be angry at this, Sylvia got shakily and mutely to her feet.

"Now sit down, both of you."

Edgar almost collapsed on to the sofa. Sylvia slowly lowered herself on to an upright chair against the wall.

"That's better," said Charles.

He bent down, picked up the shot-gun and stood it upright in the corner. Then he straightened the table, which had been moved in the struggle, righted a chair that had overturned, pulled it up to the table and sat down. He placed his revolver on the table in front of him.

"Now, let's have a little talk," he said.

Sylvia spoke for the first time since Charles had entered the room. "Talk? What—what about?"

"About you two."

Edgar was beginning to recover a little of his poise. By a great effort he managed to speak with a degree of dignity. "I have nothing to say."

"Neither have I," Sylvia said stiffly.

"Oh well, then, you may just care to listen. You'll find what I have to say quite interesting, I believe. Firstly—as you ought to have gathered, but in the, er, unusual circumstances may not have—your entire conversation in this room has been recorded. Oh, you won't see the microphone or the loudspeaker; they're rather skilfully concealed. Secondly, I have to inform you that for the past three or four weeks I've been having you both watched by quite a team of private detectives.

"I've been following my detectives' reports of your activities with intense interest and ever-growing disbelief," Charles continued. "It was quite a long time before I allowed myself to accept the incredible but ultimately inescapable conclusion that each of you was trying to kill the other. I'd first realized that something a little odd was going on when you came to see me separately the day after I told you about the Dimsdale Trust, and both fed me stories about your wishes in the matter. They were utterly at variance with everything I knew of your previous views. I just couldn't believe, Sylvia, that you were seriously thinking of selling your beloved *Elms*. No more, Edgar, could I swallow the idea that you were actually contemplating paying about twenty-five thousand pounds over the odds for a house that was no use to you. What was more, I'd seen the expression on your face when you'd learned that there was a chance of getting sixty-five thousand for *The Elms*. I was quite certain you'd made up your mind to get that money. So, frankly, when you dropped in the next day and spun me that yarn, I didn't believe a word of it. However, what really got me intrigued was the only coincidence in this whole business. The following Monday I'd meant to go back and finish off my work at *The Firs*. I drove down early and happened to stop at Hillier's Garage for petrol. I heard Hillier giving a dressing-down to a young fitter. Before he saw me and shut up, he clearly mentioned the wheel-nut on Mrs. Gascoigne-Chalmers' car and I heard the words 'could have been killed.' That made me think, so I hung about trying to get a chance to speak to the lad. Shortly after, I saw him leaving. I spoke to him and learned he'd lost his job. I got the whole story from him—Barry his name is— about how Hillier had just found all the nuts loose on one of the wheels of Sylvia's Mini, after Barry had been the last one to work on it. The boy swore blind to me that he'd definitely tightened those nuts—and I believed him. At that moment I became convinced that you, Edgar, had loosened them and that therefore Sylvia's life was in danger. I thought about going straight to warn her when she got home, but I was under the misapprehension that she loved you and wouldn't believe me. It's just not the sort of thing you can tell a wife, without proof.

"In fact, I was in a real quandary. I certainly had nothing to justify my going to the police. However, I was fairly confident that if you did make another attempt, it would be of the same general

kind: a faked accident, out of doors—though probably, after one
failure, you wouldn't be tampering with her car again. Anyway, I
was sure you'd be too cautious to try anything at home, with just the
two of you in the house.

"The best thing I could think to do was return to London and
contact a private detective I know. I told him I wanted my cousin
protected and suggested that he keep watch on you, Edgar, so as to
be ready to act if you started behaving suspiciously. But he pointed
out that if I were right about your intentions there was a possibility
you'd hire somebody to do the job for you, and it would be better to
stay close to the prospective victim. I told him that so long as he
was careful not to be seen he could stay at *The Firs*. I gave him the
keys and he drove down that same night. There was little more I
could do. I cancelled my North African trip and waited, trying to
tell myself that I'd made a mountain out of a molehill. Some days
later I had a most remarkable report from my detective."

Charles switched his gaze to Sylvia. "I thought I was hiring this
private eye to protect you. But then I heard that you'd spent Friday
afternoon at London Zoo, wearing a blonde wig, having first a long
conversation with a well-known con man, and then meeting a petty
crook called Nokes and paying him what appeared to be quite a lot
of money. You see, my detective was an ex-Yard CID Sergeant and
knew both those men by sight. On Monday you sold a valuable
painting and on Tuesday a fur coat. On Wednesday, again in your
blonde wig, you visited the man called Smith at a London hotel.

"I was now thoroughly intrigued. I began to wonder if you knew
that Edgar was trying to kill you and were planning some kind of
pre-emptive strike. Or perhaps you'd had the idea of killing him
first, and his tampering with your car had been self-defence. If so,
perhaps I didn't need to worry too much about your welfare, after
all. Maybe it was Edgar who was chiefly in danger. So—I hired a
second detective, independently, to keep an eye on him. Well, I
needn't go into everything I learned. It's all down in the detectives'
reports."

Charles reached into an inside pocket and brought out a nine-by-
four manila envelope. He opened it and extracted a number of
sheets of typescript, which he unfolded and laid on the table.

"These are duplicates, of course. You can read them yourselves,
later, if you like. However, I'll run through them briefly now."

He picked up the top paper. "One: report on Sylvia's meeting at
the Zoo with the man who called himself Smith, and with Nokes;
also of her sale of one beaver coat and one Begonzi painting; and of
her later visit to the Cogan Hotel where Smith was staying. Two:

statements by Smith and Nokes, giving full details of Sylvia's conversations with them. As I said, my PI was an ex-copper, and they wouldn't say anything to him, but he did persuade them to talk to me privately—once they knew they wouldn't be prosecuted—and I took these statements from them myself. Three: transcript of a tape recording of a conversation in a pub between my second detective and one Willie Morgan, in which Willie tells with great pride how he had just helped Mr. Chalmers by fetching from his house a valuable ornament, which was to be sold to an American millionaire. I don't pretend to understand exactly what your plan was in this case, Edgar, but plainly the idea was to kill Sylvia and somehow pin the blame on Willie.

"It was after I'd had these reports that I stopped worrying too much about the possibility of either of you harming the other. I just wanted to make sure you didn't put anybody else's life in danger. But how could I stop you? I had nothing concrete against either of you. Willie's remarks and the statements of Nokes and Smith would all be quite useless in law. I could have simply gone down to Cornfield, told you both what I knew, and warned you off. I might have frightened you—but for how long? Once a potential killer, always a potential killer—and I couldn't keep detectives watching you for ever. No, I needed evidence against you.

"The first PIs had been very good in their way; but now I felt I needed something extra. So I paid them off and went to see a friend of mine, who's head of a certain government department, and who owed me a couple of favours, for services rendered. I persuaded him to lend me one of his young operatives for a week or two—a chap experienced in the sort of work I had in mind, and who I'd already had some dealings with. This young fellow—let us for the moment continue to call him the PI—drove down with me to Cornfield on the Tuesday; because, as I wanted you both tailed, I'd decided to join in the fun and do a bit of sleuthing myself. He and I moved into *The Firs.* Needless to say, we kept very quiet, used no lights on *The Elms* side of the house, and except when we were actually following one of you, always left or approached from the other direction, taking the long route round to get to Cornfield.

"On Wednesday of last week the other chap tailed you to London, Sylvia, leaving me to keep an eye on Edgar. Later he phoned to tell me you'd hired a car—a Ford Escort—which made us virtually certain you were planning to return home in it, for another attempt on Edgar's life. Incidentally, I'd like to thank you both in passing for making it so easy for me and my men. You've been so completely absorbed in yourselves that you've both seemed to go around in a sort of single-minded trance, without the remotest awareness of the possibility that somebody might be watching you. However, that's by the way.

"You, Edgar, spent much of Wednesday in your garage, some of the time apparently sawing or hammering metal. Then you stayed indoors until about nine-forty, when you left, on foot. Well, I tailed you by the light of your torch. You walked to Cornfield, stopping on the way to leave something you'd been carrying in a dark lane. When we reached the town I watched from a distance your obvious attempts to find a car to pinch. It was quite clear then that you were going to take one to get you to London for another bash at Sylvia. It was also clear that I couldn't follow you. So I dashed off to a phone box, to ring my PI and warn him what was happening.

"Now he had booked into the Alendale hotel, and taken room 25, across the corridor from Sylvia." At these words, Edgar gave a start. Charles smiled. "Yes, that's right. Now, as luck would have it, just a few seconds before I phoned him, he'd seen you, Sylvia, creep surreptitiously out of your room, wearing that ghastly blonde wig. He'd just been going to follow you, but when we compared stories on the phone it was obvious that neither of you was going to be able to harm the other, because when you reached your respective destinations, you'd both find your birds flown. So we arranged that he'd stay at the hotel, to see if Edgar turned up there, as we expected, and I'd go back to *The Firs,* and await Sylvia's probable arrival next door.

"I'll tell you about the PI's experiences first. He kept his door open half an inch, and sat up in a chair just inside it for a couple of hours. Then at last he saw you, Edgar, wearing a stocking mask, coming along the corridor."

Charles glanced at Sylvia. Her eyes gave a quick flicker, but apart from that her face remained expressionless. Charles continued, "Now I'm not going to pretend that we've got any evidence that that was you, Edgar. But we are in absolutely no doubt that it was. You looked first at number 26, then went back and let yourself into 24, with the aid of a key. My man assumed you'd got the number wrong. He knew that a married couple were occupying that room and you'd soon discover your mistake. Sure enough, a minute or so later you emerged again. He was quite expecting you to return to 26, but then to his amazement he realized that you were coming straight towards *his* room—25. Like lightning he hopped fully dressed into bed. You crept to the bedside table and took his lighter, which he'd left there. He grasped then what your game was—that you were trying to make it look as though a professional hotel thief had been at work.

"He could have grabbed you then and raised the alarm. But he knew I wanted proof that you had attempted murder, so he lay doggo. However, he couldn't resist having a bit of fun by pretending to wake up and then keeping you crouching at the foot of his bed for about quarter of an hour. Eventually, though, he let you go. Then he jumped out of bed again, just in time to see you enter Sylvia's room. He could imagine your reactions when you found it empty. Five or ten minutes later you left. He let you leave, then slipped across and took a look inside himself—he's quite a dab hand with locks. He found his lighter, and some other things, obviously taken from No. 24. He was tempted to leave them there, just to see what would be the outcome, but he knew I didn't want Sylvia, any more than you, involved with the police in any way that might interfere with my plans for nailing her for attempted murder. So he collected them together, replaced those that had been taken from No. 24 and went back to his own room, to await for Sylvia's return some hours later."

Charles transferred his revolver from one hand to the other, then went on, "Meanwhile I had decided to try, before going back to *The Firs,* to discover what it was that you, Edgar, had left in that lane. I walked back and was hunting about in the grass, when I heard a car coming. I hid behind a tree. The car—a small Japanese one— stopped. You got out and quickly found the thing I'd been looking for. It turned out to be a package containing a pair of number plates. I decided it might be jolly useful to know what the actual number on them was. So, after you got back in the driving seat, I left my hiding place and scuttled up to the rear of the car to try and see—I had to get close, because your lights were off. When I was about six feet away you started the engine—and then suddenly the car shot backwards, straight towards me. I've since acquitted you of any intention to harm me; I think you just engaged reverse accidentally. I threw myself clear in the nick of time, fell into the ditch, hit my head on a stone—and woke up two days later in hospital in Polchester.

"I won't wait for expressions of shocked concern and sympathy," Charles went on. "The facts were that I'd been found early on Thursday morning by a farm labourer and was suffering from quite severe concussion. As a result, it was a couple more days before they let me read—and Tuesday evening before I happened to see the previous Thursday's local rag and read their report of the attempt to

run over the policeman. I knew at once who'd been responsible—
and that I was obviously the only person who did know. I also realized just how much of a menace you were, not only to Sylvia, but
also to anybody else who got in your way, and that—firm evidence
or not—I had to go to the cops with my information immediately I
got out the next day. In fact, I very nearly phoned them that night; I
should have done so. However, as things turned out, it was fortunate
I didn't. Because on Wednesday morning, before I was discharged, I
received a visit from my PI. And he brought me some of the most
interesting information I'd received of all. It concerned certain
doings of yours, Sylvia. Oh, I haven't told you his name, have I?
Well, you knew him as Warburton."

Sylvia blanched.

Charles nodded pleasantly. "Yes, he's a bright young fellow. This
fourth paper is his report of your activities last Tuesday. He tells
how he saw you buy a gallon of petrol in a can, then a box of
matches and a tin of lighter fuel at a tobacconist's in Polchester.
That made him suspicious, as he knew you were a non-smoker.
When you went to see Madge Eversleigh that afternoon, he decided
to pay a visit at the same time. While he was there he managed to
switch your matches for a rather special box of his own. He was
back there that evening, before you arrived. You see, he'd somehow
discovered that Edgar had an appointment there, and your pur-
chases, together with the matter of Madge's leaking fuel tank, had
given him a pretty good idea of what you had in mind.

"He stationed himself round the far side of the Mill, armed with
two pieces of equipment. One was a fire extinguisher. If anything
went wrong with his plan and you did manage to get the petrol trail
ignited, he could step out quickly and quench the flames before they
reached the Mill. The second piece of equipment he had with him
was—a camera."

Charles reached into his pocket for the second time and brought
from it a sheaf of glossy 5 × 3½ inch photographs. "This portfolio
of Warburton's is, I think, the highlight of my collection," he said.

He removed the clip that held the photos together and handed
them to Sylvia. "The top one was taken earlier in the day, the others
at the Mill in the evening—some through the window of the garage,
the ones of you in the open from round the side of the Mill."

With shaking fingers, Sylvia forced herself to flick through the pictures. The first showed her standing on a petrol station forecourt,
filling a can at her feet. In the second Sylvia, the can in her hand,
was approaching the Mill. In the third she was inside the garage,
pouring petrol on to the ground beneath the rear of Madge's van.

The next three showed her doing the same thing in other parts of the same area and on the stairs. The seventh showed her backing away down the path, still pouring from the can. And in the final one she was kneeling at the end of the petrol trail, a box of matches in her hand.

Charles said, "The light inside the Mill wasn't very good, even though you obligingly left the bulb lit, after Warburton had hopefully switched it on. But it's amazing what you can do these days with the latest cameras and very fast film."

For answer, Sylvia viciously tore the prints in half and hurled the pieces at him.

Charles tutted. "My, you are a harsh critic, Sylvia. I agree the composition isn't all it might be, but none the less . . . I have, of course, got the negatives of those in a very safe place."

During all this time Edgar had been making a second great effort to get his emotions under some sort of control. Now he thought he'd managed it. He spoke with a slight sneer. "I don't know what all that is about. But you seem conveniently to have forgotten your brave resolution to go to the police about me. Presumably, you quickly realized that by so doing you'd be making yourself look an even bigger fool than you had already."

Charles regarded him mildly. "Why do you say that?"

"Because, as you admitted, you had not an atom of evidence against me on that attempt to run over the policeman. It would simply be your word against mine. I've got an unblemished reputation in Cornfield. The idea that I could be convicted of anything on your unsupported testimony of having seen me in an unlit country lane, late at night—"

"I agree. That was the reason I couldn't bring myself to phone the police the previous night. But, you see, I soon discovered there was more to it than that. When Warburton came to the hospital I asked him if he'd heard anything about the attempt to kill the policeman. Now he hadn't associated that incident with you—he'd been in London at the time, remember—and I didn't tell him what I knew. But he had taken a normal interest in the case, and he'd talked to one of the local coppers whom he knows slightly. And he'd discovered two facts which interested me very much. First, the local force are up in arms about that business, and when they find the man they're set on having him charged with attempted murder. That as you no doubt know is a crime that carries a maximum sentence of life imprisonment."

Charles paused to light a cigarette. He inhaled deeply, then continued, "The second thing he'd discovered is that the police have got a clue as to the identity of that driver; to wit—his fingerprints."

Edgar gave a start. "That's a lie! I wore—" He stopped short.

"You wore gloves—is that what you were going to say? Fortunate that I put a new tape in and switched the recorder back on before coming in here, isn't it? Every little bit of evidence will add to the dossier. Yes, I quite believe you did wear gloves—from before you stole the car that night until you got home again. But you didn't wear gloves when you were making those phony number plates. You left your dabs all over them."

Edgar had gone deathly pale. Charles watched him silently for a few seconds. Then he said, "Yes, that alters things, doesn't it? Of course, at the moment you're safe, because the police haven't got your prints on file. But it only needs me to send them, say, one of the tea things you handled up at the house just now, tell them that the last person to use it was you, and suggest they compare the prints on it with those on the number plates—and you, Edgar, are finished."

Edgar seemed about to make an indignant rejoinder. But then he slumped back in his seat. He said quietly, "Then why *didn't* you go to the police?"

"For the simple reason that when Warburton visited me and told me of Sylvia's exploits at the Mill I knew for sure that she was, if anything, an even bigger threat to public safety than you, and I wanted to be able to take the police evidence against her at the same time. Now Warburton had been uncertain what to do with his evidence. He knew he ought to have gone to the police himself, but he hadn't wanted to do so before discussing this with me. He had not at that time had a chance to get the photos developed. He had the exposed spool of film with him. Obviously, we couldn't do anything about the police until we were sure the pictures were OK. For the sake of speed I decided to develop the film myself. I sent Warburton to buy some materials and took a taxi to *The Firs* in order to start rigging up a temporary dark-room. However, when I got there I discovered something that Warburton, in the excitement, had forgotten to mention to me."

For the first time Charles looked a trifle uneasy. "I went into the kitchen and saw on the table something I took at first to be an ordinary radio. I'd never seen it before and was puzzled why Warburton should have got it (there is a perfectly good radio in the house). I switched it on. And immediately I heard your voices."

Edgar and Sylvia both gave convulsive starts and stared at him, their faces studies of horror.

Charles went on, "I learnt later that Warburton had broken into *The Elms* while you were both out the previous Saturday, and planted some bugs. Since then nearly every word you'd spoken had been recorded. Needless to say, I had not authorized this, and I certainly would not have given permission had he asked. But I couldn't really blame him, as since the previous Thursday he had been doing the whole surveillance job on his own. I suppose he reckoned he needed all the help he could get. Besides, over the whole four days, he told me later, he had heard nothing remotely incriminating.

"I was about to switch the radio off. But before I could do so, I happened to hear my name mentioned. So—well, I listened. And I heard you planning to steal the old Horatio Dimsdale photo from *High Tors.*"

Edgar's face was now purple. "I've never heard anything so monstrous!" he shouted. "Deliberately eavesdropping on one's relatives."

Sylvia's cheeks were also flushed. "And you call yourself a gentleman!"

"No. I don't. I never have. There are just certain things I draw the line at. Such as robbery, the framing of innocent people for serious crimes—and murder."

Edgar subsided, muttering. Sylvia snapped her mouth shut like a trap.

Charles continued. "I must admit I found the whole conversation most interesting. I realized immediately that there was more to Edgar's plan than met the eye—something which was confirmed later when I heard one end of his conversation with the Atkins boy. The entire thing had clearly been worked out as another scheme for disposing of Sylvia. What intrigued me just as much, though, was Sylvia's ready acquiescence in the plan. You see, Edgar, I knew something you didn't—that she was plotting constantly to kill you, and so had no real interest in obtaining the Dimsdale photo at all. Although she ostensibly went along with your plan, I had a pretty shrewd idea that she was in fact going to use it as a cover for a further attempt on *your* life."

Charles flicked some ash from his cigarette. "I at once realized two things. Firstly, that neither of you was going to hurt the other—nor any third person—before today; so there was no immediate necessity of my going to the police. And that suited me fine. Because the second thing I realized was that I now had a chance of catching you both in the act—and making a cast-iron case against you.

"I didn't let Warburton in on my plan. When he arrived with the chemicals I told him to take the rest of the day off, and, while developing the photos, I continued listening in on you. I'd heard you say that you were going to phone me, so I rang Brunton and told him, when you did, not to let you know I was away, but just to say I was out. Then later I phoned you from *The Firs,* letting you assume I was speaking from here.

"I left Warburton to watch *The Elms,* came home and did some work here: bugged the room, boarded the windows and fitted a spring to the kitchen door—I had to know it would shut itself, and I could come in the back and wait in the kitchen without your knowledge.

"This morning Warburton phoned to say that you'd both left in the Rover—but that previously he'd seen you, Sylvia, sneaking the shot-gun into the back of the car. That confirmed my belief about your intentions. I instructed Warburton to stay at *The Firs* and when the Atkins boys arrived to tell them that there'd been a mistake and send them away.

"When you arrived I was hidden among the trees a few yards from here. While Edgar was climbing in I saw Sylvia take the shot-gun from the car and hide it in the bushes. When you both came indoors I slipped from my cover and unloaded it. The fact that neither of you would *know* it was unloaded meant that Sylvia would still be able to threaten Edgar with it in self-defence if he attacked her. I then hurried back to *High Tors* to await Edgar's arrival. When he later left, I hared down here across the lawn, arrived within a minute of him and listened from the kitchen until I judged it time to intervene. I opened the door an inch. But you were watching each other and didn't see me. So—I shot the bulb out, quickly reclosed the door—and the rest you know."

There was silence for about thirty seconds. Then, by a supreme effort, Sylvia rallied. "You've got absolutely no right to carry a loaded revolver round with you like that."

"Yes, I have."

"But ordinary private citizens are not allowed—"

"Agreed. But I am authorized to carry that revolver and have been for many years. Now you would be very wise to drop the subject and concentrate instead on the fact that I have enough evidence now to send you both to prison."

About to continue arguing, Sylvia suddenly thought better of it. She gave a sigh, a shrug, then said quietly, "Could we have the tape-recorder off?"

Charles hesitated, then stood up and went to the kitchen. He returned after a couple of seconds and sat down again, saying, "Right, we can talk off the record if that's what you want."

"How do I know you've actually switched it—"

"I give you my word."

"Very well." She took a deep breath. "I admit it. I have been planning to murder Edgar. But he's also attempted to murder me. So we're square. In that case, Charles, what purpose would be served in your reporting either of us to the police? After all, we both failed. So can't you overlook it all? I mean, what harm have we done?"

"Very little harm in the sense that nobody's been hurt."

"Well then—"

"But," Charles interrupted, "why is that?"

"Why? Well, because—"

"Because of some grotesquely incompetent bungling on both your parts—combined, I admit, with a little bad luck. But suppose your plans had come off? Let's talk about that for a moment." And suddenly Charles's voice was harder and sterner than it had been before.

"You first, Edgar." Edgar looked up. "You loosened those wheel nuts, knowing that Sylvia would be driving fast along the motorway and there was a strong possibility she'd veer across into the other lane and perhaps meet another car in a head-on collision. What thought did you give to the occupants of that other car? Secondly, you did your utmost to frame a harmless simpleton for Sylvia's murder, being perfectly aware that if you succeeded he'd spend the rest of his days in a criminal lunatic asylum. Next you tried to kill that policeman. Finally, you attempted to pin Sylvia's death on the Atkins boys, knowing full well that if found guilty they would get life imprisonment."

Charles turned his eyes on Sylvia. "And you, my cousin. You hired—or so you believed—a professional assassin to kill Edgar. You were quite happy when he told you that, as a blind, he intended also to shoot and wound Sir Hector Wainwright. According to Smith, you even seriously suggested he *kill* Wainwright, just to make quite sure the blind worked. However, there's only Smith's word for any of that, and although I believe him, I'll pass over it. But then we come to the incident at the Mill."

Desperately, Sylvia blurted out, "I thought he was having an affair with Madge."

Charles raised his eyebrows. "Did you really? Well, I'll take your word for that. So you're saying that if the attempt had succeeded it would have been a *crime passionnel?*"

"Yes—yes." She nodded eagerly.

"I see. Well, it's true that society and the law have tended to regard that type of crime leniently. So I suppose I could, too. But tell me, did you believe he was having an affair with his secretary, Beryl, as well—at the same time?"

Sylvia said, "I—" and stopped.

Charles shook his head firmly. "No, Sylvia, you had no suspicions of Beryl. You had nothing against her at all. Yet in order to get rid of Edgar and keep *The Elms* you were prepared to watch her burn to death—a widow with two young children."

And then they both gave a start as suddenly Charles jumped to his feet and began shouting.

"And you have the unadulterated gall to say to me, 'What harm have we done?' I don't know which of you makes me feel the most *sick!*"

He was brandishing the revolver menacingly in the air. Edgar gave a terrified yell. "Charles—be careful! What are you going to do?"

"You've got to be punished—both of you!" He jabbed in the direction of each of them in turn, with the revolver, shouting the words as he did so.

Sylvia gave a scream and Edgar scrambled to his feet and backed against the wall.

Charles went on at the top of his voice. "You don't deserve to live!"

Edgar gasped, "Charles, for the love of—"

Sylvia fell on her knees with a howl. "Oh, please don't kill me!"

Then abruptly Charles was calm. "Shut up," he said. "Tempting though it is, I am not going to shoot you. So sit down again, both of you."

Edgar subsided and remained silent. Sylvia slid back to her chair, where she continued to give hiccough-like sobs.

Charles dropped on to his chair again. He replaced the revolver on the table, put his forefinger on it and spun it like a roulette wheel. He watched it silently until it came to rest.

Edgar plucked up his courage, cleared his throat and said in little more than a whisper, "What—what are you going to do?"

Charles raised his head very slowly. "I'm not going to do anything," he said. "You're going to do something."

They looked at him in apprehension. Together, both their lips formed the word "What—?"

"First you must make some recompense. To those you've harmed, and to those you would have harmed if your plans had worked out. That young mechanic—Barry. You lost him his job, Edgar. You will see Hillier and inform him that you forgot to mention it to your wife but that you had a flat one day when you were driving her car, between the time Barry worked on it and the day of Sylvia's puncture. Say, if you like, that a little back street garage somewhere changed the wheel for you. Tell him you heard about Barry from me and you'd like the boy given his job back. Then I think Barry should have some compensation. Two hundred pounds should fill the bill. See to it."

"Yes—yes, of course, straight away," Edgar said hurriedly.

"Then there's Beryl. Give her a month off and three hundred pounds bonus. Tell her to take the kids and her mother on a nice holiday."

He looked at Sylvia. "Go round and see Madge Eversleigh. Buy one of her paintings—the most expensive one she's got." He turned back to Edgar. "Ring the Atkins boys. Tell them that your neighbour, Mr. Inchcape, will not after all be having *The Firs* painted, but that you would like them to do your house, *The Elms*. And buy Willie Morgan a colour TV set. Do you agree to all this?"

They both nodded hastily.

"I shall be checking in a week to see that all my instructions have been carried out."

Edgar cleared his throat. "Is, er, is that everything?"

"Oh, by no means. I shall, of course, be selling *The Firs* to the Dimsdale Trust. You, Sylvia, on the other hand, will reject their offer for *The Elms*. You will, however, write to them, saying that you are delighted to be having them as next door neighbours and that if they ever find themselves short of accommodation for their subjects you will be very pleased to help out—by putting them up at *The Elms*, quite free of charge. I'm sure they will be most grateful and will certainly take up your offer very soon after moving in."

Sylvia gave a strangled cry of horror. Edgar, however, had his mind on something else. "Charles, excuse me, but those private detectives of yours. Suppose one of them tries, you know—blackmail . . ."

"They can't. None of them has any evidence. The only one of them to have witnessed any actual criminal act is Warburton, who watched Sylvia's little escapade at the Mill. But there were no other witnesses, and he has no copies of the photos which he took. No, from that quarter you're safe."

"I see. Er, thank you. Thank you very much. Can we go now?"

"Go? Certainly not. I haven't finished with you yet."

"But all those things we've agreed to do . . ."

"That's just been Damages, Edgar. I've left the real penalty, until last. You see, for some time I've been trying to think what, short of being incarcerated in a slave labour camp or something like that, would be the worst punishment that could be imposed on me. And about the most ghastly fate I can think of is this: to be forced to live the rest of my days with a person who I knew loathed me and who had repeatedly tried to kill me. So this is what I sentence you to. Go home to *The Elms* and live there together, always. Don't ever separate, let alone seek divorce. Don't even take a holiday apart. I shall be having you constantly monitored and if I hear that you've disobeyed, all my evidence will go to the police—and the press. The same thing will happen should either of you die and the death cannot be proved without question to be from natural causes. I'm quite confident, however, that this will not stop either of you from continuing to try and think up ways of disposing of the other. I shall await with keen interest to learn which of you is the first to be reduced to a state of jibbering lunacy. And that, I'm delighted to say, *is* everything. Now get out of here before I throw up."

Without a word or a backward glance Sylvia and Edgar hurried from the room and from the cottage. Outside, Edgar got into the driving seat of the Rover. Sylvia took her place beside him. He accelerated fiercely away from *High Tors*.

For nearly an hour they travelled in complete silence. At long last, however, Sylvia spoke.

"Darling," she said, "I've been thinking. There's only one thing for it. We're going to have to kill Charles."

"Just what I was about to say, darling," replied Edgar.

James Anderson is the author of six other suspense novels which have appeared in hardcover and paperback in Great Britain and the United States, and have been translated into German, Italian, Portuguese, Dutch, Swedish, and Norwegian. His other novels include *Angel of Death, Appearance of Evil, The Abolition of Death, The Alpha List, Assassin,* and the highly successful thirties-style whodunit, *The Affair of the Blood-stained Egg Cosy.* ASSAULT AND MATRIMONY is his first novel for the Crime Club.

Anderson   119507

Assault and matrimony